I0824671

Halloween Folklore and Ghost Stories

Brice Stratford

To LJRO,
The Pigheaded Bride of Brixton

Also by Brice Stratford

New Forest Myths and Folklore
Anglo-Saxon Myths: The Struggle for the Seven Kingdoms

Coming soon

Christmas Folklore and Ghost Stories
Anglo-Saxon Myths 2: Legends of the Last Kingdom

If you enjoy this book, why not also try the Finding Folklore podcast, at: www.findingfolklore.org

First published 2024

The History Press
97 St George's Place, Cheltenham,
Gloucestershire, GL50 3QB
www.thehistorypress.co.uk

British Library Cataloguing in Publication Data.
A catalogue record for this book is available from the British Library.

ISBN 978 1 80399 774 2

Typesetting and origination by The History Press
Printed and bound in Great Britain by TJ Books, Padstow, Cornwall.

Trees for Life

CONTENTS

PROLOGUE

Come all ye good people, surround the fireside,
And hear now a story of Halloweentide;
Of bonfires and pixies and still-walking dead,
Of lovers whose fortunes may this night be read,
Of all that has passed and all that will come,
In the witch-heavy hours 'ere the rise of the sun.

Anonymous verse, Hampshire, 1923.

This book is written with love, and an intention to dispel a number of lazy presumptions about Halloween that are parroted endlessly in almost everything written on the subject, but which simply aren't true. They're so familiar that they're taken for granted: Halloween's an American invention, Halloween's a modern import, Halloween's actually Samhain, etcetera, etcetera.

Hogswash.

This book is designed to tear off the plastic Americana of the commercial holiday and expose the pulsing, rotting flesh of the ancient British tradition that lurks within. It is unique, in that it does not focus on America's modern Halloween, but on England's – it does not dismiss the traditional forms as dead, but views them in the context of a living and intangible cultural heritage, with direct continuity from the past to the present and beyond. It alternates between history, storytelling and gonzo folkloristics – a fitting hotch-potch for such a strange season.

Halloween, for those who care to look, is dripping in historic and contemporary ghost stories, folklore and ritual. This book includes the best of those tales that I could find, many of which have not appeared in print before, but have instead dwelt strong in oral tradition from region to region, sometimes kept alive across a county, sometimes just a village, sometimes in a single school playground or the solitary branch of a thinned-out family tree.

There is a peculiar form of arrogant exceptionalism that the English seem particularly prone to, along the same lines as believing that everybody has an accent except for oneself. It instils a presumption that we are (or should be) somehow above folk culture, archaic ceremony, and weird tradition - that these belong to more sweetly primitive, foreign climes - they don't know any better, after all, and so they can't be expected to keep up with our superior levels of logic and reform. It is due to this post-colonial snobbery that anything which hints of rustic mystery or superstitious prehistory is dismissed as belonging to the Irish, Scottish or Welsh (at a push the Cornish or Manx) - as if such backwardness is only understandable in the so-called 'Celtic' fringe, and couldn't possibly belong to our precious, streamlined, corporate-nowhere England.

Hogswash.

For beneath the anxious England of the office block and the focus group and the concrete university, there lies another England - an unselfconscious England, that does things because it always has, and doesn't stop to justify or promote itself. It is the broad and ranging, ancient England of the pub and the crumbling chapel; of the allotment and the shire; the bonfire and the wassail. This England has been around for well over a thousand years, and I believe will still remain in another thousand, long after the shiny suits and flatpack personalities of ruthless progress have withered.

England is not too good for enchantment, and the English are not above the archaic; nor should we be. Unless otherwise specified in the text, every reference and ritual that follows, all examples and each piece of evidence, are explicitly English - and all the weirder for it.

The key reference books, for those interested in reading further, are *The Stations of the Sun* by Ronald Hutton (1996); *British Calendar Customs – England, Vol. III* by Wright and Lones of the Folk-lore Society (1940); and *The English Year* by Steve Roud (2006). For those interested in the American Halloween, I recommend *Halloween: From Pagan Ritual to Party Night* by Nicholas Rogers (2002). I have tried to specify the many, many other sources I've used in the body of the text itself, but if in doubt, check the above.

If anything you find within enrages or fascinates you, then do please get in touch to discuss it further.

Enjoy.

INTRODUCTION

1

WHAT MAKES A HALLOWEEN?

What *is* Halloween?

First, the name. The general presumption is that the word 'Halloween' is simply a shortened form of All Hallows Evening, and so should properly be written as Hallow e'en. This may not be the case.

The word 'Hallow' comes from the Old English '*Halgan*' (holy), and many older, provincial forms of the word Hallowtide (referring to the wider season) retained the 'n', as Hallantide or Hollandtide – in some examples, it is called Hallowen, and Hallowen Eve and Hallowen Day are referred to. The Halloween spelling, then, likely developed as a continuation of the linguistic Halgan/Hallan/Hallowen shift, rather than as a specific contraction of 'evening', or as a reference to a single day.

Originating in the dialects of northern England and southern Scotland, today the word 'Halloween' refers both to the night of All Hallows Eve (31st October), but also to the wider halo of the Halloween period – the word 'Christmas' is used in a similar way: for both the day and the broader season.

The preference for this specific form (where before there had been many local variants) began after the Scottish poet Robert Burns published a verse of the same name in 1759. It became hugely popular during the 1800s, and ubiquitous across the English-speaking world over the twentieth century.

All Hallows Eve is, of course, followed by All Hallows Day, which is then followed by All Souls Day. Known together as Allhallowstide, this triptych is a 1,000-plus-year-old Christian festival season, maintained still by the Catholic Church, to honour the saints without committed feast days, and to pray for them to intercede on behalf of souls in Purgatory. Continental Europe still observes it fervently, as do most other Catholic countries globally, and it is still defined for them today by church services and religious custom.

So. How did the Catholic All Hallows become the semi-secular, folk-spiritual, pseudo-pagan season of Halloween?

Contrary to popular belief and much misinformation, it was not invented by or imported from America, nor does it really originate in a pre-Christian 'Celtic' festival called Samhain (pronounced Sowen) or a pre-Christian Roman festival for the goddess Pomona.

When the English Reformation tore Catholicism from the state, and the Anglican Church divorced from the Pope, the official and authoritarian observance of All Hallows in England ceased.

But All Hallows did not die.

Instead, it forked off into a second form of observance. The rituals and the practices continued, still celebrated and performed by the common folk, but without the guidance or control of any church authority, and without restrictive interpretations or rigid explanations. It folkified into strange and distinctive, organic paths that were powered by The People, and which resulted in broad and beautiful divergences from region to region. Country lore and rustic superstition began to blossom, without any form of officialdom to uproot it when it sprouted; strange practices not sanctified by any Church started to spread. The customs around the dead crystallised and developed in instinctual folkways, varying from village to village and, truly unleashed from the religion that birthed and bound it, the British rewilding of All Hallows there commenced.

Over the 500 years that followed, so formed our modern Halloween. I do not mean that our modern Halloween is only 500 years old – the secular British Halloween is not a separate holiday to the historic Catholic Allhallowstide, any more than the modern Catholic Allhallowstide is. Both have direct continuity with the historic version, and both can claim those roots as their own.

English, Irish, Scottish and Welsh emigrants to America eventually took Halloween with them, of course, and (as often happens in America) the holiday became genericised, simplified and commercialised; covered in candy and nylon and popularised through Hollywood.

But it is not American.

In this book I will try to prefer Hallowmas and Allhallowstide when referring to the wider Halloween season, and All Hallows Eve/Day when referring to the specific dates. I'll use other names as the mood takes me, however, so keep your wits about you.

Most calendars consider that Halloween is exclusively 31st October, but that's a rare observance in practice. In England today (and certainly throughout my childhood), the main festivities tend to occur on the Saturday beforehand and then stretch on at least until the day itself (I write this on Friday, 27th October 2022 – tomorrow, the main village parties are all being held, and decorations will stay up through the 29th, 30th and 31st October, and most likely linger until Bonfire Night and beyond).

It is not unheard of (and in the United States it is established as the norm) for the entirety of October to be given over to the Halloween season. In Britain, it usually starts later, but often spills into the Guy Fawkes festivities of 5th November. Parts of the country take it even further, and still celebrate 'Old Halloween' at Martlemas, on 11th November.

For those unfamiliar, in 1752 Britain changed from the old Julian calendar to the current Gregorian calendar – in doing so, leap years were established, and everything was moved forward by about eleven days. As a consequence of this change in calendars, all festivals in the UK forked in two and now have the 'new' date of observance, which is the regular date associated with them, and the 'old' date, which is eleven days hence. Thus, the celebration of Halloween is expanded from 31st October all the way through into mid-November, with the season ending on St Brice's Day (Old All Souls Day, 13th November).

British Popular Customs tells us that as far back as 'the reign of Charles I [1625–49] the young gentlemen of the Middle Temple were accustomed to reckon All Hallow Tide the beginning of Christmas', and Halloween plays this role still today: a liminal, transitional festival that carries us from the lazy late summer and early autumn harvest, through into the chill festivities of winter. It is no wonder that many of the traditional associations are shared, and that ghosts feature heavily across both (*The Nightmare before Christmas* being an obvious expression of this).

As the practices of Halloween vary from region to region, it is this inclusive, expansive Hallowmas season that I'm writing my book about – late October to mid-November, from around 28th October until 13th November. This, in England today, is the secular or folk season of Allhallowstide, within which we, of course, find All Hallows Eve itself, as well as All Hallows Day, All Souls Day, Bonfire Night, Martlemas, St Brice's Day and more.

If any of these names are unfamiliar, fret not. All will be revealed.

2

THE MANY DAYS OF HALLOWMAS

The English Halloween Season, then, is made up of the following:

LATE OCTOBER – PUNKIE NIGHT

Punkie Night is a trick-or-treating custom in Somerset which has held various dates in late October, but is currently settled on the last Thursday of the month. It involves Jack o' Lanterns made of mangolds (punkies), and a procession is held. Outside of Somerset, Punkie Night is usually just the day that the Jack o' Lanterns are carved.

28TH OCTOBER – BAKING DAY

Though Halloween events and decorations are often unveiled throughout October (moreso the older the month grows), the 28th is the earliest specific day to have a Hallowmas tradition. This is the day that the batch cooking of soul cakes began (these will be explained later), to be ready for the festivities that follow.

30TH OCTOBER – MISCHIEF NIGHT AND RINGING NIGHT (THE FIRST)

One of two Mischief Nights, and two Ringing Nights. In some areas bells are rung and great noise is made, in others youths roam the community causing mayhem and playing pranks – convinced that normal laws do not apply until daybreak.

31ST OCTOBER – ALL HALLOWS EVE

The crux of it all.

1ST NOVEMBER – ALL HALLOWS DAY

The day follows the eve, as we all know, and thus All Hallows Day (also All Saints Day) follows on from Halloween proper. This is also All Souls Eve, and the observances between all three are very much shared – historically, All Hallows Day used to see more celebration than the Eve in England, and the trick or treating custom of Souling was often centred around it.

2ND NOVEMBER – ALL SOULS DAY

All Souls Day is here. Soul cakes are eaten, souling plays performed, Old Hob rides.

4TH NOVEMBER – RINGING NIGHT AND MISCHIEF NIGHT (THE SECOND)

The night before Bonfire Night is, just as the night before Halloween, both a Mischief Night and a Ringing Night, for exactly the same reasons and with exactly the same practices.

5TH NOVEMBER – BONFIRE NIGHT

Also Guy Fawkes Night or Fireworks Night. Effigies are burned on bonfires, fireworks parties are thrown, revelry and mulled drunkenness holds sway, and in some places (mainly Sussex and Devon), wild parades are still performed, with flaming tar barrels carried by brave young men or dragged along streets. The Shebbear Stone is turned, and we are all kept safe from the Devil.

11TH NOVEMBER – MARTLEMAS

Old Halloween, which some hold as the true date of the thinning veil. It is also properly termed St Martin's Day, and in England we call it Martlemas and eat goose. Before daybreak Wroth Silver is collected, and later on Fenny Poppers are fired. Tying it back to the dead, this is also Armistice Day, in which we remember those who have died in Britain's wars, with a two-minute silence held on the eleventh hour of the eleventh day of the eleventh month. Parades and wreath-laying ceremonies at churches and war memorials are common. The nearest Sunday is usually Remembrance Sunday, on which similar services are also held.

12TH NOVEMBER – OLD ALL SOULS EVE

The old date of All Hallows Day and All Souls Eve, with customs repeated.

13TH NOVEMBER – ST BRICE'S DAY

St Brice's Day, interconnected with Martlemas. Historically, the infamous Stamford Bull Run was held. The day is thus associated heavily with beef, and it is traditional to eat it – either stewed in beer or as a roast in the English style. In the old calendar this is All Souls Day and customs repeat, especially in parts of Somerset with connections to the historic Brice family. It is now six weeks until Christmas Day, and the Halloween season has concluded. Time to get ready for Yule.

To briefly summarise, then: celebration of the established Catholic Allhallowstide ceased to be controlled by the Church in England after the Reformation in the 1500s. Thereafter, it rewilded and strangeified, with different customs developing in different regions.

In 1606, Bonfire Night was established in England on 5th November, beginning a nuanced relationship with Hallowmas that I will detail later. Over the coming century, the word 'Halloween' began to form. In 1752, the change in calendar gave us a second Hallowtide, which sits alongside and melds with St Martin's and St Brice's Days on 11th and 13th November.

Over the 1800s the word 'Halloween' became known across Britain. Bonfire Night, by then the highlight of the Hallowmas season for many, reached such peaks of wildness that it had to be tamed - from around the middle of the century. This resulted in the division of a Mischief Night and Ringing Night immediately beforehand in some areas, and the creation of the Bonfire Boys and similar groups in Sussex. Bonfire Night was then secularised as the century progressed, and as the 1900s drew nearer Halloween was exported to America.

In 1919, Armistice Day was added to the cocktail, and in the 1980s (with the release of the film *E.T.*), a more generic and commercial Americanised version of Halloween was popularised, and celebrations became less regionally distinctive.

But what defines it? What actually *is* Halloween?

The season boils down to about seven elements, each of which has a committed section in the book that follows. Among these, there are an array of customs, themes and traditions that remain an intrinsic part of Halloween today, and which have been so for the 1,000 years or more since All Hallows first began.

The most important is death and **The Dead**. Alongside this, we find **Trick** (pranks, raucous revelry and misrule) and **Treat** (the giving of food and alms), **The Flame** (from bonfires to Jack o' Lanterns), **Defence against the Dark Arts** (be they witches, spirits, pixies or worse), **Divination** (usually related to love and marriage), and finally, the late harvest and slaughter of **Bloodmonth**.

All seven arrive early, and all are recognised in the coming chapters. Other, more recent, innovations (haunted houses, pumpkins) remain rooted in these older associations, and as is so often the case, we find that the things we think at first glance are new are merely the latest incarnations of things far older.

It is this blend of custom, belief and superstition, at this particular moment of late autumn – that cusp between the life of harvest and the death of winter – that makes 'Halloween' an entire season as opposed to merely a day. Still, it exists again beyond that. It is a feeling, a concept, an aesthetic – one naturally developed and unselfconsciously self-aware.

It is the thinning of what we know to be thick and solid and safe; the strangening of the familiar and mundane. It is woven through the winter, and its tendrils reach past Christmas and into New Year, though at All Hallows Eve it is at its most unsoftened and intense, without the rich gifts and fellowship to counterbalance.

You would be forgiven for finding this an unfamiliar way of approaching the subject, but do bear with me, for I take you now beneath the hood of Halloween, into the deep, dark, cobwebbed recesses and dusty, forgotten nooks within, which remain in surprisingly good working condition, despite the generations they have spent obscured behind a mask.

Light the fire in the hearth, then, and pour yourself a glass of port. Make sure the rest of your household will not disturb you, nor friends pierce your quietude. Deactivate your telephone, check once more that all doors are locked, and step with me through the dust and ash and confusion of Allhallowstide, for speak we now of Halloween.

We shall begin, as all things do, with death.

THE DEAD

3

THEY SAY THE CHURCHYARDS YAWN

> They say the Churchyards yawn at Halloween, and do stretch forth their slumberers who onward creep, confused in waking dream awry; and thus, they say, the dead do walk.
>
> Anonymous note from a commonplace book, Hampshire, 1789.

Halloween, from the very start, has been defined by death.

At Halloween today, as at Halloween five centuries ago, ghosts walk, the dead must be appeased, and contact with the otherworld is rife; it is the time when the bars that bolt the doors 'twixt life and death are slid back, that free movement between them may briefly reign. This is the very essence, the core of the season – this temporary melding of the present with the past.

Of the many and many customs and traditions that have accumulated at this date over the last millennium, all of them stem from this one core element of The Dead. I'll detail each of these connections – some direct and obvious, some further removed – in turn, when I reach the relevant chapters. For now, we speak of the dead themselves, and Halloween's relationship with them.

To do so properly, we first must speak of distant origins and dates, and other such dry things. We've established the broad evolution of Halloween, and now must dig into the roots. Forgive me, for we will move swiftly on to the good stuff, but this foundation is where our story starts.

The festival of All Hallows began, some time before the mid-fourth century AD, in the churches of the Mediterranean as a date to celebrate the uncountable numbers of dead saints who didn't get a concerted feast day of their own. Though the date chosen for this was 13th May, over the next century different countries chose different times of year: in Syria, it was during Easter week, in Greece, the Sunday after Pentecost. In AD 609, however, the Roman Church formally nailed it to 13th May, and everyone else followed suit.

Except for us.

Approximately 1,300 years ago, give or take a lifetime, the Anglo-Saxon Church decided not to. Nobody knows why, or when exactly. All we know is that at some point in the 700s, by the time of Alcuin of York (AD 735–804), the English had bucked the international trend and started to hold All Hallows Day on 1st November, with the Eve on 31st October.

Thus it has been ever since.

The Irish and Scottish Churches did not, and for them, the All Hallows date remained as 13th May, with 1st November apparently already holding another event, generally known as Samhain (*sowen*). As this is just the Irish language word for November, however, it is hard to distinguish between references to a specific festival and references to the month itself.

A brief digression on the subject of Samhain.

Though an astonishing amount of fanciful stuff has been written about Samhain, there is almost no evidence whatsoever of its existence beyond the surviving name, and no hard evidence at all of what it consisted of. All references we have to a festival of Samhain date to well after the Christian period and well after the establishing of All Hallows on that date. There is almost no pre-Christian evidence at all, and none that indicates it had anything to do with the dead, witchcraft, magic, fire or the supernatural. The earliest traces of all these associations comes from the Christian festival of All Hallows itself, centuries later.

Much of the back projection of medieval Halloween onto a supposed pre-Christian festival comes from romanticism and a naive presumption that the Victorian Church must have been essentially the same as the medieval Church (and so all that is not comfortably Victorian must thus not be Christian). This combined with a hefty amount of anti-Catholic prejudice, specifically the Protestant slur that Catholics are pagan, and anti-Irish prejudice – whereby Gaelic people were primitivised as backward, ungodly and immoral. This is completely ahistorical. Not only is modern Ireland far more religious (and far more Christian) than modern England is, but Ireland was Christianised literally hundreds of years before England.

To get it into perspective, when England started holding All Hallows on 1st November, it was within living memory of our last pagan king (Arwald of the Isle of Wight, d. 686), and at a time when there would still have been practitioners of Anglo-Saxon paganism (we know such people existed during the time of Bede, who died in 735). Ireland at that point, conversely, had been Christian for almost 400 years, Wales for even longer. Scotland for about 200.

The churches who first mimic our November All Hallows are not Celtic or Gaelic, but German (specifically that of Alcuin's close friend, Arno, Bishop of Salzburg, and another in Bavaria). The practice then appears to have spread through northern Europe, until in 835 Pope Gregory IV, through the Emperor Louis the Pious, officially announced All Saints Day as belonging to 1st November. As Hutton says, 'this makes nonsense of [any] notion that the November date was chosen because of "Celtic" influence; rather, both "Celtic" Europe and Rome followed a Germanic idea [of Halloween]'.

There are plenty of stories in Irish literature that refer to events as taking place at 'Samhain', but they were written down in their surviving forms by Christian monks, hundreds of years after All Hallows was established. The bulk of the folklore was only recorded in the 1700s and 1800s, around 1,000 years after All Hallows, and these customs are mirrored by those recorded in English folklore of the same time, where there is no recorded history of Samhain at all.

Anyway.

By the 700s, England was holding All Hallows on 31st October/1st November, and by the mid 800s everyone else was doing likewise. At this point, it was nominally still about the saints.

A major anxiety of the time, especially in recently Heathen England, was that one's cherished parents, grandparents and great-grandparents were now all suffering in hell due to their paganism. Thus, the notion of purgatory was established as an alternative to hell, and with it the ability for the prayers of the living to eventually rescue the Heathen dead from torment.

One of the key interactions that people had with saints, then, and one of the main practices of the All Saints festival, was praying to them for intercession on behalf of the souls of the dead, generally one's ancestors or loved ones, to help those in purgatory achieve paradise. It is this element, in particular, that is considered heretical in Protestantism, and which resulted in the post-Reformation Church's hand-washing of Allhallowstide.

Pretty well from conception, then, All Hallows had expanded beyond merely the saintly dead, to encompass all those whose souls might appreciate extra support. The addition of a committed All Souls Day was more or less inevitable. Much obscurity attends its origin, and all we can readily say is that various places in various countries soon began to celebrate some version of it, with varying degrees of formality – presumably designed, in part, to help refocus the attention of All Hallows back onto the saints themselves.

The Catholic tradition of the origin of All Souls is thus: a travelling pilgrim, on return from his pilgrimage to the Holy Land, was caught in a terrible storm and forced to take refuge on a rocky island. There he found a wizened hermit, who told him that amongst the cliffs there was a deep chasm that opened up into Hell itself, through which huge flames ascended, and where the groans of the tormented were distinctly audible. As the tradition goes, the pilgrim then travelled to Odilo, Bishop of Cluny, to inform him, and Odilo took no hesitation in establishing the next day as All Souls.

The first formally constituted Soul Mass Day was indeed established by Odilo, Bishop of Cluny, in 998, but it was held in February (again, likely to try to distance the two observances). It is probable that the tradition was originally that Odilo himself had seen the hellmouth, and as tastes changed over the centuries this was pushed arm's length onto a pilgrim, and then still further onto a hermit, turning it into one of the most influential friend-of-a-friend stories in history.

All Souls would remain variable and non-standardised over the next two centuries, during which time it gradually cohered to 2nd November, immediately following All Hallows, and combining with it to make Allhallowstide, the festival of the dead.

But when did they learn to walk?

This particular development is a strange one. The vast bulk of evidence for overtly supernatural associations dates to after the reformation, but there are hints here and there that such ideas may have already existed.

But you have, I feel, earned a break from this dense and vague tapestry of presumption and pedantry over fragments from a millennium past, so before we analyse the earliest trace of the Halloween undead, let us enjoy firmer ground and look at the most recent.

Let us discuss the haunted house.

4

THE GENESIS OF THE HAUNTED HOUSE

'Beware all ye who enter here. Approach at thy peril. Knock and be damned.'

Whether it's a domestic home that's dressed for a party or trick-or-treaters, or one of a spate of more recent immersive scare attractions, a characteristic aspect of Halloween today is that of the 'haunted house'.

The concept of a house that is haunted is, obviously, an old one. Supposedly genuine accounts of such things go back to antiquity, and acknowledged fakes likewise have been around for hundreds of years – since well before the eighteenth century we find records of criminals and smugglers confabulating them, encouraging superstition to discourage the curious from investigating their hideouts or stashes.

There are two key developments from this broader notion of 'a house that is haunted' to the modern Hallowmas stalwart. Firstly, there's the point at which haunted houses become specifically associated with Halloween, and secondly, the point at which haunted houses become social opportunities and entertainment attractions rather than serious sources of danger.

Let's start with the latter.

Ghost-themed illusion displays, designed to scare and thrill the audience, were a part of touring shows throughout the nineteenth century – initially in England, but spreading quickly to the rest of Britain and then on to America, themselves a logical enough development in the sideshow culture that had produced endless conjurors, magicians and freak shows across the West. From these scare displays came two fresh concepts: first the 'haunted house' attraction, and then the 'ghost train' ride.

A major element in the development of this show was the illusion known as Pepper's Ghost, named after the scientist John Henry Pepper

(1821–1900). It essentially involves a specially designed stage with a hidden room, which is separated from the main space by an angled sheet of glass or transparent plastic. Using bright lights, a figure in the hidden room will appear translucent and projected, via the angled glass, onto the stage. Though the reflective concept had been recognised since the Renaissance, it wasn't until 1858 that an engineer named Henry Dircks would come up with the idea of building special stages to enable the effect to be performed on a human scale, and in turn, to produce a new form of theatre.

Dircks's ideas were costly and impractical, however, and he found disinterest everywhere he went until he showed the concept to John Henry Pepper, in 1862. Pepper immediately saw the potential and went into partnership with Dirck, redesigning the system so that the entire effect could be produced by merely adding an angled sheet of glass to a pre-existing orchestra pit. In December that year, they gave the first public performance – a scene from Charles Dickens's *The Haunted Man.*

The effect was an instant hit, and 'Pepper's Ghost' was soon touring the UK, then Europe, then America, in various guises and from different producers. A string of patent and copyright disputes followed, and it all became very acrimonious and bitter for all concerned. The illusion is still regularly used today, and remains one of the key approaches to presenting ghosts in live performances.

A little over fifty years later, in 1915, the first haunted house attraction was built, as 'Ye Haunted Cottage'– a supernatural twist on the carnival fun house, by Orton & Spooner (the world-renowned Burton-on-Trent fairground ride manufacturers) for Flora Collins née Ross, the Wrexham-born wife of Walsall MP and funfair impresario Pat Collins.

Extraordinarily, this tiny original attraction (and bona fide piece of history) is still fully operational, and barring the odd period of maintenance, it has been in active use since it was first constructed over a century ago. Its various features (vibrating walls, uneven floors, unexpected puffs of air) are still entirely steam powered.

Today, this first ever haunted house can be visited at the steam-powered amusement park and museum, Hollycombe Steam in the Country, near Liphook in Hampshire (the fairground itself is actually in West Sussex) – they acquired it in 1991 and restored it in 2017. It still bears its original Edwardian design, with just a couple of additions made to the exterior in the 1920s and 1930s (Lon Chaney as the Phantom of the Opera, and Boris Karloff as Frankenstein's monster). Supposedly it has, in the intervening years, accrued an additional haunting: fairground workers have reported it mysteriously activating in the middle of the night, strange noises coming from it which aren't part of its usual functions, and unfamiliar figures inside who aren't supposed to be there.

Fifteen years later, English architect Joseph Emberton had the idea of expanding the static Haunted House attraction into a larger 'dark ride', in which the audience was carried along a specific, timed journey by rail. Dark rides were named not for any dark themes, but rather for the low lighting states they utilised. These were peaceful, gentle journeys through beautiful, exotic locations. They were well known in America, especially those made by the Pretzel Company, and a common example is the Tunnel of Love, or Disney's 'It's a Small World'.

In England the potential for fear was first realised, and the world's premier ghost train was built in 1930 at the Blackpool Pleasure Beach. It was a success. So much so that others soon followed at Dreamland in Margate, Pleasure Beach in Great Yarmouth and Pleasureland in Southport. In 1936, Blackpool Pleasure Beach commissioned Emberton to build an even larger, more extravagant version of his original ride, and success was cemented.

Over the following decades the ghost train and haunted house attractions became more and more popular, replicated across Britain, Europe, America and the world. The live actors and special effects of the earlier Victorian London ghost shows were soon introduced, and thus was born the modern scare attraction. Probably the most famous of these would be Disneyland's 'Haunted Mansion', which opened in 1969 – a huge-scale version of Emberton's Ghost Train concept, replete with Pepper's Ghosts and other stage effects throughout.

But when, specifically, were they twinned with Halloween itself?

As these scare attractions had developed through the twentieth century, so too had domestic Halloween parties begun to echo them. Grotesquely carved mangold-wurzels and turnips had long been an element of All Hallows, with pumpkins added by the late nineteenth century, and these would all have formed some part of the standard decorations for Halloween. Masks (or 'false faces') and costumes were worn by this time, and their aesthetic would likely have been incorporated, and the divination customs that we'll detail later indicate that candles and decorative foliage would have been present also.

It was inevitable that, as the haunted house/ghost train aesthetic was popularised, it spilled over into the domestic sphere, and the traditional parties and games of Halloween grew to encompass scares inspired by the increasingly familiar fairground attractions. But when did they first acquire their seasonal associations? How far back can we find evidence for haunted houses specifically at Halloween?

The answer is 1649, and the time has come to tell you the story.

5

THE DEVIL OF WOODSTOCK

In mid-October of 1649, a team of civil servants arrived at the town of Woodstock in Oxfordshire. It had been about eight and half months since King Charles I had been beheaded by the fundamentalist Puritan government who had now taken total control.

This team of surveyors had been travelling the land, recording and evaluating the late king's holdings to ensure that all remaining royal pockets were properly picked and profited from. That which couldn't be reused or sold was to be destroyed, and one of their first acts in Woodstock was to seek out and uproot an ancient tree in the high park, known to the locals as the King's Oak (as it had been since time immemorial).

The royal oak was torn down, not merely chopped – no stump or remnant was allowed to be left as memorial to the recently purged kingship. The roots were dug up, and the workmen closely watched to ensure that none took wood away that could be used as relic or souvenir. The timber was then hacked to fragments and taken by the commissioners, on 16th October, to the King's Estate and Manor House, where they took up lodging in order to start the meticulous work of accounting for the property of the deceased.

Captains Crook, Hart, Cockaine and Carelesse were the men responsible, and with their messenger Captain Roe, their secretary Mr Brown, and two or three servants whose names have not survived, they happily took up residence. The royal bedchamber and adjoining withdrawing room were converted into a dormitory and kitchen; the Presence Chamber was where they conducted their business and held their meetings, the Council Hall became a brewhouse and beer-cellar, and the grand dining room was turned into a log store, filled with the hewed remains of the ancient King's Oak.

Having so thoroughly taken residence, the captains settled in for a well-earned rest in the newly defaced grandeur of the once-royal bedchamber. All went off merrily, bellies full of fine beer from the Council Hall, toes warmed by fire from the burning of the venerable oak. The next day, they woke and set about the business of their stay, as the servants finished setting up their offices and accommodation. Later they went to sleep, much as they had the night before. Initially.

In the middle of the night, they woke to violent knocking at the door of the bedchamber.

The men were gripped with a paralysing fear as, unseen in the pitch black, they heard the knocking stop, the handle turn, the door open and something enter the room. They lay awake, each of them, barely able to breath as the thing stepped heavy and loud about the bedchamber, pacing around the space for half an hour before stopping.

The beds they had salvaged from the rest of the house were large four-poster ones, and they slept in them two to a bed with the curtains down – more like tents than what we think of as beds. It was immediately outside the bed of Captains Hart and Carelesse that the heavy steps had stopped.

Writing this almost 400 years later, I can only imagine what might have been going through the minds of Carelesse and Hart as this unfolded. Being civil servants, of course, the men kept meticulous note of the events that would unfold, and it is thanks to the detailed journal they dictated that I can tell you all that I am about to so clearly. Though the material occurrences are described explicitly, the emotional trauma that resulted can be glimpsed only in the margins.

The thing that had stopped at the bed then crept beneath it. Though it behaved in the manner of a dog, it had the look of some strange bear, and was of a size far greater than either. From under the bed, it began to gnaw and bite at the structure from beneath, tearing and rending at the feather bedding itself. After an interminable period, the gnawing stopped. It was then that the bed was heaved up on one side, held a while, then dropped to the ground. And again. And again. Each time higher than before, sometimes one side, sometimes the other.

On and on this went for half an hour, until suddenly it stopped, and the thing moved on from Carelesse and Hart to crawl beneath the servants' bed and do likewise, and then on to do the same to all who lodged in the withdrawing room. After more than two hours, the creature walked out as it had come in, slamming the door loudly, with inhuman strength. Throughout this time, not a single one of the nine men had said a thing, and each bed assumed itself to be the only one so assaulted.

Come morning light, the men told each other their experiences. They checked the beds and found the mats scratched, but the bed-cords whole. There was talk of it being a wild animal that had gained access somehow, but the quarts of beef stored in the kitchen area remained untouched, though fully accessible.

The next night was worse.

Just as before, they were woken in the wee small hours. They heard the great clefts of the King's Oak dragged about and slammed down. They heard them roll, heavy about the room. They heard the chairs and stools tossed about and thrown, and after an hour of torment they heard the great, bear-like thing enter the withdrawing room, where lodged Mr Brown, the secretary, two of the captains and two of the servants. The creature paused for breath.

The creature screamed.

It stalked on into the bedchamber, and under the beds again it went, and again did heave them up, and again. And those in the beds clung tight to the bed posts to save themselves from falling into its arms. The beast lifted the bed in its entirety and rocked them like a cradle, shaking them hard for nigh on half an hour. It returned then to the withdrawing room and did likewise to the others, standing at the foot of the bed and heaving it up and letting it drop, and again, and again, hoisting it so high that those inside near fell out, head first.

After two hours of this, the thing exited as it had before; slamming shut the door with a mightier force than any living thing.

These visitations were repeated without relenting. The next night it stamped so hard about the bedchamber that the room itself shook, and it beat a brass warming pan from the withdrawing room 'as loud and scurvy as five untuned bells rang backwards'. According to the account we have, the captains affected strained humour at 'the Devil in the pan'.

The next night, the contents of the house flew about, smashing into walls and going through from one room to another then back again, as if thrown. Captain Hart was grabbed at the shoulder and shaken awake, then hit in the head with a trencher of bread until he and all the others hid beneath their sheets as more trenchers flew about the room – when Hart peeked out again, he was bombarded with them. (Trenchers, for those who don't know, are edible plates made of hard-baked bread, and not something you want hurled at your face with force.)

The next morning, they found their trenchers, pots and spits strewn about the floor, and dents and gouges covering the walls as if beaten with hammers. Still the captains stayed. Every night grew worse, and the full diary (which I shall not repeat here) is worth reading. Suffice it to say that the feigned humour soon dissipated, and the fear and distress of the captains became overwhelming, though still they tried to complete their work.

Meanwhile, the great monster nightly was seen or heard stamping and stalking about the rooms, hurling things about. The wood of the King's Oak took on a life of its own, flying about the heads of the servants, sometimes while lit.

On the 25th of October, a lawyer named Richard Crook arrived but was so startled that he fled the next day. Night by night, events intensified. On the 28th, each captain in turn found himself crushed by an unseen force, in something like sleep paralysis, one after the other, while each in turn grabbed a sword and ran to the next to try and help him, as fires were blown out and terrible blows were heard on the roof and stones hurled about the house by invisible forces.

Finally, they persuaded their Ordinary Keeper to lodge with them, and to do so with his large dog, a mastiff bitch, for protection – the first night with the dog (29th) there was no disturbance at all. They woke confident and relieved, and went to bed on the 30th certain that all was over, and that they would not need the Ordinary Keeper to bring his mastiff back.

All was not over.

About midnight, 'something knocked at the door as with a [black]smith's great hammer ... with such force as if it had cleft the door'. There then entered, once again, 'something like a bear' that 'seemed to swell more big and walked about the room, and out of one room [and] into the other; treading so heavily, as the floor had not been strong enough to bear it'. For the next two hours the beast smashed the room, attacked the beds and hurled glass and other objects at the captains. The night was the worst it had been, and come the morning they began to discuss leaving permanently, though as they still had work to carry out they eventually settled on one final push – they would bring the mastiff back, and more people to lodge with them as protection. They resolved to try another night.

So it was, that everything reached its peak on All Hallows Eve:

> **Octob. 31.** This night, the fires and lights prepared, the Ordinary Keeper and his bitch, with another man persuaded by him, they all took their beds, and fell asleep. But, about 12 at night, such rapping was on all sides of them, that it wakened all of them. As the doors did seem to open, the Mastive bitch fell fearfully a yelling, and presently ran fiercely into the bed to them in the truckle bed.

As the thing came by the table, it struck so fierce a blow on that, as that it made the frame to crack; then took the warming pan from off the table and stroke it against the walls with so much force as that it was beat flat together, lid and bottom; now were they hit as they lay covered over head and ears within the bedclothes; Captain *Carelesse* was taken a sound blow on the head with the shoulder blade-bone of a dead Horse (before, they had been but thrown at when they peept up, and mist,) Brown had a shrewd blow on the leg with the back bone, and another on the head; and everyone of them felt severall blows of bones and stones through the bed clothes, for now these things were thrown as from an angry hand that meant further mischief; the stones flew in at the window as if shot out of a Gun, nor was the bursts lesse (as from without) than of a Cannon, and all the windows broken down.

Now, as the hurling of the things did cease, and the thing walkt up and down, Captains *Cockaine* and *Hart* cried out, *In the Name of the Father, Son and Holy Ghost, What are you? what would you have? what have we done that you disturb us thus?* No voice replied (as the Captains said, yet some of their servants have said otherwise) and the noise ceast. Hereupon Captains *Hart* and *Cockaine* rose, who lay in the Bed-chamber, renewed the fire and lights, and one great candle in a candlestick they placed in the door, that might be seen by them in both the rooms; no sooner were they got to bed, but the noise arose on all sides more loud and hideous than at any time before, in so much (as to use the Captain's own words) it returned and brought seven Devils worse than itself; and, presently, they saw the candle and candlestick in the passage of the door, dasht up to the roof of the room, by a kick of the hinder parts of a Horse, and after, with the Hoof trod out the snuffe, and so dasht out the Fire in the Chimnies.

As this was done, there fell, as from the sieling, upon them in the Truckle beds, such quantities of water, as if it had been poured out of Buckets, which stunk worse than any earthly stink could make. And, as this was in doing, something crept under the High Beds, tost them up to the roof of the House, with the Commissioners in them, until the Testers of the Beds were beaten down upon them, and the Bedsted-frames broke under them. And here, some pause being made, they all, as if with one consent, started up, and ran down the stairs until they came into the Counsel-Hall, where two sate up a Brewing, but were now fallen asleep; those they scared much with wakening of them, having been much perplext before with the strange noise, which commonly was taken by them abroad for thunder, sometimes for rumbling wind; here the Captains and their company got

> fire and candle, and everyone carrying something of either, they returned into the Presence-Chamber, where some applied themselves to make the fire, whilst others fell to Prayers, and, having got some clothes about them, they spent the residue of the night in singing Psalms and Prayers; during which, no noise was in that room, but most hideously round about, as at some distance.
>
> It should have been told before, how that when Captain *Hare* first rose this night (who lay in the Bed-Chamber next the fire) he found their Book of valuations crosse the embers smoaking, which he snacht up, and cast upon the Table there, which, the night before, was left upon the Table in the presence, amongst their other papers. This Book was, in the morning, found a handful burnt, and had burnt the Table where it lay; *Brown* the Clerk said, he would not for a 100 and a 100l. that it had been burnt a handful further.
>
> This night it happened that there were six Cony-stealers, who were come with their Nets and Ferrets to the Cony-burrows by *Rosamond's* Well, but with the noise this night from the Mannor-house, they were so terrified, that, like men distracted, away they ran, and left their Haies all ready pitched, ready up, and the Ferrets in the Cony-burrows.

Finally, the men fled. They moved their belongings to the rooms above the gatehouse, where they stayed a single night. According to the reports:

> They were also the same night much affrighted with dreadful apparitions ... the Gate-keepers wife was in so strange an agony in her bed, and in her bed-chamber such noise (whilest her husband was above with the Commissioners) that two maids in the next room to her, durst not venture to assist her, but affrighted ran out to call company, and their Master, and found the woman (at their coming in) gasping for breath: And the next day said that she saw and suffered that, which for all the world she would not be hired to again.

The commissioners left Woodstock the following morning. A few plucked up the courage to return the next Sunday to correct some errors in their book of valuations. They were visited much as before.

Captain Cook joined them on the Tuesday:

> ... and how he sped that night the gate keepers wife can tell if she dareth, but what she hath whispered to her gossips, shall not be made a part of

> this our Narrative, nor many more particulars which have fallen from the Commissioners themselves and their servants to other persons; they are all or most of them alive, and may add to it when they please, and surely have not a better way to be revenged of him who troubled them, then according to the Proverb, tell truth and shame the Devill.

None of the men, from Wednesday onwards, ever set foot there again. Though many others, of a wide variety of backgrounds, beliefs and sensibilities, would go on to stay in the same rooms, none experienced any hint of the devilling that had befallen the surveyors. The structure itself was badly damaged during the remainder of the Civil War and the ruins were torn down in 1723, after Blenheim Palace had been constructed nearby.

The first published account of these extraordinary events was the extended verse, *The Woodstock Scuffle; or Most Dreadfull Apparitions that were lately seene in the Mannor-House of Woodstock, neere Oxford, to the great Terror and Wonderful Amazement of all there, that did Behold them*, from 1649. It's worth noting that this poetic version works well as a subversive Royalist folk song, and was likely composed and published (during the Interregnum itself) to be performed as such.

The case was outlined in further detail after the Restoration, in its own pamphlet of 1660/61 by Thomas Widowes (posthumously). We have it given in yet more detail, including diary entries, in Robert Plot's *Natural History of Oxfordshire* (1677), then again in the *Saducismus Triumphatus* by Jon Glanville (1700).

In April 1747, almost 100 years after the original events, a long submission appeared in *The British Magazine*, which appears to debunk them totally. Titled 'The Genuine History of the good Devil of Woodstock, famous in the world, in the year 1649, and never accounted for, or at all understood to this time', the anonymous author of the piece claims to have recently discovered a handwritten manuscript titled the '*Authentic Memoirs of the Memorable Joseph Collins of Oxford, commonly known by the name of Funny Joe, and now intended for the press*'. He claims that he is soon to publish the book in its entirety, and that among its pages he's found a section in which 'Funny Joe' claims to have been responsible for the hoax:

> Joseph Collins, commonly called Funny Joe, was himself this very devil;– that, under the feigned name of Giles Sharp, he hired himself as a servant to the Commissioners;–that by the help of two friends–an unknown trapdoor in the ceiling of the bedchamber, and a pound of common

> gunpowder—he played all these extraordinary tricks by himself;—that his fellow-servants, whom he had introduced on purpose to assist him, had lifted up their own beds; and that the candles were contrived, by a common trick of gunpowder, to be extinguished at a certain time.
>
> The dog who began the farce was, as Joe swore, no dog at all, but truly a bitch, who had shortly before whelped in that room, and made all this disturbance in seeking for her puppies; and which, when she had served his purpose, he (Joe Sharp, or Collins) let out, and then looked for. The story of the hoof and sword he himself bore witness to, and was never suspected as to the truth of them, though mere fictions. By the trapdoor his friends let down stones, fagots, glass, water, etc., which they either left there, or drew up again, as best suited his purpose; and by this way let themselves in and out, without opening the doors, or going through the keyholes, and all the noises, described, he declares he made by placing quantities of white gunpowder over pieces of burning charcoal, on plates of tin, which, as they melted, exploded with a violent noise.

The letter goes on to claim that Funny Joe further admitted to having used his advanced knowledge of chemistry (of a type unknown in 1649 but more widely understood by 1747) to create a number of other illusions with gunpowder and advanced fireworks.

This explanation, appearing almost a century late, was accepted and embraced almost universally and taken at face value as objective fact. Any mention of the Devil of Woodstock in print today explains condescendingly that the whole thing was a hoax by that famous Joseph Collins, and oh what silly fools those olden-timey folk were to believe it.

Joseph Collins does not appear in any contemporary Oxfordshire birth, marriage or death records. There is no reference to him or to Funny Joe anywhere in the written record outside of this one letter. The supposed memoirs were never published and do not survive in any archive.

If you analyse the explanations given, issues arise. Supposedly, a secret trap door in the ceiling not only existed but was kept secret from all, before and since, except for Funny Joe (how did he know of it?). It was unnoticed even by the building surveyors whose entire job and purpose was to inspect, survey and value properties, and is not mentioned in their survey (which survives).

Supposedly, all of the servants were in on it, meaning they were all local and all friends of Funny Joe, who used a fake name, even though the surveyors were not local and would not have known him. Why? Did his accomplices use fake names too? Why? The fact that nearby poachers ('cony catchers') also bore witness is unexplained (surely, if all of Lucky Joe's friends were in on it and acting as servants then word would have got around beforehand?)

The giant bear-dog hybrid monster is explained as simply a regular dog, but one behaving strangely as she had given birth in the room the previous day – but the surveyors had been there for two days by then. The bizarre addition of extra details not included in the original accounts, which are then explained by (then) modern chemistry, seems an obvious straw man argument – and how Joe could have made such advanced scientific discoveries (and never revealed them to anyone, or sought to profit from them) is completely unexplained. Various other details, such as sleep paralysis and invisibility, likewise remain completely ignored.

Finally, and perhaps most prosaically, the phrase 'for the press', in the sense it is used in the title of the supposed memoirs, was slang that only began to be used in the 1680s. If Funny Joe was at least 20 when the Republicans took over in the Interregnum (had he been any younger, he'd not have been likely to hold any great loyalty to the old regime), and about 30 when the Woodstock events occurred, he would have been into his 60s when 'for the press' began to be used in that sense. This seems an unlikely linguistic innovation for an elderly (by the standards of the time) man, and it is more likely to have been phraseology of the letter writer himself in 1747.

The strange conclusion seems to be that the letter debunking the haunting is, itself, a hoax. Alas, the hardest cynic will happily believe complete and obvious flim-flammery so long as it supports their cynicism, and thus it has been accepted uncritically ever since.

Sir Walter Scott published his own story inspired by the tale, *Woodstock, or The Cavalier. A Tale of the Year Sixteen Hundred and Fifty-one*, in 1826. This ensured the story's survival, though it is little known today. A detailed introduction, discussing the sources and including large reproductions of the original texts, appears as a preface in editions from 1832 onwards. I recommend it as further reading.

The tale of the first Halloween haunted house contains far more questions than answers. I am glad. Good confusion always beats bad explanation, though few enough see things this way, and as a rule, tawdry explanations are embraced enthusiastically so long as they allow preconceptions to go unchallenged. This is something we will see repeatedly in the stories this book contains, starting with the chapter that follows.

6

THE RICHMOND GHOSTS

Let's discuss a distinction between two types of story in this book. Some are tales of terrible acts at All Hallows Eve – deeds so striking they burned themselves into the season when first they were carried out and so became entwined with it, producing ghosts which haunt the Hallowtide as memorial to what has come before, be they victim, perpetrator or both. Others, like the Devil of Woodstock, are different; these are hauntings without a clear, worldly origin or instigator. These are ghosts and beings who were born of Hallowmas itself, and begin life as an explicit encounter, with any story or explanation coming second – they were not entwined with the season, but grew from it directly. These are the sort that most often get dismissed as hoaxes, in part because the lack of any origin story makes them essentially inexplicable (odd as it may seem, a clear narrative is usually enough to satisfy people, even if they remain cynical of theactual events within it).

So it is with the Richmond Ghost. Or one of them, at least.

Much as we take the credulity of olden times folk for granted, in the majority of historical accounts the first presumption is scepticism. People know what bedsheets and shadows are, and in the past were far more used to the flickerings produced by firelight than you or I, and far less likely to be gulled by them. Just as many enjoy stories of ghosts, and just as many more believe them, when an encounter is thrust upon the public, just as many people are desperate to believe that there's a good, solid earthbound explanation at the bottom of it.

It is likely for this reason that, lacking a narrative of its own, the baseless 'explanation' for the Devil of Woodstock has been grasped at so uncritically and by so many. Most people do not want their perceptions challenged or their world views rocked. When an excuse to dismiss comes along, which allows them to maintain unaltered the view that's served them thus far, more often than not, they will take it.

The vast majority believe or disbelieve based on bias and prejudice. Either they automatically believe accounts of hauntings because they long ago committed to believing in ghosts, or alternatively, their logic rigidly goes that 'there is no such thing as ghosts, therefore it is not a ghost, therefore it is a hoax' – both conclusions will be reached regardless of context or evidence.

As it is almost impossible to prove a negative, and as most sightings are long past the potential of any real investigation, such hauntings can be termed 'Schrodinger's ghosts' – as the reality of them is purely experiential and subjective. Until the point that they are proved unambiguously to be either genuine or fake, they exist simultaneously as both real and unreal, both prankster and spirit. True to those who believe, untrue to those who disbelieve, with neither position rooted in anything beyond the self.

Speaking of ghost sightings in these terms allows us to put to one side the messy matter of truth or fiction and to take an account on its own merits. It also allows those with a predisposition in either direction to suspend their belief or disbelief and focus on the story as we have it. We can acknowledge compelling evidence and dismiss shoddy theories, regardless of the directions such things may point in, as we are no longer discussing the nature of objective reality or life after death – merely the quirk of a Schrodinger's ghost.

A particularly good example of a Schrodinger's ghost can be found in the Halloween season of 1801, in the town of Richmond in Surrey, today a suburb of Greater London. The astute among you will notice parallels with the infamous and far better-known Spring-Heeled Jack, who would first appear to terrorise London thirty-six years later, at Christmas of 1837. But Richmond's ghost is a Halloween ghost, and blazed the trail that would later be followed by Jack and many others.

Unlike at Woodstock, initially this was a case of an itinerant haunting – a traveller-botherer, or spectral visitant, who came to houses door to door as trick-or-treaters do, rather than being restricted to a single dwelling place. This is an extremely obscure case, barely spoken or written of today (indeed, it may not have been written about at all), though it caused a severe stir two and a bit centuries ago. It unfurled, as I have said, towards the end of October 1801.

The first mention I can find is in the *Morning Post* of 28th October that year, where we are excitedly informed that 'the inhabitants of Richmond, in Surrey, have been for some time in a state of alarm at the appearance of a ghost in that neighbourhood, which shews itself to several persons under a variety of forms'.

The 'variety of forms' is an interesting element, as the article goes on to describe two very different ghosts that, for some reason, have been assumed to be the same creature in different guises – why they are not considered to be two separate beings is never specified (ghosts, after all, are often like buses – you wait ages for one, then two come at once). The first 'is all black, with a long tail, bearing the human form', while the second 'appears in white, with black face and black hands' – the article implies multiple encounters with both forms, but does not specify which in the brief selection that follows:

> To one lady it appeared a few nights since at her bed-chamber window, on a moonlit night; the church bell was at the moment striking the hour of twelve. The lady was found by the servants (whom she had called to her assistance by ringing the bell) in a swoon, and was with difficulty restored to her senses. A young girl, walking near the [Richmond] Theatre at a late hour, was tapped on the shoulder by the ghost; she was so much frightened as to be confined to her bed ever since. Two ladies and a gentleman were walking by the water side on Friday evening last, when one of the ladies suddenly exclaimed, 'There it is now!' This exclamation had such an effect on the gentleman, that the ladies, notwithstanding their fright, were obliged to support the gentleman to the town, or he would have fainted.

The paper goes on to tell us that 'the town is all in confusion, and two guineas reward has actually been offered to any one who can discover the ghost'. That's approximately £200 today, so certainly worth exchanging gossip for; and so, it seems, was the case, as the article concludes by telling us that 'a lady, an inhabitant of the place, has left it in consequence of one of her sons being accused of *knowing the ghost*'.

Things apparently continue, and the Richmond ghost quickly becomes the talk of the chattering classes. The wry and gossipy society paper, *The Porcupine* of 30th October comments that 'the Richmond Ghost [occupies] so much of the conversation of our females and fashionable *petits maitres*, that they can scarcely find time to say their prayers'. The article goes on to refer to the 'two guineas reward for the discovery of the *Ghost with a Black Tail*'.

The *London Courier* confirms that, as of 7th November, 'The *Richmond Ghost* continues to excite much alarm in that neighbourhood', but by Martlemas Eve, circumstances had, according to the *Oracle and Daily Advertiser* of 10th November, 'completely *exorcised* the *Richmond Ghost*, who now lies (as the Village Gossips say) buried in the Red Sea "full fathom five"'.

The full story of the ghost's undoing (and consequent loss of Schrodingeral status) is given at the end of the month in the *London Courier* on 28th November, where it's referred to as 'The Kew and Richmond Ghost', and we are told of a subtly different modus operandi:

> The neighbourhood of Kew has of late been extremely alarmed by the report of a ghost having been seen in different places about the fields, whose nocturnal visits to the pale glimpses of the moon excited such terror, particularly among the females, that hardly one could be prevailed on to stir out at night, the spectre, all in deadly white, being sure to meet them at some convenient gate or turning: those who did not believe in such supernatural appearances very properly resolved to detect the imposition, and for the better doing it, offered [£20] reward [given in the original text as '20l.', this is probably an exaggeration rather than a genuinely increased reward from the 2 guineas already mentioned] to any person that would apprehend the ghost, either alive or dead; when lo! a few evenings since, a labouring man, defying the Devil himself, seized the spectre, who, as a proof of his being corporeal, offered the man [£40] to let him go; but this was refused, and on an investigation taking place, it appears that the imposter is the son of a gentleman in that vicinity, who had clothed himself in a white sheet, to carry on the farce; a custom that would certainly be more 'honoured in the breach than the observance.

That seems to be the mystery solved, though an unnamed 'son of a gentleman' is an extremely common (and completely un-evidenced) explanation for such things, often given when no other materialises. This is quite aside from the fact that a young man in a white sheet (presumably his face and hands would have to be painted black, though this is not specified) hardly explains the sightings of the other form – a black, humanoid figure with a long tail and nothing white at all.

Though this is the last mention I can find of the ghost of 1801, it would not be the last haunted Hallowmas for Richmond. A little over a century later, in the Halloween season of 1903, things began once again to go bump in the night.

Known today as The Duke, on Duke Street, back then the pub was called the Cobwebs Hotel (before that it had been The Grapes), and was famous for the thick spiders' webs that festooned the bar and the huge vine that grew through the roof, on which various objects, including skeletal hands (apparently genuine), shoes and other remnants of executed criminals were hung.

It sounds fantastic.

According to the *Portsmouth Evening News* of 24th August 1904, it was at the end of October in 1903 when 'mysterious tappings and noises were heard [in the hotel …] and strange lights appeared in the dead of night'. The phenomena intensified throughout Allhallowstide, and on into Christmas and the New Year, to the extent that the decision was made to close the more than 300-year-old inn and rebuild much of it, expanding the property into a more recently built adjoining one and retaining only a small portion of the original structure.

This made matters worse.

The ghost, it seems, did not appreciate the building work – the strange sounds and mysterious lights soon began in the new premises, louder and more frequently than before. And it didn't end there. According to the report of the landlord, Mr George Luff, as quoted in the article a few months after the move:

> There have been a lot of mysterious noises here in the night lately […] This house has three floors. The second consists of drawing, sitting and dining-rooms, and the third is used for sleeping purposes. About two o'clock on Monday morning [21st August] we were all frightened nearly to death by hearing piercing shrieks proceeding from the second floor, and as I went down to investigate I saw mysterious reflections of light here and there. I called to my manager, who had hurriedly jumped out of bed, and we went carefully through all the rooms, but failed to find anything out of the ordinary. Whilst we were searching a loud knocking came to the front door, and when I went down I found a policeman who had heard the shrieks, and who wanted to know what was the matter.
>
> Near here there is a tradesman who employs a number of young ladies, who sleep on the premises, and they heard the noise, and hurried to the windows, which command a view of this house. They saw a blue light and a white figure moving about, they say, in my front room, and their mistress afterwards came to me and complained that her girls had been frightened by a ghost on my premises. After my previous experience in the old house […] I began to regard the thing seriously, and I have placed the matter in the hands of the police.

The piece goes on to confirm the landlord's story, and that 'some of the young ladies were very much scared. They generally agreed that the apparition was clothed in white, and appeared to be carrying a powerful lamp or light.

It was only visible for a few minutes, but said one young lady, the screams were piercing.'

The manager gave his own account in an interview with the *London Evening News* of the same date:

> Twice shortly after midnight, just when I had gone asleep, I have awakened to hear noises such as I have never heard before in my life. They are sounds which are so foreign to any experience that I have had, that it is impossible for me to describe them.
>
> I have found myself in a cold sweat shivering all over. As soon as my eyes have become accustomed to the darkness, I have realised that there was someone in the room besides myself. I have waited, restless, not daring to speak, to see what would happen next.
>
> Presently something has stolen out of the gloom and flourished brilliant lights in my face. Then a wild non-human being has gradually appeared. Spellbound, I have not dared to move.
>
> Screeching and moaning, it has wandered round the room and then vanished. I have then got out of bed, searched the room all over, rushed down into the vault, and explored every nook and corner, but all to no purpose.
>
> The only theory I have to explain for the presence of the ghost is that it is the wraith of the sailor who many years ago was robbed and murdered in this inn. It is either his ghost or that of Kate Webster, whose hand hangs up in the back room. Kate, you know, murdered her mistress in Richmond by boiling her in a copper, and then heaving her body over into the Thames.

The piece cites George Luff as confirming the manager's story, and mentions that 'the other night Mrs. Luff, the landlord's wife, left alone to herself, was nearly terrified to death by the screeches'. It tells us the 'strange affair has caused a sensation in the district, and curious crowds are flocking all day to the hotel'.

The news spread rapidly, and the Cobwebs Hotel was soon so inundated with people hoping to see the ghost that the landlord came to regret having said anything to the paper at all, and began actively debunking the sightings to the many who asked him about it, in hopes of discouraging the attention. By the following day, reports that the ghost was fictitious had been enthusiastically disseminated, far too widely to be by chance. The *Portsmouth Evening News* of 25th August 1904, reported:

> The ghost which was alleged to have been seen at a house in Richmond on Monday morning has not, so far as can be gathered, put in a reappearance. The residents of the house, or those of them who had nerve enough, sat up on Monday and Tuesday nights, in the hope of solving the mystery, but they were disappointed.
>
> Meanwhile those who live in the neighbourhood are sceptical, and the opinion is held by some that the 'ghost' had its origin in a practical joke on the part of some high-spirited individual anxious to provide a little amusement. The police are keeping an extra watch on the house for anyone who may be anxious to repeat the 'joke'.

The *Morning Leader* of the same day was more forceful in its debunking, and crowed gleefully that the ghost had been 'killed by cold print':

> All yesterday the new Cobwebs Hotel was stared at by visitors and residents; and the bar attendants, the manager, and the landlord were plied with questions.
>
> It was more in sorrow than in anger that the last-named, Mr. Luff, was heard to reply to the forty-fifth inquirer that the rats, disturbed from their long tenure of a portion of the old Cobwebs, must have been guilty of the piercing shrieks which startled the household early on Monday morning.
>
> It might have been rats alone, or rats in collaboration with their natural enemies, the cats. It is well known that noises of a very human description are frequently heard from these creatures.
>
> During Sunday night and Monday morning (when the ghost 'appeared') plateleyers were busy on the line from Richmond to St. Margaret's; and the air carried the sound of their blows, as of the firing of guns, just across Richmond-green to Quadrant-rd.
>
> Poor ghost – R.I.P.!

The oddly smug tone of this rather vague explanation implies the case is closed, but rodents and railway workers hardly seem to account for eyewitness reports of spectral figures and blue lights, or for any of the events of the preceding ten months (not to mention the fact that neither cats nor rats are at all 'well known' for sounding like humans). This theory was taken a step further in the *Eastern Evening News* of the same date:

> The ghost that has been harrowing Richmond with fear and wonder will harrow it no longer, for it appears that the spook at the Old Cobwebs Inn,

> Richmond, has been laid by the heels. As far as the 'noises' are concerned, Mr. Luff, the landlord, has many explanations. Sounds have been heard at night, he admits. But the old house that stood on the site of the present gorgeous structure was pestered with rats, which have, in all probability, moved next door. Here, therefore, is another explanation.
>
> It is further suggested that the 'screechings' may be just the midnight communings of several owls that haunt a barn at the back of the public-house. On the other hand, a neighbouring parrot of mischievous tendencies is being charged with the disturbances, and, taken altogether, there is every reason to suppose that the ghost is nothing but a conglomeration of the noises of the night which, what with owls, rats, and banging doors, are not conducive to sleep.

On the same date, the *Daily Mirror* posted an entirely different and even more tenuous explanation, but with an equal amount of patronising certainty and snide derision for any who dared maintain curiosity in the ghost:

> Here is the probable explanation. Next door to the Cobwebs Hotel building operations are taking place. A house, half erected, stands surrounded with its heavy scaffolding. The noise was occasioned, it is thought, by a heavy beam falling.
>
> The strange, ghostly light and the unearthly creaking was nothing supernatural. It was simply a heavy coffee stall, with ungreased wheels being pushed along the narrow and somewhat uneven road.
>
> The coffee stall was surmounted by a brilliant lamp, and its flickering rays shone into the windows of the dark street, to an accompaniment of groans and squeaks on the part of the wheels.
>
> If the startled young ladies really saw a ghostly figure it was probably that of the manager of the hotel, who got up in his night garments to see what all the noise was about.

If indeed it was a hoax, I would assume that none of these contradictory explanations are entirely correct (from stray parrots to ungreased coffee stalls), even if elements of them may be, and posit that the manager most likely spread the fictitious story for increased publicity after the rebuild (perhaps the punters had not been flocking to the new premises as much as they had the more characterful original), but the extra attention was immediately regretted by the landlord, who then actively persuaded papers to nip it in the bud (note how the *Eastern Evening News* takes care to emphasise how 'gorgeous' the new structure is).

The wrinkles in this, of course, are that the manager's account of witnessing a ghost is so accurate a description of a sleep paralysis hallucination that it is unlikely to have been entirely made up, and the girls across the street are not likely to have been in on it, even if it was. Either way, none of the theories offered for debunking seem compelling enough to fully explain it away, and the ghost remains in Schrodinger's clutches.

No more is written of the Cobwebs Hotel's brief reputation of haunting, but nevertheless, there is a third act to our drama.

On Halloween of 2005, three teenagers were walking through Richmond. On their way to a house party, they had just come out of the tube station when a strange figure appeared about 100 yards in front of them, stock still, and with its back awkwardly turned. The figure 'to start with was sort of all in white, but then that got really bright and everything was blue, but then that died down and faded like it was all a light, and then he was all just in black in, like, a hood'.

I spoke to one of the three, who wishes to remain anonymous, in September of 2023. He told me that the strangest thing about the figure was how transfixed they all were, unable to take their eyes off it; that though they didn't realise it at first, while the figure was present they saw nobody else – no cars, passers-by, shopkeepers, revellers – nothing. On Halloween night of 2005, Richmond could not possibly have been so deserted.

After a brief time the black, caped figure turned strangely, but did not show a face, and then disappeared. At this instant they heard an ungodly, terrifying scream that lasted longer than seemed possible, then the streets returned to their usual bustle and the three boys blinked at each other, astonished at what they'd seen, terrified at what they'd heard. They hurried on to the party, drank some courage, and soon were convincing themselves it had just been a strange costume.

A girl at the party apparently overheard them, grabbing my informant by the arm, looking him in the eye and asking him directly, 'Did you see it too? Did it scream?'

After a pause he simply replied, 'Yes.'

The girl began to cry. When they asked her what the matter was, she showed them her arm, freshly bruised and badly scratched. 'It wouldn't let go', was all she would say. She left the party soon after. None of them knew her or saw her again, and all present were drunk.

Other sightings filtered amongst their friendship group over the following week, all similar to their own, with no further direct, physical encounters to match the unknown girl's. Some claimed to have seen it atop a local bonfire at Guy Fawkes Night, others, while on a bus home from school. After a couple of weeks nothing more was seen or heard, though the experience has stuck with my informant ever since.

He contacted me directly over social media, in response to a call-out I had posted asking for details of any first-hand accounts of the supernatural at Halloween. As you can well imagine, I received and receive a great deal of nonsense with these call-outs, and a lot of grandiose gibberish from people who simply want attention. I am well aware that this could all be a fiction, and I'm usually hesitant to take unsubstantiated, solo accounts seriously enough to include in a book, but there were a few things that stopped me from dismissing this as that.

First, the disturbing and very real fear that came over the man as he was telling me his story, patchy and vague as it was. Second, he claimed (and I believed him) to have no notion of any previous Richmond haunting – indeed, though there is the remotest of possibilities he may have come across the haunting at Cobwebs (it is mentioned briefly on one or two websites and in a book on haunted pubs), he could not have come across the ghost of 1801 unless he happened to have found it in the newspaper archives himself. The figure, both in white and in black, the bright blue light – while these are not entirely uncommon they are still distinctive, and the coincidence is worth noting. I made a point of mentioning nothing of these other stories to him, and of prompting nothing in his statement.

The road on which the tube station in Richmond sits is the Quadrant. It is just by the corner of Duke Street, where Cobwebs was, and around the corner from the Richmond Theatre, in the vicinity of which the ghost of 1801 was first seen. The Cobwebs ghost first appeared at Halloween exactly 102 years after the Halloween ghost of 1801. The most recent ghost first appeared, likewise, at Halloween – exactly 102 years after the one at Cobwebs. All of them were first encountered within just a few hundred yards of each other. Each was independent of the other, and none of the witnesses or reporters seem to have been aware of any of the other sightings.

If the pattern continues the ghost should next rear its head at Richmond in 2107 (I will not be there to see it, but perhaps you will). The most chilling of the coincidences is a description my informant gave me of his cloaked figure that I haven't shared with you yet.

He described it as having a long, black tail.

TRICK AND TREAT

7

GOODING, GUISING, SOULING AND TREATING

All elements of Halloween stem from death.

This is a fairly obvious statement where haunted houses and walking ghosts are concerned, but perhaps less so when we come to that cornerstone of the season, the trick-or-treat. Ask the average Halloween enjoyer today, and they'll tell you it's about sweets and plastic masks and dressing up and jollity, and (if pushed) that it's a fairly recent American thing that came over in the 1980s. A potential for pranks to go too far might exist, or for children to be scared by grotesque costumes (and the elderly by an increase in nocturnal visitors), but that's the extent of the custom's morbidity.

Nevertheless, the death is there for those who know how to look.

The practice of ritualised begging on holy days or festivals was widespread until very recently – today, the only large-scale, nationwide examples are at Christmas (carolling and mummers plays) and Halloween, with some other regional examples (such as pace egging at Easter in parts of northern England) and very little else. Until the middle of the twentieth century, however, there were many other examples – Clementing, on St Clement's Day (23rd November), Catterning on St Catherine's Day (25th November) and Thomasing on St Thomas Day (21st December). Today, these are extremely obscure, and generally, where practised, they're restricted to a small community or to a particular trade or special-interest group.

A broad term for such house-visitation practices is 'gooding', and all share a similar formula – a small ritual or simple rhyme, phrase or song performed in the doorway of a home in exchange for food, drink, coal, candles or money – a socially acceptable way of apportioning alms and charity without any accompanying stigma, embarrassment or wounded pride. Many of these gooding customs also incorporate costume, masking or other forms of disguise, in which case they're also referred to as 'guising' customs. While sometimes the person beneath the outfit is completely concealed, often the disguise is just a token costume or face paint, and does not really obscure the identity of the 'guiser' – Hutton tells us that in Uttoxeter in Staffordshire, the guisers were working men who 'went round pubs with blackened or reddened faces, performing a rhyme and passing round a hat for pennies', with similar guisers found in Hertfordshire, Bradford and elsewhere.

Nevertheless, the paint allowed a symbolic separation of the individual in that context, from the same individual in a day-to-day context, thus making such behaviour socially acceptable and giving others the opportunity (should it be necessary) to behave as if they did not recognise the guisers when out of costume – literally saving face for all concerned. In many communities, guising would have ceased to serve the function of literal disguise early on, if it ever did; costumes and masks are also fun, and it would be naïve to think that this wasn't a significant part of their appeal.

Guising customs exist in every country of the British Isles, and on many dates of the year – they are not exclusive to Halloween, nor to England. The term 'guising' simply refers to any gooding practice that involves a costume, much as 'fancy dress' refers to any form of costuming, and not specifically the costuming of Halloween. Many make the mistake of thinking that guising *became* trick-or-treat, but this is to misunderstand the term – rather, guising is a broad category that many seasonal customs fall under, not a specific seasonal custom like trick-or-treat.

There is, however, a clear precursor to and origin for trick-or-treating.

Just as the gooding traditions of St Clement's Day were Clementing, those of St Catherine's Day, Catterning, and those of Thomas's Day, Thomasing, so those of All Souls were known as Souling. 'Soulers' would travel from door to door and sing a song or chant a rhyme, both to announce their presence and to ask for a ritualised treat, often edible – originally, this treat was the triangular 'soul cake' (which we shall speak of further in the committed chapter), but over time it became commonplace to offer alternatives in the form of any food, drink, money or similar, with 'soul cake' often merely a metaphor or nickname for these seasonally appropriate alms.

As is usual with these sorts of folk practices, the rhymes collected from across England vary enormously in the details, but are generally based on recognisably similar core lines and structures. An indicative version recorded at many places in the nineteenth century goes:

Soul, a soul, a soul cake,
Please, good missus a soul cake
An apple, a pear, a plum or a cherry
Any good thing to make us all merry.

Here, the initial request for a soul cake has been followed with suggestions of alternative or additional donations that are also acceptable. By this time, it was commonplace for alternatives to be given, especially to adults – sometimes money, sometimes beer, sometimes fruit, depending on the circumstances of the household. This clear outlining of the proposed transaction neatly echoes that of the later phrase, 'trick or treat', and in other rhymes we can see that the connection to the original soul cakes has disappeared altogether, such as in this one from Staffordshire, as recorded in the *Folk-lore Journal* of December 1896:

Soul soul, for a apple or two
If ye've got no apples, pears'll do,
Up wi' the kettle and down wi' the pan.
Give us a big 'un, and we'll be gone.

The rising role of the apple here is worth noting, as apples were a common aspect of Hallowtide, due to their prevalence in late autumn. A completely fanciful and discredited idea, once popular, is that Halloween was an ancient Roman festival to the Goddess Pomona (a goddess of orchards). No evidence for any such festival exists, and though it used to be touted as an origin for Halloween, it's sheer hogswash; anyone who starts to tell you about it can be politely ignored in everything else they have to say.

Robert Hunt, in his 1902 *Popular Romances of the West of England*, tells us:

> The shops in Penzance would display Allan apples, which were highly polished large apples. On the day itself, these apples were given as gifts to each member of the family as a token of good luck. Older girls would place these apples under their pillows and hope to dream of the person whom they would one day marry. A local game is also recorded where two pieces of wood were nailed together in the shape of a cross. It was then suspended with 4 candles on each outcrop of the cross shape. Allan apples would then be suspended under the cross. The goal of the game was to catch the apples in your mouth, with hot wax being the penalty for slowness or inaccuracy. [...]

> The ancient custom of providing children with a large apple on Allhallows-eve is still observed, to a great extent, at St Ives. 'Allan-day', as it is called, is the day of days to hundreds of children, who would deem it a great misfortune were they to go to bed on 'Allan-night' without the time-honoured Allan apple to hide beneath their pillows. A quantity of large apples are thus disposed of the sale of which is dignified by the term Allan Market.

The practice certainly existed in the nineteenth century, and the selling of Allan apples is still conducted in Penzance, and very likely elsewhere.

Originally merely a gooding custom, souling began to incorporate costume and mask in various regions at least as early as the seventeenth and eighteenth centuries, and thereafter developed into a fully fledged form of guising in many parts of Britain – though, in others, it remained unmasked, and more akin to Christmas carolling. We can see this transition in many seasonal customs, and it is important to remember that there is rarely a hard line between guising and gooding, and most examples of one, sooner or later, will also provide examples of the other.

The earliest reference to something we can recognise as souling is from the late 1400s, in which soul-bread is the only foodstuff given out, and it is engaged in by those in need of alms. In other times and regions, it is practised mainly by women (especially widows and the elderly), and often in the nineteenth century either by children (which was generally considered sweet and positive) or by men (which was tutted at, as motivated by beer and debauchery).

An account of the latter, and of the dangers that the soulers could face which might encourage disguise, can be found in the *Norwich Mercury* of 19th November 1873:

> MR. REGINALD CORBETT, the master of the Cheshire Hounds, has been committed for trial on the charge of shooting a boy named Tomlinson. Mr. Corbett resides during the hunting season at Daleford, Delamere Forest, and on All Hallows' Eve, the 1st inst., a party of men and boys went to the hunting box of Mr. Corbett, and chanted a ditty about 'souling time.' They then commenced a glee, and it being near midnight, the defendant and some of his domestics went out of the house to expostulate with the 'soulers.' Two of them were chased off Mr. Corbett's premises into the high road, and the defendant called out that unless they stopped he would shoot them. As they did not stop, he fired, and shots struck Tomlinson on the leg.

The trial was reported in the *Sheffield Independent* on 28th November 1873:

> The trial of Mr. Henry Reginald Corbett, charged with having unlawfully and maliciously wounded John Tomlinson, labourer, at Marton, on the 1st inst., by shooting him, took place on Wednesday at the quarter sessions at Knutford. The facts that Mr. Corbett is highly connected, is a magistrate of Shropshire, and is master of the Cheshire hounds, imparted a great amount of interest to the case.
>
> John Tomlinson said he went along with some companions to Mr. Corbett's house on the night of the 1st of November, being All Souls' Eve, for the purpose of 'souling,' or serenading, in accordance with a local custom. After they had sung 'The Gentlemen of England,' they rang the bell, in order to obtain a contribution of money or refreshment. There was no answer, and they then started 'Now pray we for our country.' Having finished that song, they rang again, and in few minutes afterwards the door was thrown open, and Mr. Corbett and a number of other people rushed out, one of the party shouting out, 'Go at them.' Mr. Corbett had a gun in his hand, and overtaking one of the 'soulers,' who had fled in surprise, demanded what the devil they were doing. Their object was explained to him, whereupon he let go the man he had caught, and shouted. 'Run, run, or I'll shoot you.' Witness had by that time got outside Mr. Corbett's grounds, and was on the public highway. While standing there, he saw Mr. Corbett approach with his gun, and on being challenged to stop else he would be shot witness ran off, but had proceeded only a few yards when he heard the report of a gun, and felt that he was shot. He cried out, and then Mr. Corbett and one of his men came up, and led him back to the house. He had been receiving surgical attendance ever since. Mr. Corbett afterwards sent him £25, and said he would pay the doctor's bill.

The jury pronounced Corbett guilty of common assault. The verdict elicited applause from the court and the magistrates fined him £100, alongside taking sureties totalling £1,000 from Corbett and two others (presumably his staff) ensuring their good behaviour for twelve months.

This case well illustrates the regionally diverse nature of English Halloween practices, whereby rustic and working-class locals would consider their own customs so long established that it didn't occur to them that others may be unfamiliar, and incomers or outsiders could be so ignorant that they had no frame of reference that any customs might be occurring at all. It also offers useful evidence of at least two specific songs that were used, 'The Gentleman of England' and 'Now Pray we for our Country'. 'Now Pray we for our Country' is extant, written by A. Cleveland Cox (1818–96).

The 'Gentlemen of England' song is itself the 'ditty about souling time' – likely some variation on the traditional one that is recorded in many versions throughout the country. The most complete I've found was published in the *Northampton Mercury* of 1st December 1849. Take note of the first line:

You gentlemen of England pray you now draw near
To these few lines, and you soon shall hear
Sweet melody of music all on this evening clear,
For we are come a-souling for apples and strong beer.

Step down into your cellar, and see what you can find,
If your barrels are not empty we hope you will prove kind;
We hope you will prove kind with your apples and strong beer,
We'll come no more a-souling until another year.

Cold winter it is coming on, dark, dirty, wet, and cold;
To try your good nature, this night we do make bold;
This night we do make bold with your apples and strong beer,
And we'll come no more a-souling until another year.

All the houses that we've been at we've had both meat and drink,
So now we're dry with travelling, we hope you'll on us think;
We hope you'll on us think with your apples and strong beer,
For we'll come no more a-souling until another year.

God bless the master of this house and the mistress also,
And all the little children that round the table go;
Likewise your men and maidens, your cattle and your store,
And all that lies within your gates we wish you ten times more;
We wish you ten times more with your apples and strong beer,
And we'll come no more a-souling until another year.

I raise the case of Corbett and the soulers, not only as it gives an indication of the process of souling and the danger of outsiders reacting badly to localised customs, but also in relation to the following from the *Huddersfield Daily Examiner* on 11th March 1994:

> A WOMAN who threw a bowl of scalding water over an eight-year-old boy playing trick or treat was today ordered to pay him £750 compensation. Yin Yin Man, 34, originally from China but who now lives in Victoria Way, Huntington, York, was unaware of the Halloween tradition and thought she was seeing a 'ghost' when neighbour Daniel Cooper knocked on her front door wearing a spooky mask and fancy dress. Man admitted causing actual bodily harm at York magistrates court. As well as the compensation order she was given a conditional discharge for a year and ordered to pay £40 prosecution costs.

The more things change, the more they stay the same.

The process by which souling becomes trick-or-treating is an interesting one, and we shall explore it in more detail over the coming chapters. Though there is no glib, simple algorithm to explain it, it isn't so inexplicable as one might think, and I hope to make this and much more clear by the time we finish. Either way, we can take comfort from the fact that trick-or-treat, under various names, has been a part of the English Halloween for over 600 years, and that it shows no sign of waning.

Before we dig deeper into the dry facts, however, I think the time has come for another story. Are you sitting comfortably?

Then I'll begin.

8

LEST SOME THING SHOULD FETCH THEM

One particularly strange souling tale comes from the area around Cannock Chase in Staffordshire. Souling is a strongly held custom in those parts, and so it was that in 1824, on the brisk, bright afternoon of 1st November, three children went out from their home in Milford to spend an hour or two travelling door to door around the neighbouring farmsteads.

They were young, very young – two boys aged 4 and 6, and a girl aged 5. The trio wandered, as all children did, from house to house, singing the familiar chant on its opening. Milford was not a large place, and the children knew it well.

Hours later, they had disappeared.

The official story, as printed in the *Morning Advertiser* of 9th November 1824, goes as follows:

> STRAYED CHILDREN. – On Monday afternoon (the eve of All Souls), three children, a girl aged five, and two boys aged four and six, set out from the houses of their parents at Milford, near Stafford, on an expedition to the surrounding farm-houses, to beg for 'Soul-cakes,' or, as substitutes (so the young mendicants sing on such occasions), 'an apple, a pear, a plum, or a cherry,' according to the customary usage.
>
> As night came on without bringing home the little ramblers, their parents began to entertain fears for their safety, and made enquiries after them amongst their neighbours; but no tidings could be learnt; and hour after hour passed on, but no children appeared.

> A search on a more extended scale was then commenced by the parents, who continued roaming about after their lost offspring during the whole night, without discovering the least trace of them. In the morning they were joined by several neighbours, who, with the most laudable activity, took different routes, some over Cannock Chase, others to Rugely, Penkridge, Cannock, Stafford, &c. hoping to meet with the wanderers; nor, we are happy to state, were these benevolent exertions unavailing.
>
> About noon, the eldest boy was descried alone on Cannock Heath; he was in a pitiable state of exhaustation [*sic*], without one of his shoes, and he had walked about until his stocking foot had nearly worn away; he could not tell where his brother and the little girl were, for, said he, 'I left them in the night sleeping together on the ground, and I went to look for my lost shoe.'
>
> No doubt being entertained that the other two were somewhere on the heath, several neighbouring farmers sent their men to engage in the philanthropic task of seeking them. The number of persons scattered about the heath, including several women and two or three respectable farmers on horseback, was augmented to fifty; and about three o'clock one of the horsemen had the satisfaction to discover the two little creatures lying in each other's arms in an opening of the furze which surrounded and formed a sort of cradle for them.
>
> They were in an extremely debilitated state; and were unable to support themselves. On being asked why they had not made a noise and cried, they said, 'they durst not cry, lest some thing should fetch them.'
>
> The spot where they lay was near Hednesford, six or seven miles from their home, and two miles from where the eldest boy was found. If they had remained another night exposed to the weather, death would have been inevitable; the extremities of their bodies were already become benumbed, and their garments were thoroughly soaked with wet. It is needless to add, that the parents were overjoyed to receive the little fugitives again into their bosoms (whom they had given up for lost). We understand the two boys have regained their usual strength, but the little girl remains weak and poorly.

I met with Eric Bromley, a retired Stafford welder, back in 2019. He told me of his childhood before the war, and how his grandfather had known of an elderly local man who claimed to have been one of the two boys lost on Cannock Heath all those years ago.

The story the old man gave was a very different one to that in the paper.

As he told it, the souling had begun normally enough, with the young trio bouncing between the familiar farmsteads. It was then they caught glimpse of one they'd never seen before.

The strange house seemed just a little way further off, and appeared to glint in the distance as they walked towards it. On arrival at the grand building, they knocked at the great, tall green entrance and waited what seemed like an age.

The door swung wide, and there before them were the most beautiful people the children had ever seen, and when their souling song was sung they were applauded, and beckoned in to join the beautiful people in their feast. In went the children, deep into the house, whose corridors seemed to stretch on for longer than made sense, with half-heard hints of revelry echoing from the various rooms.

Finally they came to a large dining room, in which were all manner of richly dressed guests, all eating the finest of meats and the sweetest of fruits. The children were asked what they wanted most, and responded that they wanted their soul cakes.

The beautiful people stopped still and silent, and the elder boy was handed meat, which he took, hesitantly. The children were asked again what they wanted, and again replied that they wanted their soul cakes. The girl was given wine, and the children were again asked what they wanted. At this stage they had started to feel uneasy, and as the girl started to sip some of the sweet drink, for a third time the youngest boy told them that they wanted their soul cakes.

The people round the table started to scream.

But no longer were they beautiful. Shrivelled now, hunched and wrong. The food they ate no longer was rich nor sweet, but rotten and stale. The house, no longer tall and fine, grew earthen and dank about their ears.

The elder boy dropped his meat. The girl spat out her wine. The children ran.

They ran and they ran, through tunnels of filth, past weeping holes, until they found the green door, now merely a rough scrap of wood, but just as they went to burst through, one of the strange, withered people grabbed at the older boy's shoe, gripping him tight to pull him back down. The boy wrenched his foot free and off the three went, bursting out of a hole in the ground and running and running and running until it was safe to collapse.

The three roamed then, lost and confused, the boy hobbling, the girl growing ever sicker, the sounds of the strange people from the hole in the ground calling after them, begging them, offering treats and riches and

more besides. Though it had felt like they'd been there mere minutes, it was dark now, and cold, and seemed as if hours had passed.

Finally, they found their patch of furze, made a small bed and huddled together shivering. The rest is as the article gives it.

Though the children told their tale to anyone who'd listen, it was dismissed, understandably, as nonsense. They were never again allowed out souling, nor did they have any desire to.

Only once did they return to the mound they had fled from, at Allhallowstide the following year. They found it yawning open to them once more, and from within the barrow there shone an otherworldy light, beckoning, inviting. Though tempted, none of the three re-entered, and none of the three visited again.

While this could easily be the drink-fuelled fiction of a bored old man from 100 years ago, it contains too many archetypal fairy-tale tropes to ignore – the triple demand of soul cakes breaking the spell; the aesthetic illusions of fairyland; the strange passage of time; the subterranean dwelling; the fact that the boy who held the meat (but did not eat) lost a shoe in escaping, the girl who sipped wine but did not swallow grew sick, while the boy who did neither was fine – all fit with the legend that eating or drinking in fairyland keeps you stuck there forever; even the fact that the Cannock Chase area has a number of Bronze Age barrows and an Iron Age hillfort – earthworks that are known to connect with fairy lore.

Whether it is a tall tale from an elderly local who'd brushed up on obscure stories, a surviving piece of oral folklore dating back to the original event of 1824 or some combination of the two, this Cannock Chase tradition is now preserved, and you can draw conclusions at your leisure.

The Halloween relationship with fairies is something we'll revisit in due course. For now, let's focus on soul cakes.

9

SOUL, A SOUL, A SOUL CAKE

We've already mentioned the widespread soul-caking verse that goes:

Soul, a soul, a soul cake,
Please, good missus a soul cake
An apple, a pear, a plum or a cherry
Any good thing to make us all merry.

Often, however, the following lines were added:

One for Peter, two for Paul,
Three for Him who made us all.

According to some accounts, this addition was either saved for, or repeated on receipt of, an explicitly *triangular* soul cake, with the rhymer pointing to the different corners in turn as they counted through the three.

Historic descriptions have the cakes as coming in two main forms, either round or triangular, though there is also at least one reference to them being square. In Warwickshire (*Observations on Popular Antiquities*, John Brand, 1777) and Northamptonshire, they are referred to as a kind of seed cake (*Glossary of Northamptonshire Words and Phrases*, Anne Elizabeth Baker, 1854), in Yorkshire as small fruit cakes (*The Dialect of Mid-Yorkshire*, C. Clough Robinson, 1876) and as 'oat cakes' by Thomas Blount in his *Glossographia* of 1674.

Interestingly, while Francis Kildare Robinson in A *Glossary ... of Whitby, etc.* (1876) describes them as 'sets of square "farthing-cakes" with currants on top [...] given by bakers to their customers' (and mentions that 'it was a practice to keep some in the house for good luck'), George Young's *History of Whitby* (1817, p. 882) states that 'they are chiefly small round loaves, sold by the bakers at a farthing each, chiefly for presents to children. In former times, it was usual to keep one or two of them for good luck; a lady in Whitby had a soul-mass loaf about 100 years old.' This gives us a vague idea of their development in one locality over around sixty years, whereby the form and composition may change, while the core concept and practice remain relatively static.

Soul cakes, then, are usually round, though historically were triangular, and can sometimes be found square. Confusing. In terms of content, there are three main varieties evidenced, that of the seed cake, the oat cake or the fruit cake. The Folklore Society's fairly definitive 1940 *British Calendar Customs (England: Vol III)* explains that 'their composition varied according to locality, but they were usually light in weight and texture, somewhat like Madeira cake, but spiced; milk and eggs were important ingredients [...] usually, soul-cakes were flat and round in plan but sometimes they were more like buns'.

The earliest (and only) surviving traditional recipe that's explicitly for soul cakes is a nineteenth-century English one from Weston-under-Lizard in south Staffordshire, copied from the manuscript book of a 'Mrs. Durant' in *Bye-Gones Relating to Wales and the Border Counties* (J.H. Clarke, 1909–10, p. 37). It is given as follows:

Flour, 2 lbs.
Butter, 4 oz.
Sugar, 8 oz.
Eggs, 2
Barm [yeast or leaven], 2 tablespoonfuls
Spice [nutmeg and mace are appropriate]
Saffron
New milk (to make it into a soft dough)

Put all the ingredients together, except the sugar and spice and let the mixture be left before the fire for half an hour; then add the sugar and spice, mix well, make into flat cakes, mark each one and bake.

Though there is no indication what the mark might be, most soul cakes in practice bear a cross cut into them like a hot-cross bun, a crosshair, or a sun wheel – the origin of this is unknown.

Even though no other historic recipe specifically for soul cakes has come to light, we certainly do have period-appropriate recipes for oat cakes and seed cakes. The seventeenth-century reference does not, it should be noted, refer to a modern oatcake, which tends to be crisp and biscuit-like, but instead would be closer to what we think of as a muffin, just with a larger proportion of oat flour to regular flour. A representative recipe for oat cakes is given in a manuscript from around 1700 (MS7788 in the Wellcome Library), and it includes spices that connect it with our later soul cake recipe:

> Take a Quart of fine oatmeal, as much wheat flower, a Quart of milk & water, 9 yolks and 4 whites of eggs, a little sack [a fortified white wine, sweet sherry works as an easy substitute], one nuttmegg grated, a little beaten mace, 3 spoonfulls of ale yeast, and a little salt, stir altogether and put in halfe a Quarter of a pound of sugar. Sett it by the fire to Rise and bake them on a stone or in a frying pan.

John Brand refers to seed cake versions of the soul cake in 1813, as do various others, and the following recipe for 'Little Seed Cakes' is from Charlotte Mason's *The Lady's Assistant for Regulating and Supplying Her Table* of 1777:

> One pound of flower well dried, one pound of sugar sifted; wash one pound of butter to a cream with rose-water; put the flower in by degrees; add ten yolks and four whites of eggs, one ounce of carraway-seeds; keep beating till the oven is ready; butter the pans well; grate over fine sugar; beat the cakes till just as they are set into the oven.

If we compare the three, we find similarities – the seed cake replaces the spices of the other two with carraway seeds, and the oatcake mixes oatmeal in with the flour – but beyond that there is minimal difference. The yellowing and 'marking' of the nineteenth-century version is what makes it the most distinct, and this is a development that we see echoed across most twentieth-century versions.

What none of these three recipes include is any fruit, though it would be a simple thing to add the currants that are described as belonging to some versions, and it seems likely that is all that would be needed for that variation.

In terms of the shape, the one reference to square versions seems to have described a large tray having been baked, which is then cut into squares for serving, as with brownies. It is of note that this is an example of the cakes being baked in large quantities by a professional baker.

In a domestic setting we see round cakes referred to in terms of baking or feasting, with triangular cakes most often referred to in contexts of collection by gooders. The key here, I think, is the large cross that is customarily carved into the round loaf. If one takes a circular soul cake and breaks it along these lines, then a single circular cake elegantly divides into four triangular cakes, like a pizza. In terms of practicality, this has obvious advantages.

A related cake/bread tradition, which almost certainly developed and migrated organically from the soul cake, is the Bonfire Night tharf cake or parkin tradition of Yorkshire and Lancashire, and rather than lump them all together, I will save that discussion for a later chapter.

In October of 2023, English Heritage had a well-meaning but characteristically misguided campaign to 'revive' the soul cake, with lots of press releases about how it was a forgotten medieval treat. They invented and publicised a new recipe 'inspired by history', which was essentially just a biscuit with raisins – seemingly ignorant of the historical recipes above, their new version has misinterpreted the 'oat cake' reference into something like a cross between a modern oatcake and a raisin shortbread. They also, rather naively, seemed to be ignorant of the fact that this tradition had not actually died out, and parts of Yorkshire, Staffordshire and Somerset (and probably other areas I'm unaware of) still bake and disseminate soul cakes of the nineteenth-century style, and never stopped.

This is an excellent example of the academic or institutional top-down approach that, despite having the best of intentions, tends not only to fail, but also to distort. Folk culture and ritual must come from the ground up, be grassroots by definition and be engaged with by people who are actually part of the community, not as a PR campaign by marketing and events managers for museums. This is intangible, living cultural heritage – not a historic costume to be worn artificially for an exhibit. Had it been successful, English Heritage's biscuit version could have obliviously overwhelmed and wiped out the genuinely surviving true soul cake traditions that still hold on.

Subtle, regional developments and survivals of these traditions are rife, and generally very obscure, lasting well beyond the point at which mainstream heritage-tourism bodies and arms-length academics have officially declared them dead. Much damage can be done by this sort of arrogance.

The origins of the custom are obscure, and certainly precede both the gooding custom of souling and the Reformation itself. The earliest clear reference we have to soul caking at Hallowtide is from John Mirk's 1511 tract *Festyvall*, which contains the entry, 'We read in old time good people would on All Hallowen Day bake bread and deal it for all Christian souls'. Already considered a relic of 'old time' in 1511, we can then comfortably date it at least to the 1400s.

There is, however, a tantalising and compelling piece of evidence to indicate that the 'old time' referred to may indeed be much, much older than 1511. By almost 1,000 years.

The Venerable Bede, in his masterly *The Reckoning of Time*, written in AD 725 (some time before All Souls was established), tells us that the pre-Christian Anglo-Saxons called February '*Solmonath*', or Sol-month, and explains it as meaning the '"month of cakes" [called *sols* in Old English], which they offered to their gods in that month'. This is all the more compelling when we consider that the original date for All Souls, when established by Odilo in AD 998, was in February.

It is plausible, then, that soul cakes, or '*sol*' cakes, originated as baked offerings to Anglo-Saxon gods (often themselves ancestral figures) or literal ancestors, that the practice then survived the Christianising of the country and was latterly appropriated into a February All Souls Day custom in the late 900s, before being moved into November alongside the festival itself. This might explain the lack of any clear, widely accepted epistemologically Christian explanation of the caking practice.

This becomes even more interesting when we see, again from Bede, that to the Heathen Anglo-Saxons, November was '*Blotmonath*', or Bloodmonth, meaning 'the month of sacrifice, because our forefathers, when they were Heathens, always sacrificed in this month, that is, that they took and devoted to their idols the cattle which they wished to offer'. Was the soul cake offering actively moved to November to help phase out surviving customs of animal sacrifice? Pure supposition, of course.

The existence of similar customs in other European countries might indicate that the custom spread from England after Christianisation, or even that the attested Anglo-Saxon practice was itself a non-unique survival of an older form of pan-Germanic, and possibly even Indo-European, paganism known across the Continent.

In western Flanders, children set up street altars and begged passers-by for money 'for cakes for the souls in Purgatory'. In the Flemish part of Belgium, little cakes called 'soul-bread' were baked with white flour and eaten hot with a prayer for souls in Purgatory – it was believed that a soul was delivered for every cake eaten. In Antwerp, the cakes were coloured yellow with saffron to suggest the Purgatorial flames. In southern Germany and Austria, little white, oval loaves were baked and usually named after 'souls'; in Tyrol, they were given to children by their godparents, and those left over after dinner remained on the table and were said to 'belong to the poor souls'. All of these are Germanic cultures, which would have shared pre-Christian beliefs with the original Anglo-Saxon tribes.

Leaving aside for now the shaky potential that trick-or-treat might stem from a genuine, if much altered, Christianised-then-secularised survival of Anglo-Saxon (or earlier) Heathenry, let's get back onto firmer ground, and harder evidence post-Reformation..

Thomas Blount, in his *Glossographia* of 1674, writes of the All Souls Day:

> ... custom of Soul Mass cakes, which are a kind of oat cakes, that some of the richer sorts of persons in Lancashire and Herefordshire (among the papists there) use still to give the poor upon this day; and they, in retribution of their charity, hold themselves obliged to say this old couplet: God have your soul,/ Bones and all.

John Aubrey, writing not much later, noted them as a popular custom in Shropshire and the neighbouring counties, and not restricted merely to 'papists' – they were piled on a household table into a 'high heap of soul cakes', and visitors would come and take one, with the rhyme 'A soule-cake, a soule-cake, Have mercy on all Christen soules for a soule-cake'.

By the nineteenth century the practice was still widespread, most especially in those English counties from Lancashire southward to Monmouthshire, and the Welsh counties that bordered them. It also spread out across into scattered parts of north Wales, on one side, and Derbyshire, Staffordshire and Yorkshire on the other, as well as down into Somerset and Hertfordshire, and with scattered instances even further afield. It was by this time that the gooding element had taken over from the cake itself, as previously discussed, though the cakes were still sometimes baked and were known of in most places.

The exact meaning and symbolism of the soul cake (or soul bread, soulmass cake, saumas bread, dirge loaf, etc.) is hard to define, but of particular note when speaking of the development of Halloween. Once clearly an acceptably Catholic practice, after the English Reformation the custom continued unshackled by Church involvement. Just as with the festival as a whole, then, the understanding and interpretation of the cakes was able to grow undirected, and to take root organically as folk culture.

As the season was defined by praying for souls in Purgatory, it seems from various eighteenth and nineteenth-century accounts that the cakes were thought of as physical manifestations of this. It is worth emphasising that it's impossible to determine to what extent these beliefs were held, the degree to which they were actively enacted and engaged with, or even whether some may have pre-dated and originated the custom.

The simplest interpretation is of a basic transaction – that the poor agree to go home and pray for the dead family of the wealthy in return for receiving a soul cake. This also seems the least likely in terms of practicality, and there is no evidence of such post-prandial prayers ever having taken place (or even of their being expected).

Some considered that the giving of the cakes, as an act of Christian charity, was done *on behalf of* the deceased, and so such good works, even if relatively modest, would cumulatively count in their favour. For others, the cakes were seen as a representative embodiment of the prayer itself, given to and eaten by the visiting gooders and guisers, who, when they did so, were a symbolic embodiment of the soul that the prayer was intended for – by the process of eating it, they ensured that the soul absorbed the prayer itself.

Another belief that arose was the inverse of this: the idea that souls were literally trapped within the soul cakes, and the baking of them somehow took a soul from Purgatory, whereby the eating of them either set it free (presumably for a better destination) or absorbed it into one's own body, so that it could benefit (or suffer?) by proxy from the good works that the eater then carried out over the rest of their lives.

In this latter sense, then, when people in strange costume come to your door, they are doing so as a symbolic representation of your ancestral dead. When you give them a treat, you are giving that treat as a symbolic offering. While you are literally giving chocolate to a child in a costume, on a symbolic (or, dare I say, spiritual) level, you are making a sacrificial offering to your ancestral spirits, and though the physical remnants of that offering are consumed by hyperactive infants, the 'spirit' of the offering is consumed (and benefited from) by the souls of the dead.

Though it's a bold claim to say that this is a survival of any pagan ancestor worship, it is certainly a custom which reflects (or came to reflect) an instinctual human impulse towards the honouring of dead relatives, and after the Reformation in England, it was this aspect which was most able to develop (or redevelop) along such deeply ingrained folkways – much as we see in the Mexican Day of the Dead (for which evidence of any pre-Christian origin is considerably more sparse, despite what the tour-guides may tell you).

This idea of eating prayers or souls on behalf of the dead through the proxy of food is but a small step to the similar practice of eating sins.

A Sin Eater was usually an outcast member of a community who lived apart, ostracised and looked down on, even feared. When someone in the area died and had been unable to confess their sins beforehand, or perhaps had never been baptised, this individual would be called for, and would sit by the fresh corpse as food was placed on or passed over it. In so doing, the food would absorb the sins of the deceased, and as the Sin Eater consumed it they would absorb those sins in turn, leaving the dead individual absolved and ready to go to Heaven.

The mechanics are complicated and unspecified. Presumably, the Sin Eater would have to hope that, when they died, either they were able to confess *all* their accrued sins (although, as they would be ignorant of many, this may not have been possible) or that another Sin Eater would take their place and absorb in turn all that they themselves had.

The Sin Eater tradition has been victim of the same misrepresentation that much of Halloween has, and most articles and search results will tell you that it is Irish or Scottish, because this fits in with an exoticised image of those countries as (ironically) being somehow more un-Christian than the rest of the British Isles. In fact, the only historic accounts of Sin Eaters at all come from western England, northern Wales and the border counties in between. The reason I emphasise this is that these are also some of the counties most engaged in the soul cake custom – this enticing fact has been obscured by the primativising superiority complex that projects such things away from a supposedly more advanced England and artificially onto a supposedly backward Celtic fringe.

The oldest surviving reference to Sin Eating, from the 1600s, has it taking place in Herefordshire, England. The *Morning Herald* of 2nd November 1822 quotes the seventeenth-century diarist John Aubrey as writing about it in 'some miscellanies of his among the Lansdown Manuscripts, at the British Museum'. Aubrey describes the custom as old, but still ongoing in his own time:

> In the County of Hereford was an old custome at Funeralls, to hire poor people, who were to take upon them all the sinnes of the party deceased. One of theme, (he was a long lean ugly lamentable raskal), I remember, lived in a cottage on Rosse [Ross-on-Wye] highway. The manner was, that

> when the corpse was brought out of the house, and laid on the biere, a loafe of bread was brought out and delivered to the sinne eater over the corpse, and also a mazar bowl [a broad, flat bowl for drinking from], of maple, full of beere (which he was to drink up), and sixpence in money: in consideration whereof he took upon him, *ipso facto*, all the sinnes of the defunct, and freed him or her from walking after they were dead.

Already, we can see the Sin Eater is considered wretched, low and apart from society. The fact the bowl he drinks from is of maple wood may also have some significance (but if so, I do not know what). The 1926 book *Funeral Customs* by Bertram S. Puckle specifies that the Sin Eater:

> ... lived as a rule in a remote place by himself, and those who chanced to meet him avoided him as they would a leper [...] when his purpose was accomplished they burned the wooden bowl and platter from which he had eaten the food handed across, or placed on the corpse for his consumption.

The English antiquarian John Bagford (c. 1650–1716) includes the following description of the sin-eating ritual in his *Letter on Leland's Collectanea* (as cited in *Brewer's Dictionary of Phrase and Fable*):

> Notice was given to an old sire before the door of the house, when some of the family came out and furnished him with a cricket [low stool], on which he sat down facing the door; then they gave him a groat which he put in his pocket, a crust of bread which he ate, and a bowl of ale which he drank off at a draught. After this he got up from the cricket and pronounced the case and rest of the soul departed, for which he would pawn his own soul.

All accounts seem to agree on the extreme stigma against the Sin Eater, and that he (in all accounts, the Sin Eater is male) is often associated with evil, black magic and devilry. According to the *Cardiff and Merthyr Guardian* of 1st October 1836, 'one curious belief was current, that he was none other than "The Wandering Jew" – the man who spit on his Saviour, and cannot die'.

The practice dwindled severely during the nineteenth century, and the last Sin Eater on official record finally concluded his vocation in the first few years of the twentieth century. He lived, worked and died in the English county of Shropshire, in the village of Ratlinghope, where his grave can still be visited (it was restored in 2010 after a fundraising campaign by the local vicar). Richard Munslow was his name: born 1833, died 1906. He alone appears to have bucked the trend of the outcast, and was instead a well-known and financially successful farmer.

A theory some in the church there have posited, to justify such an unseemly pastime in someone otherwise so respectable, is that he only turned to the archaic practice after three of his children died in one week from scarlet fever in 1870 – they hold that he must have revived it, as surely no good Christian village could have had a living tradition of such a thing so deep into the modern age. The theory is, of course, pure supposition. It seems to me to be motivated less by evidence or likelihood, and more by wishful thinking.

The novel *Precious Bane*, written by Mary Webb in 1924, contains a scene of sin eating in which the words spoken over the body are recorded (and, interestingly, are formatted in italics in the book itself, in contrast to the rest of the speech given – this usually denotes a quotation, and every other italicised example in the novel is an excerpt from a pre-existing text or saying). Webb was a Shropshirite, and regularly visited Ratlinghope, and so it is plausible that these words are accurate, and a memory of Munslow's own ceremony:

> I give easement and rest now to thee, dear man. Come not down the lanes nor in our meadows. And for thy peace I pawn my own soul. Amen.

If indeed these words reflect the living tradition, then it indicates that an element of sin eating was not only to save souls from damnation, but to stop them from rising after death and tormenting the living. This hitherto unrecorded aspect of the unquiet dead connects us directly back to Hallowtide and the traditions surrounding it, and when combined with the similar geographic spread of soul caking is difficult to ignore.

10

OLD HOB AND THE CHESHIRE SOULING PLAYS

The *Miscellanies of the English Dialect Society* for 1876 tells us that 'On Caking day, which in Bradfield is the first day of November, boys and young men dress themselves like mummers and go to farm houses collecting money'. The overlap between guisers and mummers is considerable, and the terms are often used interchangeably.

The costumed guising and gooding traditions of the Halloween season reach their absolute pinnacle in Cheshire, where folk performances of mummers plays are incorporated into the customs as Souling Plays, Soul Cake Plays or Soul Apple Plays. Every year, an array of groups perform for two weeks, from Halloween until Martlemas (or St Brice's Eve on 12th November). Though today October 31st is the most popular of these dates, historically November 1st or 2nd were the preference. In many respects, they follow the same essential structure as the Christmas mummers plays that are prevalent across the entirety of England, but with the regional variation in scripts that is to be expected, and a few specific identifiers that set them apart.

These plays are performed at pubs, country houses, fairs and social events by local amateur performers (think Shakespeare's 'rude mechanicals'). In the past, they were performed in exchange for food or drink, though today charity collections are more common.

The broad plot of mummers plays, or 'quack doctor plays', as they are more accurately termed, is that a champion (often St or King George) is introduced, a challenger appears, they fight, one of them is killed, a doctor is called for and the deceased is brought back from the dead. In many cases, 'Old Beelzebub' is involved.

Usually, there then follows an array of different characters who introduce themselves sequentially with a brief verse, before asking for money and singing a song. Costumes are usually ragged, rough, folky and surreal – often made from extraordinary quantities of rag strips to disguise body shape and with head gear to obscure faces.

Souling plays, unlike other mummers, also incorporate a puppetry figure known as Old Hob, described in Vol. 1 of George Ormerod's 1819 *History of Cheshire*, as 'the custom of carrying a dead horse's head, covered with a sheet, to frighten people ... between All Souls day and Christmas' (in the Antrobus play, the character is called Dick and has an accompanying Driver – in the Alderley Play, performed exclusively by the Barber family, he was Young Ball). This unnerving figure consists of a jawbone fixed to a pole, with the remainder of the skull resting atop it, using the natural joints. A lever is then attached to the back of the skull, where the vertebrae meet the head, so that the upper part can be snapped by its operator. It is then carried aloft with a blanket or cape obscuring the puppeteer. The skull can be decorated with bows or ribbons, painted designs or balls for eyes (in Antrobus, it's coloured black).

Often, Cheshire groups who didn't have the wherewithal to enact full plays would simply travel door to door with Old Hob, causing mayhem – if two gangs happened to pass each other en route, the tradition was that each must then try to steal the other's skull. Sometimes, a candle would be lit inside and, according to Michael Billington's 2018 *The Story of Urmston, Flixton and Davyhulme*, in the early 1900s men in Warburton went out souling with lanterns at night, with one of the men wearing a horse's skull called the Old Warb, visiting farmers' houses for drink and money.

This has obvious overlaps with the Jack o' Lantern and trick-or-treat tradition, and we will discuss this again in a later chapter – an older name for Jack o' Lanterns was, as it happens, Hobby Lanterns (or Hobbedy/Hob o' the Lanterns), and this custom is one of the points at which the Halloween treat traditions intersect with those of the Halloween trick. We will return to this later.

The horse skull custom has, in the past, been prevalent throughout much of England and south Wales, and still survives in many contemporary examples. The best known is the Mari Llyd of southern Welsh Christmas custom, though the near-identical figure of Old Hob remains relatively obscure. The only difference is one of nationality and that Hob comes out earlier than Mari.

There are many other ongoing English examples of similar hobby horse traditions – such as Padstow's 'Obby 'Oss, Kent's Hoodening, the Bull Broad of the Cotswolds, the Derby Tup of the East Midlands, the Old Horse of the north-east and the Old Ball of Lancashire – but most are held around Christmas or Mayday, and only Old Hob belongs to Hallowtide.

Though a lot of silliness is spoken of about these figures and the plays, and their origins are certainly obscure, they are almost certainly not 'pre-Christian in origin' in any meaningful sense, as a lot of twentieth-century romantics like to believe. This was one of many lazy myths propagated by the (again) well-meaning but deeply misguided 2017 Cheshire Souling Project by Minerva Arts. Like many academic and arts industry approaches to folk culture, it presented a living piece of ongoing heritage as something dead, discarded and forgotten that they, with their entitled, disconnected and boardroom-authorial voices, were going to 'revisit and revitalise'. Predictably, several of the souling groups on whose patch they were obliviously treading got a little annoyed (not least because they renamed them 'Soul Plays', exploited them to shallow political ends, and ignored both the extant tradition and the preceding 50 years of scholarship). Folk culture is not a top-down affair, and if an academic or 'creative practitioner' wants to avoid patronising appropriation then they should start their dabblings not with the Arts Council or the university, but with the pub or the village hall.

The authority on the Cheshire Souling plays, in particular, is one Duncan Broomhead, who is also responsible for the Duncan Broomhead Collection, one of the major folk-play archives (consisting of scripts, accounts, field recordings, pictures and much more besides, collected over the past sixty years or so from the front lines of English folk performance). He has made it his life's work, and I had the honour of meeting him as part of some mumming I did at the Old Red Lion Theatre Pub back in 2017. (If interested, further details on Duncan's collection and on souling plays in general can be found at mastermummers.org and folkplay.info - Broomhead's work builds on that of Alex Helm (1920-70), who moved to Congleton after the war and became a foundational researcher of the Cheshire plays. For a thorough exploration of the field in its entirety, I highly recommend the 2020 book *Mummers' Plays Revisited* by Peter Harrop.)

Mummers plays were found across the whole of England, with some overspill into Scotland, Wales and Ireland, from the 1700s (with possible precursors in the 1600s) up until the First World War (1914–18). Most villages had their own variant of the script, and the plays were often performed by young men from the locality, with parts passed down orally through the generations, sometimes within just a single family. The huge numbers of young men aged 16–30 who were killed during the war was devastating to small communities and their folk customs, and many ceased completely thereafter.

There were a handful of exceptions.

A few mumming groups kept performing, and increasing numbers of folklorists and folk music enthusiasts set to work tracking down retired performers and recording their scripts in the 1930s. In the years after the Second World War, many revived, and continue to do so annually. Today, most areas are served by a group of mummers at Christmas or Easter.

Though a small number of these Christmas and Easter mumming groups maintained the pre-war continuity for later revivals, the tradition of Hallowtide souling plays exists unbroken thanks to a single man, who deserves more credit than he gets.

Major Arnold Whitworth Boyd (20th January 1885–16th October 1959) was a countryman, ornithologist and amateur naturalist, who lived in Cheshire his entire life. Born in Altrincham, from 1902 he lived in the broader parish of Antrobus. When the First World War came, he did his duty, barely out of his teens. Afterwards, he returned home to Antrobus and married the wonderfully named Violet Conybeare in 1919, living thereafter at Frandley House.

Boyd had grown up with the souling plays and refused to let them die out. He wrote down the script for the Antrobus play, encouraged the old players and began co-ordinating performances. By the end of the 1920s he had ensured that, after a break of little more than a decade, the Antrobus Soul-Cakers were back doing the needful every season. Today, he lies in the graveyard of Antrobus's St Mark's Church. Pay your respects, should you be passing, especially if it's Halloween.

Based at the Antrobus Arms Pub, the Antrobus Soul-Cakers continue to perform at various sites around Cheshire – a group that has existed for centuries (possibly as early as the late 1600s) and which (one hopes) will outlast you or I. They have inspired many other revivals in the intervening years, and at time of writing there are active soul-caking gangs at Alderley, Antrobus, Halton and Warburton (and probably others).

Sometimes one man really can make the difference.

11

THE PIG-HEADED BRIDE OF PIPE

The tiny village of Pipe and Lyde, in the middle of Herefordshire, is an unassuming little place, with a population of 333 at the 2021 census and (or so it would seem) no real claim to fame barring the grave of James Honeyman-Scott, the guitarist of the Pretenders. The church there is worth a look, with a twelfth-century nave, thirteenth-century tower and fourteenth-century chancel (largely rebuilt by F. Kempson in 1874).

Nearby is a pub that used to be called the Rose Garden Inn, or the Rosie. I was told the strange tale of its ghost by the magnificent Rachel Spink, not long after her 105th birthday on Bonfire Night of 2019. As Rae told it, around Halloween and Guy Fawkes Night every year, people used to report strange encounters with a veiled woman in white when travelling home from the pub. Others said the strange figure would follow them from Pipe, always at a distance. Some claimed to have seen the woman in white tapping at the window – once the spectre had the attention of an unsuspecting witness she would slowly remove her veil to reveal a hideous pig's head.

Rae recalled one popular playground story whereby the woman in white was ethereally beautiful and would beckon men to her, seductively taking them in an embrace, only to terrify them at the last by pulling back her veil for a kiss. Others spoke of hearing her grunting in the darkness as they travelled along the road.

According to Rae, there once had been 'a very old painting' of the pig-headed woman in white, which hung on the wall of the pub, and another rougher sketch of the same scene nearby. She remembered it as depicting the figure near the church, on a road, and rather grotesque, but could give no clearer recollection.

I asked around in various Hereford pubs, and while a handful of older drinkers found the tradition dimly familiar, no further facts could be added. No mention of such a thing is made in any of the books on Herefordshire folklore, most of which are rehashes of Ella Mary Leather's seminal work of 1911, *The Folk-lore of Herefordshire* – I thus came to the conclusion that this strange creature was most likely a mid-twentieth-century development, perhaps encouraged to drum up business for the pub (many such cases), with the 'very old painting' either being the original inspiration for the story, or simply not very old at all.

Having exhausted all relevant sources, some years later, I came, by chance, upon an obscure account from the *Hereford Journal*, reproduced in the *Morning Chronicle* of 12th November 1825:

> A GHOST!! – Considerable alarm has been excited amongst the credulous in the vicinity of Pipe, in this county, by the reported appearance of one of those unearthly visitors y'clept a *Ghost*, whom, some assert, comes in the enticing garb of 'a fair lady in white,' veiled and adorned as a bride, but sometimes her shoulders are decorated with a pig's head, instead of the human face divine; other reports give still stranger shapes to the disquiet spirit. The favourite resort of the visitant is near the yew and ash, on the high road between Holmer and Pipe Church, where it was lately *most positively* seen in the shape of – a donkey. It is probable some mischievous wag has been playing his pranks, to create all this nonsensical apprehension, and we hope measures will be adopted to discover and punish him for his folly.

As we've seen before now, the report immediately presents it as a hoax – if it was, it seems to have been such a successful one that it survived in the oral folklore of the area for about 200 years before I heard it, unrecorded and unpublished by folklorists.

Hutton's *Stations of the Sun* (which I reference throughout this book) details a certain Welsh Halloween custom, namely 'the belief that the most fearsome spirit abroad in the night took the form of a tail-less black sow, *yr Hwrch Ddu Gwta*'.

> In north-western Denbighshire, children running home from the [Halloween bon]fire would scream 'the tail-less black sow take the hindermost'. In Anglesey they had a rhyme:

A Tail-less Black Sow
And a White Lady
Without a head
May the Tail-less Black Sow
Snatch the hindmost.
A Tail-less Black Sow
On Winter's Eve,
Thieves coming along
Knitting stockings.

> It was said that menfolk on the island would pretend to be the pig, grunting in the darkness, to get the youngsters home faster. All across the north of the principality during the 19th century, down to and including Montgomeryshire, *yr Hwrch Ddu* was said to sit on stiles upon this night, waiting for victims. Who this being might have been is a complete puzzle.

Hutton goes on to explain that there are no obvious origins or earlier examples of similar figures in Wales, and tentatively concludes that it 'may have been a folk-devil evolved from the early modern period onward'. Elements of this, both the hideous pig head coming from a long, white dress (or sheet?) and the grunting pursuit of youngsters, are vaguely reminiscent of hobby horse traditions, but these few shreds of evidence are not enough to draw any real conclusions.

The parallel with the Pig-Headed Bride seems obvious, and it appears that the 'tail-less black sow' and the 'white lady without a head' of the Anglesey rhyme have become merged into (or even, potentially, derive from) a single figure sharing these attributes. Herefordshire does, of course, border Wales, though it seems strange that this single example should be tied to such a small locality in the very centre of the county and relatively far from the Welsh border. Interestingly, the newspaper report seems to have come from around 11th November – 'old' Halloween.

Rae had one more pub reminiscence to share with me, describing a curious dent in the bottom of the front door, and strange scratches here and there on the interior walls. As she recalled (and this was from childhood), the damage to the door was said to be from the Pig-Headed Bride charging to gain entry, and the scratches on the walls a memento of the one time she succeeded. As a young woman, she'd once met a man who claimed to have encountered the bride on Halloween night - his hair turned entirely white with the shock, and fleeing back to the pub with his story, he was rewarded with drinks on the house for weeks afterwards (perhaps not an unbiased witness, after all).

In 2018, the Rosie was more or less gutted by new owners Dan and Vicky Weager, who painted the building grey, threw up cheap new interiors in a starkly modern style, and renamed it the 'Secret Garden'. Any pictures of the Pig-Headed Bride that might have survived were thrown away or destroyed. They went into liquidation soon after Halloween in 2022, citing difficulties post-covid, and the place was bought by the local Wobbly Brewing Company and reopened on 25th October 2023, just in time, again, for Halloween.

The mystery of the Pig-Headed Bride of Pipe, and her relation to *yr Hwrch Ddu Gwta*, is one that has yet to be fully resolved. What is certain, however, is that in the story we have, again, found a plausibly centuries-old Herefordshire Halloween tradition that has survived authentically in oral folklore, and which (were it not for Rachel Spink) would almost certainly have been lost forever, like the historic interiors of the 'reimagined' pub.

12

TRICKING, MISCHIEF AND THE LORD OF MISRULE

We have discussed the Treat at length. Now we talk of Trick.

The association of the season with revelry is well established, and Halloween parties are still today known for the sort of wildness that only masks and costumes can bring out. Historically, it was on All Hallows Eve that the Lord of Misrule was chosen and crowned, his reign lasting from then until Twelfth Night (5th January) or Candlemas (2nd February). As Philip Stubbes describes, in his 1585 *Anatomie of Abuses*, 'The wilde heades of the parishe conventynge together, chuse them a grand Capitaine (of mischeefe) whom they ennobel with the title Lorde of Misrule'. He describes them as dressing colourfully, tying bells to their legs to 'go to the churche (though the minister be at praier or preachyng) dauncying and swingyng their handercheefes'.

The Lord of Misrule has many parallels, such as the Catholic Boy Bishops, the Bean King (a bean was baked into a cake and whoever got that slice was crowned king for the day), the ancient Roman mock-kings of Saturnalia, and the Mock Mayors that still exist in villages around England today (which we will mention again later). Essentially, he is a figure of fun, elected ironically and put in a (usually ceremonial) position of authority over social festivities, often a jester figure himself.

The courts of Edward II and III had Bean Kings at least as early as 1315, and we find equivalents (called Prester John and King Balthazar) in Oxford colleges from the early 1400s. Later that century, Henry VII had both a Lord of Misrule and an Abbot of Unreason in his court. Lords of Misrule rocketed in popularity under Henry VIII, spreading on to aristocratic estates, Cambridge University, and various parishes and other institutions.

John Stowe describes the office in his 1603 *Survey of London*:

> [I]n the feaste of Christmas, there was in the kinges house, wheresoeuer hee was lodged, a Lord of Misrule, or Maister of merry disports, and the like had yee in the house of euery noble man, of honor, or good worshippe, were he spirituall or temporall. Amongst the which the Mayor of London, and eyther of the shiriffes had their seuerall Lordes of Misrule, euer contending without quarrell or offence, who should make the rarest pastimes to delight the Beholders. These Lordes beginning their rule on Alhollon Eue [Halloween], continued the same till the morrow after the Feast of the Purification, commonlie called Candlemas day: In all which space there were fine and subtle disguisinges, Maskes and Mummeries, with playing at Cardes for Counters, Nayles and pointes in euery house, more for pastimes then for gaine.

The Lord of Misrule survived Henry VIII, but was abolished as an official figure of the royal court after the death of Edward VI in 1553. The practice continued at the local and aristocratic level for over a century, but was dealt something of a death blow by the social inversions of the Civil War and concomitant Interregnum (not to mention the fact that Christmas itself was banned), with the last high-profile appointment, apparently a one-off, in 1661. The practice survived in private Twelfth Night parties and in the related mock mayors, though by this point it had lost its Halloween association.

But the misrule of Halloween survived the loss of its lord.

In 1605 was established the first official Guy Fawkes Night. This rough celebration very soon took over the mantle of wildness and chaotic intensity that had typified the Lord of Misrule's reign, and extreme pranks and raucous hedonism were very much the order of the day. So much so that, from the mid-1700s, there were increasingly high-profile calls to curb its excesses and rein it in.

The carnival street parties, flaming tar barrels, impromptu bonfires in the public highways, bull-baiting, drinking, fighting, vandalism, costumes and masks of Bonfire Night all eventually proved too much for Victorian sensibilities, and from about the 1830s to the 1870s it was successfully tamed, with increased police presence and intermittent bans (the great exceptions were those domains of the Bonfire Boys, but we'll discuss that later).

From the latter portion of the nineteenth century Bonfire Night became an increasingly private affair, smaller scale and less wrapped up in mayhem. But people still needed an outlet (a purge, if you will), and running parallel to the century-long taming of 5th November – or potentially even as a direct consequence – an interesting development occurred that has not before been given proper attention.

The first evidence we have of Mischief Night dates to before 1790, when records from St John's College, Oxford refer to a school play concluding with 'an Ode to Fun which praises children's tricks on Mischief Night in most approving terms'. Initially, up to the early 1800s, it seems exclusively to have been the night before May Day (30th April, when it was also sometimes called May Yule) and was most popular in (if not exclusive to) the north, especially parishes in Yorkshire and Lancashire.

During the early to mid-1800s, however, we find increasing evidence of the practice in other districts on other dates, often the night before Shrove Tuesday, occasionally on Christmas Eve or New Year's Eve, more rarely on the night before All Fools' Day, and most commonly (after May Eve), on the evening before Bonfire Night. Thereafter, this date of 4th November becomes extremely well established (though isolated regional variants remain – in some areas, the date was chosen by children in secret).

Local newspaper archives provide extensive evidence for each, and all of the earliest references on each of these dates claim it as being a long-established tradition at that time and in that area. The Lahore *Civil & Military Gazette* of 23rd November 1930 tells us that there 'are whole towns in West Yorkshire and Lancashire which celebrate between the 5th and 12th of the month in "Mischief Nights"'. The *Derbyshire Times* of 28th December 1907 tells us, 'Christmas Eve at Tideswell has always been known as "Mischief Night"', and the *Sheffield Daily Telegraph* of 29th December 1932, tells us the same was true for Bradwell. The *Manchester City News* of 7th May 1910 reminisces about past Mischief Nights on 1st March, and the *Armley and Wortley News* of 2nd January 1891 describes the Armley New Year's Eve as Mischief Night, explaining that it 'was honoured in the customary style [...] Bands of young people paraded the streets dressed in fantastic costumes; mummers visited people's houses as usual; and various pranks were indulged in by the roysterers.' The *Liverpool Weekly Courier* of 5th September 1903, reporting a case of vandalism at a railway station on 21st August, confirms, 'it had been Churchtown Fair that week, and there was a "mischief night"'.

Despite these examples, the overwhelming majority of Mischief Nights are, from about the 1830s, held on the eve before Bonfire Night. The *Yorkshire*

Post and Leeds Intelligencer of 5th November 1903 confirms that 'much of the horse-play that used to usher in the celebration of Guy Fawkes' Day has now happily disappeared, but "mischief night," as it is known, is still associated with a good deal of practical joking', and regardless of the date chosen, the pranks are more or less the same.

Mischief Night (also today called Miggy or Mizzy Night) developed as a raucous, informal time for children and youths to roam the streets causing havoc; a night when it was (and in some places still is) genuinely believed amongst the perpetrators that ordinary laws do not apply. As the *Westmorland Gazette* of 11th November 1848 puts it (quoting from the *Early Days of Samuel Bamford*, No. 3):

> MISCHIEF NIGHT ... when 'as there is a time for all things.' Any one having a grudge against a neighbour was at liberty to indulge it, provided he kept his own counsel. On these occasions it was lawful to throw a neighbour's gate off the angles, to pull up his fence, to trample his garden, to upset a cart that might be found at hand, to set cattle astray, or to perform any other freak, whether in the street, house, yard, or fields, which might suggest itself, or be suggested. The general observation in the morning would be, 'Oh, it's nobbut th' mischief neet.'

The *Wakefield and West Riding Herald* of 20th October 1883 draws the connection explicitly:

> We have no longer a lord of misrule, but we have a 'mischief night,' or rather mischief nights, when the boys bent on bonfires on the 5th of November embolden each other to steal, take and carry away anything to which they can lay their hand that is ignitable, especially timber in the shape of fences. This annual custom has too long been tolerated, and it behoves the police to put it down.

A particularly horrible Mischief Night tradition existed in the vicinity of Manchester, where once lived the Radcliffe family, one of whose members was believed to be implicated in the Gunpowder Plot. The 'Notes and Queries' section of the *Manchester City News* for 21st November 1885 describes it thus:

> At Barton Moss a custom prevails on the 4th of November of scouring the neighbourhood in search of stray cats and dogs, and when a good supply is collected the villagers assemble at midnight at the north-east corner of

> the Moss (close to the Manchester No. 2 target) and stretch a line between two trees. Each cat is then tied tail to tail with a dog, and the pair are thrown over the line, where they are allowed to fight until first blood is drawn, when they are released and another pair is thrown over in their place. This union of dog and cat is held to be symbolic of the infamous union between the Radcliffe family and Guy Faux. These mischiefs, as they are called, are generally attended by the young people of both sexes, even the fair daughters of the good families in the districts not objecting to accompany their gallant lovers to see the poor victims of the sport tortured. When the line is cut down, parkin is distributed by the town crier, after which one solitary sky-rocket is fired, and then all go home.

This tradition is the exception, and the vast majority of observances seem to have been relatively harmless door-knocking or handle-gluing type things. The removing of garden gates seems to have been a mainstay from the eighteenth right up into the late twentieth century across all Mischief Nights. Some variation exists depending on the date (when held around Christmas, there was often the addition of mumming and other Yuletide customs, when around Mayday, there were garlanding pranks associated with May rituals), but the bulk of the customs were standard across all Mischief Nights in all places and dates.

According to the *Leeds Mercury* of 5th November 1930:

> [In] clothing factories where large numbers of young girls are employed [...] practical jokes were much in evidence [...] quite dignified persons eventually found that they had been walking about with a leering face chalked on the back of their overalls [...] mysterious objects were found in the linings of hats and coat-sleeves were tied up. Guys or little dolls were made up out of linings. These and similar tricks were winked at by the authorities.

The *Yorkshire Evening Post* of 5th November 1921 tells us:

> 'Mischief night' was well and duly celebrated in Leeds last night, and many groups of children paraded the streets, indulging in a little harmless devilment. Many girls wore their brothers' clothes, and vice versa [...] in one street alone there were no fewer than four fires burning merrily.

Sometimes, children went too far, of course, and the perceived lawlessness is no exaggeration. The *Bolton Free Press* of 18th May 1844 tells us that 'Joseph

Thornley and Thomas Lambert, crofters, of Horwich were [...] charged with removing [...] about forty gates [...] On being asked what their motive was for such conduct, they said it was "mischief night," and did not know they were doing wrong'.

There are many, many other examples, even into the twenty-first century – a feature for the regional BBC North Yorkshire from 31st October 2006, called *Confessions From a Mischief Night Brat*, explicitly states that 'when I was a kid I actually thought it was legal – "coppers can't arrest you on miggy night." That was the folklore.'

A century and a half after Thornley and Lambert were found guilty, we have someone writing in to the *Huddersfield Daily Examiner* of 30th November 1994:

> I have just learned that two old ladies living in a quiet residential district of your town have been the victims of 'Mischief Night' vandalism. The guisers (as they are called in this part of the world) rang the ladies' door bells, but gave them no time to answer and decide for themselves whether it was to be 'trick or treat.' The following morning the ladies found that their gates had disappeared. The gates were later discovered on waste ground some distance away and considerably damaged.

The longevity of this specific prank is extraordinary.

There is some evidence that, through Mischief Night, a traditional Bonfire Night association with the supernatural also existed, with a ghostly variety of prank that did not exist for the original May Day version. In a short story called 'My First Burglary: A Confession' by 'W.D.L.' (first published in the *Leeds Mercury* but quoted here from the *Hampshire Advertiser*, 3rd January 1891), some young men staying in Yorkshire are trying to think up a good trick to play on the village for the 4th November Mischief Night.

'Let's raise a ghost in the churchyard,' one suggests.

'Bah!' comes the reply, 'that game is played out; even these thick-headed Yorkshiremen are up to that trick.'

The spectral tradition is further confirmed in an article from the *Leeds Mercury* of 5th November 1907 bemoaning the once-common pranks that were falling out of fashion there:

> Spirit-rapping and knocking at 'other folks' doors seems to be the only mischief now indulged in. No more do ghosts made of turnips and smuggled sheets raise your ire, no more are the door knobs of a row of

> houses firmly secured one to another, and no more is the policeman lightly tampered with, or the night watchman toppled on the road with his box on top of him [...] Instead, jumping crackers are fastened to the cat's tail, and 'cannons' thrown after nervous and apoplectic old gentlemen.

The turnip Jack o' Lantern here mentioned has overt Halloween connotations, and the *Clitheroe Advertiser and Times* of 30th October 1936, goes into more detail while speaking of the common tricks of 'half a century or so ago':

> Perhaps the most ingenious was the illuminated 'death's head.' This was made by extracting all the pulp from a big Swede turnip. The 'face' was carved and the ghastly features illuminated by a candle. Hidden behind a fence, in ill-lighted thoroughfares or dark lanes, the 'face,' attached to a fishing or other light rod, would be suddenly dangled by some young imps in front of unwary pedestrians, who, as my correspondent says, would be 'scared stiff.'

The *Leeds Mercury* of 10th December 1929 further gives us the details of a case of assault between two women in Great Barugh, north Yorkshire:

> WOMAN AS 'GHOST'.
> 'Mischief Night' in a North Riding Village.
> [...]
> One night Mrs. Turner and Mrs. Best were going up the lane when they saw something white in the hedge bottom. It turned out to be Mrs. Wilson with a white sheet over her head.
>
> Next day Mrs. Turner was leaving the village, and it was alleged that Mrs. Wilson aimed a blow at her with a poker, beat the poker on a shovel, and shouted, 'Hip, hurrah.'
>
> Mrs. Wilson admitted putting a white counterpane over her head to frighten Mrs. Turner, as it was 'mischief night.' She alleged that Mrs. Turner had thrown 'crackers into her house'.
>
> The Bench dismissed both summonses.

It is worth noting that, although officially on 5th November, Bonfire Night observances are often held up to three days before or after, especially if the 5th falls on a Sunday or a weekday, and the same is true of Halloween itself. This closeness leads, in practice, to a real mutability of dates and an inevitable blending.

Bearing in mind that all the mischief nights thus far discussed have been held on the evening before a more established festival, it should come as no surprise that by as early as the mid to late 1800s, Halloween (being All Hallows Eve) is itself referred to as Mischief Night in some localities, and celebrated as such, along with all of the masks and costumes and chaotic pranks already mentioned. We have testament to this from *The History of Honley* by Mary Anne Jagger. Writing in 1914, she confirms not only that in Yorkshire, 31st October was called Mischief Night, but further specifies that it had been at least since she was a child, and that the origins of the tradition were beyond memory. Mary Jagger was born in 1849.

Costumed revelry abounded and:

> ... numerous tricks [...] were practised upon people on this night of All Hallows' E'en. When younger, I have known doors taken off hinges, gates opened in fields so that cattle could stray ... Also posts, doors, and other property were often whitewashed, and door latches tied. In case of long-standing feuds between families, the night served as a pretext for petty revenge either in one shape or another.

The *Burton Observer and Chronicle* of 24th October 1935 confirms that in 'some parts of the country Hallowe'en has fallen from its former high state to the extent of degrading the day with observances known in many places as "mischief night".' The *Warwickshire Advertiser* of 26th October 1951 speaks of 'Hallowe'en, Mischief Night and Bonfire Night' as interconnected, and bemoans their post-war slump, 'Where are the pranks of other days? The ghostly processions with turnip lanterns, the dressing up and the mischievous games?'

In the *Penistone, Stocksbridge and Hoyland Express* of 5th November 1932, All Hallows Eve and All Hallows Day are referred to as Mischief Night and Caking Night respectively, and it informs us that 'observances this week have been confined to "dressing up" by the youngsters who visited various parts of the district and received "parkin" from residents who still prepare for the occasion'. The same paper, on 8th October 1938, warns that children will likely use their wartime gas masks as Halloween costumes at 'mischief night'.

Deep into the war, the *Gloucester Journal* of 30th October 1943 reminds us:

> Hallow E'en was also called 'Mischief Night' and perhaps the fact that people played all sorts of tricks on one another, such as taking gates and doors off hinges, leaving gates open, whitewashing doors and tying latches,

may have given rise to the belief, on the part of those who didn't do such mischief, that witches were the cause of the trouble.

The *Runcorn Weekly News* of 2nd November 1952 acts as further testament to the popular experiential blending of Halloween, Mischief Night and Bonfire Night into a contiguous season. It is a small step for Mischief Night to go from being *the* wild night before the 5th, to simply *a* wild night before the 5th, with:

> ... parties of diverse types to mark [...] All Hallows Eve, or as it is sometimes termed 'Mischief Night' [...] and of course Guy Fawkes night [...] With their 'duck apples' and their ghost stories and jokes against each other they are able to have a thoroughly entertaining evening without bringing any hurt to any unsuspecting member of the public.

The celebrating of Mischief Night somewhere between 30th October and 5th November continued in the north, the Midlands and parts of the south-west throughout the rest of the twentieth century, with annual reports of the (sometimes extensive) damage caused, and the police efforts to reduce it (generally a locality will have Mischief Night either on 30th/31st of October, *or* 4th/5th November, not usually on both).

The *Formby Times* of 4th November 1999 moans that the 'fun's gone out of Hallowe'en' due to harmless trick-or-treaters giving way to pranks and petty vandalism 'from local idiots who claim to be keeping alive the spirit of "mischief night"', though the *Hull Daily Mail* of 29th October 1994 still believed 'Mischief Night on October 31 can be a night for a lot of fun that everyone can enjoy'. The *Scarborough Evening News* of 6th November 1996 confirms 'up to £10,000 worth of damage was caused in a Mischief Night attack on public park' on 4th November.

By the 1940s, the English Mischief Night had spread to America and joined with Souling, to become a part of their Halloween celebrations also. It is the melding of these two traditions, Souling and Mischief Night, that essentially create the modern Halloween – though the American version has certainly popularised it here, the evidence is clear that this regional combining of the traditions had already occurred in England by the time it was exported to America, and the modern Halloween is a homegrown holiday, not an import.

Today, mainly in parts of Yorkshire and the vicinity of Liverpool, Mischief Night still occurs as a major night of mayhem, chaos and police activity, usually on 31st October, 4th November or one of the days around them. As well as Mizzy and Miggy, it's also called Mischievous Night, Chievous Night, Tick-Tack Night, Corn Night, Gate Night, Micky Night and Trick Night. Surges of 999 calls are reported annually, outrage reigns in local papers, and it shows no sign of stopping.

In America, Mischief Night became specifically rooted to 30th October, and became known as Devil's Night in Detroit and the surrounding areas from the 1960s to the 1990s, during which time dangerous violence and arson became de rigueur. Elsewhere in America, 'Mischief Night' was sometimes the term used for 31st October until 'Halloween' became ubiquitous around the 1960s.

The elegance of the term 'trick-or-treat' in reducing and containing the chaos of the two main Halloween elements, the trick of Mischief Night and the treat of Souling, into a single, neat, transactional exchange perfectly expresses the modern Halloween as an organic melding of them both. This may account, in some small, subconscious way, for its success in becoming so well established.

The phrase itself is a recent addition, and a rare Canadian contribution to the Hallowmas season. Canadians started saying variants of the phrase as part of their Souling and Mischief Night customs in the early portion of the twentieth century, and the first written evidence for it is from Ontario in 1917 (which, likewise, is where the first written evidence of guising in North America occurred, in 1911). The pleasingly alliterative construction spread across Canada, then infiltrated the USA during the early middle of the century. By around the 1960s, the popular phrase was the standard term for the practice in America, and it finally spread to the rest of the Anglosphere in the 1970s and 1980s, particularly aided by the release of *E.T.* in 1982.

Thereafter, having previously been restricted to regional variations in the north, the Midlands, and the south-west, the practice of mischievous gooding and guising at Halloween (whatever you want to call it) was popularised and revitalised across the whole of the United Kingdom, perhaps permanently.

A trick and a treat, indeed.

13

FOR WHOM THE GATE TOLLS

As night fell on 27th October 1782, John Newman huddled by the fire in the toll-house and tried to get warm. He was not an old man, but at 40, he no longer felt young, and no longer kept out the cold as once he had. John was the keeper of the toll-gate at Hutton, on the road from Brentwood to Billericay in Essex. His life had been harder than some, but easier than many, and he had a reputation for generosity and charity, sometimes to a fault.

He'd been happy to find the job as the night toll-keeper, but it was not a job in high demand. Though it gave him somewhere to sleep, it was a fitful sleep at best – ever waiting to be disturbed by the ring of a bell or the knock of a door, signifying that some nocturnal traveller was keen to pay the toll and gain passage onward.

It was a Sunday night, and John's belly was still full (though not so full as it could have been) from the day's roast. He had carefully apportioned out cold cuts enough for two meals, as was his habit, one for the Monday (which he was already looking forward to) and another for Tuesday. John was not a wealthy man, and it was perfectly likely that he would not see fresh meat again until the following Sunday, so such simple pleasures did not stem from gluttony.

It was as he warmed his hands and contemplated tomorrow's beef that three hard knocks came at the door. John sighed. Again came three hard knocks. 'Hold!' called John, as he forced his limbs to standing and wrapped up his greatcoat, taking the lamp as he did and pulling back the bolts of the thick, high door, as three more impatient knocks beat themselves against the wood.

Poor John Newman would regret doing so for the rest of his short life. As reported in the *Oxford Journal* of 9th November 1782:

> On Monday the 28th of October last, about Nine in the Morning, John Newman, Collector of the Tolls at the Turnpike at Hutton, in the County of Essex, was found most inhumanly wounded and bruised, quite speechless, and seemingly insensible, in which Situation he languished till Wednesday morning [the 30th], when he died.

He was found in his bed, the door shut. His night greatcoat was covered in dirt, as if he had been writhing on the ground, and was hung in its usual place. So, too, was the key to the great gate, which was unlocked and set open. According to the report, 'much blood was seen upon and about the toll gate'. The money collected in tolls (about 20 shillings) was missing, as were John's savings, alongside a silver watch he'd been given by his father and the buckles from his shoes. It all totalled between £10 and £15 in value, did the life of poor John Newman.

John Newman took two days to die. He finally found release the night before Halloween, to the sounds of children's mischief outside the window. The following day, on Halloween itself, the Trustees of the Essex Turnpikes held an emergency meeting in which they agreed to offer a reward of £40 for the capture of whatever person or persons tricked their way into Newman's trust, and beat him to death. The Crown authorities also offered £100 reward for the capture of the perpetrator or perpetrators, alongside a full pardon for any non-murderous involvement. That £140 comes to about £20,000 in today's money.

As the story goes, the culprits were a rough and dishonourable trio. A conman from Great Waltham called William Ketley had scoped and found poor John, ascertained that he'd be an easy mark, and when and how would be best to go about doing the deed. The muscle was a man named Samuel Pegram, from Fyfield, not quite 30 years of age. He was a ruffian and ne'er-do-well who, alongside his wife, Frances, had a reputation for all manner of crime and cruelty. All spent and drank and ate freely the day after the murder, and the day after that. On the day that John Newman finally died, they were too drunk to realise or care.

Then came All Hallows Eve.

That night, Samuel and Frances had been drinking and revelling as usual, stumbling home from their hostelry of choice and collapsing in boozy embrace. As the clock turned to midnight, three loud knocks came at the door.

'Nobody's home!' Sam shouted, as Frances cackled. The knocks came again.

'No soul cakes here, bugger off!' he bellowed back, getting angry. The three knocks came again.

'I've nothing for you, damn your mischief!" screamed Sam as he leapt to the door and swung it open, only to find, of course, nobody there. Nor was there anyone in the street.

Sam looked up and looked down. All was still, not a soul in sight. Confused, he closed the door and returned to his dribbling wife, feeling more sober than he had a minute ago, and less inclined to Frances's merriment. 'Somebody playing a trick, children I should think,' he mumbled, half to himself. But as he walked away, the three knocks came again, louder now, more violent than before – instantly, he lurched back and flung open the door.

Just stillness in the cold Halloween air. Not a soul in sight.

Scared now, he shut the door, bolted and barred it. The knocks came again.

'Be away with you!' he shouted, but it did not go away.

'Who is it?' asked Frances.

'Nobody, just tricksters, ignore it.' But he could barely be heard over the banging, and he ushered her out of the room, slamming shut the door behind them. As soon as he did, the knocking began at that door too.

'They're in the bloody house!'

Samuel grabbed Frances and pulled her upstairs, dashed into their room and threw her onto the bed, again slamming the door behind them, which again instantly began to receive great, loud blows from the other side. Sam shoved the bed up against it, grabbed all he could to barricade.

Soon the banging was coming from the window shutters as well, from the walls, the roof. From everywhere.

It stopped as the sun rose. Once it had, they ran out, wild-eyed, and woke the neighbours to ask them if they'd seen anything. Nobody knew what they were talking about. They'd all slept soundly, no noise at all.

Soon enough, the night disturbances seemed to belong to another life, too strange to exist in the light of day. They dismissed it as a bad batch of gin. Tried to catch up on some sleep.

After an uneasy nap, Samuel sought out William Ketley, and found him bedraggled in the Green Man Inn, just outside Great Waltham. Ketley was laughing and weeping in turns, hunched over a drink, great bags under his eyes, babbling. He too had been kept awake through the night, but not by banging. By whispering.

It was fine enough when others were about to talk, or give noise and comfort and distraction, but as soon as Ketley was alone – as soon as the noise stopped – that was then it started.

'But who whispers to you? What do they say?' Ketley just looked at Samuel, with a face of hatred and pity.

When Pegram left the pub he was shaken – Ketley cackling away, screaming mischief. Samuel went home to his wife. At midnight, the banging started again. All went as before. No rest was had, no explanation found. They spent the day drinking and took rooms at the Black Bull Inn at Fyfield.

Happy, drunk and in each other's arms, they settled down for the first good sleep they'd had in days, in the unfamiliar but comfortable bed. Samuel held Frances tight, they shared a smile, and he drifted into merry unconsciousness with the warmth of his wivvery wife by his side.

They woke to someone at the door. Bleary-eyed and half-asleep, Samuel got up to open it, expecting to find the landlord or a serving boy. Not a soul in sight. Just the gentle creaking of an empty ale house at midnight. Very slowly, Samuel closed the door. He looked at Frances, and she looked at him. Neither spoke.

It all began again.

Samuel and Frances barrelled out of the tavern, fled down the street through the night, every door they passed banging as they did so, ever louder. On they ran, and on, until they were far from any house, far from any building and far from any door. When all before and behind them was road, and all they could hear was the sound of the rain that fell about them, they sank to their knees, half-weeping, half-laughing.

Then they saw him.

Distant, walking towards them down the road.

Samuel and Frances were too far gone and too, too relieved at their respite to care for some passing traveller. Frances noticed how bloody and bruised he was first. How dirty his coat. They returned the way they had come, unwilling to pay the toll to stop the knocking of the doors.

No knocking came the next night. Nor the night after that. Hallowmas came and went, Martlemas came and went, Christmas came and went.

It was around New Year of 1783 that Ketley was arrested. He'd been taken, babbling about whispers, and when his rooms were searched, he was found in possession of extensive stolen property from a number of people, obtained through various frauds, cons and deceits. Half-mad by this stage, he grabbed at his arresters and begged to confess, told them all about Newman, all about Samuel, all about Frances.

The happy couple, of course, had put it all out of their minds come New Year's Day. Truly inexplicable experiences have a tendency to fade from memory as soon as they're no longer inhabited – just as a trip abroad feels like it never happened once you get back home. Copious revelry 'twixt Halloween and New Year certainly helped. The authorities found them easily enough.

On 15th January, Frances was let free, there being no real evidence to hold her, and her role as accomplice a vague one at best. Samuel, however, would be charged and held until trial on 8th August, alongside Ketley – who was himself a changed and happy man, pious and rested.

Ketley was found guilty of various frauds and cons and sentenced to nine months for it, which he took with a smile. It was decided not to pursue him for anything to do with John Newman, despite the confession. Samuel, too, having been held for the best part of eight months, was let off completely free. He was ecstatic.

Samuel and Frances revelled and celebrated, treated themselves to as fine a time as could be had, and put the entire sordid affair out of their minds completely. They had gotten away with murder, and never again would they think twice about that damnable Newman.

Until All Hallows Eve, of course, when the knock came at the door.

And so it was again on All Hallows Day, and so it was again on All Souls Day. Wherever they went, whatever they did, the beating at the door was endless, and the only thing worse than the banging was the bloodied, battered figure of John Newman, who was waiting should they flee, and the dreams that Samuel had of what would happen should ever they meet.

Hallowmas passed. Martlemas passed. Their luck passed.

For they had indulged in no shortage of theft and untruth since gaining their freedom. As November progressed, they found themselves with a hunger that could not be fed and a thirst that could not be slaked. The beef of St Brice's Day, the goose of Martlemas – though both were had in their plenty, they were but as ash to their lips. Friends avoided them, accidents occurred, money dried up. When they broke into a watermill to steal a load of flour, on the 27th of the month, it was just a week and a day until Frances was jailed.

Samuel went on the run, but he didn't last long. Everywhere he went he felt watched, uneasy; as if someone was standing too close to him. When talking to people, they would not hold his eye, kept looking around, as if another was with them. Barmaids would bring two drinks then take one away, confused; strangers making pleasantries would nod and say, 'Good morning to you both', as they passed him on the streets. Samuel began to wither.

There are different stories of what happened to him in the end. Many say he was driven mad and killed himself. Others that he served more time in jail, but was eventually released with Frances, and the pair carried on as ever they had done, with the diminishing returns that are the lot of such lives. Some say that he lived out his days in a bleak half-life, ever under threat of madness when Halloween rolled around each year, and with it came the knocking.

Still more say that, when the time was right and he could bear it no more (or perhaps when the avenging revenant finally allowed), he took himself far from any house, one All Hallows Eve, and watched and waited until he saw the bruised and bloodied figure, and waited patiently as he walked the slow and aching walk to meet him. To repent of his mischief, and finally pay the toll.

The Black Bull inn still stands, and rooms can still be rented there – reports of phantom knocking and spectral figures in the pub date back at least to the turn of the century, and are still reported regularly. The Green Man is now the Galvin Green Man, and was named Pub of the Year for 2022 (don't ask me by who) – though there have been accounts by punters sat at the bar of inexplicable whispers since the 1950s (and as recently as 2023), they don't like to talk about that sort of thing anymore, thankyouverymuch.

A number of people I spoke to in the area claimed, likewise, to have experienced phantom knocks at their doors around midnight on Halloween. Some ascribe them to the lost and wayward soul of Samuel Pegram, doomed to knock every year at All Hallows, until some offering may finally be given that will set his wretched soul free. But it's probably just some mischief. Children playing tricks.

John Newman was buried on 2nd November 1782, at St Mary the Virgin Church in Shenfield. Pay your respects next All Souls Day, should you ever pass that way. I'm sure he'll think it quite the treat.

THE FLAME

14

BONFIRES, TAR BARRELS AND TAPERS

> It was as if these men and boys had suddenly dived into past ages, and fetched therefrom an hour and deed which had before been familiar with this spot. The ashes of the original British pyre which blazed from that summit lay fresh and undisturbed in the barrow beneath their tread. The flames from funeral piles long ago kindled there had shone down upon the lowlands as these were shining now. Festival fires to Thunor and Woden had followed on the same ground and duly had their day. Indeed, it is pretty well known that such blazes as this the heathmen were now enjoying are rather the lineal descendants from jumbled Druidical rites and Saxon ceremonies than the invention of popular feeling about Gunpowder Plot.
>
> Moreover to light a fire is the instinctive and resistant act of man when, at the winter ingress, the curfew is sounded throughout Nature. It indicates a spontaneous, Promethean rebelliousness against that fiat that this recurrent season shall bring foul times, cold darkness, misery and death. Black chaos comes, and the fettered gods of the earth say, Let there be light.

The above passage, from *Return of the Native* by Thomas Hardy, is what revives in my mind whenever I am present at a bonfire. Though it's true that he overstates, perhaps, the directness of the link from Hallowmas fires to those of Druidry and Wodenism, in doing so, he perfectly encapsulates the deeper, atavistic and experiential truth of the feeling of primal connectivity that they inspire, which is beyond and beneath reason, and all the more powerful for it. Though today we are used to thinking of Bonfire Night as unrelated and unlinked to Halloween, it not only sits firmly within the broader Hallowmas season of 31st October to 13th November, but as we've already touched on, it has been interacting with All Hallows since its inception.

Halloween bonfires are an old custom, and historically were not limited to 31st October alone, but spread fluidly into the days before and after. In one sense, it's little wonder that the shrinking days and lengthening nights, combined with wetter air and dropping temperatures, should result in fire wherever possible, and communal fire as a preference. Flames were a common aspect of festivities for this reason; as William Henderson's 1879 *Notes on the Folk-Lore of the Northern Counties* tells us, 'It is unlucky to let the fire out on Hallow E'en night. The same holds good for New Year's Eve, Midsummer Eve, and Christmas Eve'.

According to Hutton, English parish accounts of the early 1500s specify that at Hallowmas 'many churches laid in extra supplies of candles and torches, to be carried in procession and to illuminate the building'. In Bristol in the 1470s, every mayor was expected to entertain the councillors, gentry and local dignitaries at All Hallows before Evensong, with 'fires and their drinkings with spiced cakebread and sundry wines'.

We find an interesting survival of this from Anna Eliza Stothard, in *The Borders of the Tamar and the Tavy* (1879), where she tells us that in Devon and other parts of the west of England, people would commonly go souling on All Hallows Eve 'to beg fire at the doors of the rich' (often accompanied by a small monetary donation).

In the Lancashire parish of Whalley, as J. Weld's 1913 *A History of Leagram* tells us, Catholic families still assembled at the midnight between All Hallows and All Souls in the early nineteenth century, to carry out a fire rite known as 'teenlay'. The ritual consisted of local families gathering on hills near their homes, with one of the group holding a large bunch of burning straw on the end of a fork. According to Hutton, the rest 'knelt in a circle around and prayed for the souls of relatives and friends until the flames burned out'.

Charles Hardwick confirms, in his *Traditions, Superstitions and Folk-lore* of 1872, that prior to the waning of the practice in his time, 'it had been very common and at nearby Whittingham such fires could be seen all around the horizon at Hallowe'en'. The location of such teenlay customs often took on a related name, such as Purgatory Field or Purgatory Farm, and the fact these names are so widespread across northern Lancashire testifies to a broad distribution of the practice.

John Brand's 1777 *Observations on Popular Antiquities* testifies to his witnessing the 'hills throughout the country illuminated with sacred flames

[...] under the name of Teanla fires [...] connected with superstitious notions regarding purgatory'. He also mentions another purpose, and one that has nothing to do with the post-Catholic practice of prayers for the dead – in the region of Fylde, farmers would, at Halloween, circle their fields 'with a burning wisp of straw at the point of a fork [...] to protect the coming crop from noxious weeds'.

Though northern Lancashire was a stronghold of Catholicism, which might help explain the survival, the vicinity of Derby in Derbyshire was not, and yet we find the practice there also. The *Gentleman's Magazine* of November 1768 notes that every year on All Hallows Day people would light fires known as 'tindles' on common land in the area, and that the rite had something to do with purgatory and the dead. In W. Holden's 1944 article on tindles for the *Derbyshire Archaelogical and Natural History Society Journal* 65, we find that tindle fires were still an element of the Derbyshire All Hallows a century later, in 1868.

Teenlay was not restricted to the north, either. In 1638, the antiquary Sir William Dugdale recorded at the end of an almanac that at Hallowe'en (probably in the Midlands county of Warwickshire), the head of the family used to carry a burning bunch of straw round a field, saying, 'Fire and Red low / Light on my teen low'. According to Doris Joan-Baker's 1977 *Folklore of Hertfordshire*, a certain Purgatory Field in Gosmore, located in the chalk hills in the northern portion of the thoroughly southern county of Hertfordshire, was so named due to 'former assemblies of men there at Hallowe'en to pray for the souls of the departed until a fire burned out'.

Examples of Halloween fires are certainly not restricted to England, and can be found in the lowlands of Scotland and parts of the eastern Highlands from at least the 1500s, though apparently not in the western Highlands or the islands. In Wales, references exist from the early 1700s, though they're probably older. There they were known as '*coel-cearths*' and were found in the north and centre of the country, along the border with England, but not in the south. They existed also in the Isle of Man (recorded in the early nineteenth century, where they were called '*Sauin*' and fended off witches and fairies), but do not appear to have been an Irish tradition, with the only two examples there both being recent introductions: one in the Protestant areas of north-eastern Ulster, heavily populated with Scottish immigrants who likely introduced the fires in the nineteenth century; the other in Dublin, where the fires dated only to the mid-twentieth century.

Most accounts of these fires postdate the introduction of Bonfire Night, and it is just as likely that from the late 1600s onwards Hallowmas fires came to be influenced by Bonfire Night fires as it is that the opposite is true – there is evidence of costume wearing and masking at Bonfire Night before any such practice is recorded as defining Halloween. The popular idea that these fire traditions date to an earlier, pre-Christian festival of Samhain has no meaningful evidence to back it up (though communal fire, as we have discussed, will always *feel* atavistically pagan).

A good example of this potential for back-influence can be found in the Halloween celebrations at Balmoral in 1876, as detailed in the *Woodbridge Reporter* of 9th November:

> Hallowe'en was celebrated at Balmoral Castle, with unusual ceremony, in the presence of her Majesty, Princess Beatrice, the ladies and gentlemen of the Royal household, and a large gathering of the tenantry. The leading features of the celebration were a torch-light procession, the lighting of large bonfires, and the burning in effigy of witches and warlocks. Upwards of 150 torchbearer assembled at the castle as dark set in [...] refreshments were served to all, and dancing was engaged in round a huge bonfire. Suddenly there appeared from the rear of the Castle a grotesque apparition representing a witch with a train of followers dressed like sprites who danced and gesticulated in all fashions. Then followed a warlock of demoniac shape, who was succeeded by another warlock drawing a car, on which was seated the figure of a witch, surrounded by other figures in the garb of demons. The unearthly visitors having marched several times round the burning pile, the principal figure was taken from the car and tossed into the flames amid the burning of blue lights and a display of crackers and fireworks.

What this describes is far nearer to a Bonfire Night celebration, and the piece goes on to refer to 'these strange innovations', specifying that the only 'old time honoured custom characteristic of Hallowe'en [...] that was not forgotten amidst the excitement of the novel ceremonies and the weird burnt offering' was the traditional toast to the health of Her Majesty. It makes clear that these elements were not, in 1876, considered a traditional part of the Scottish Halloween, and 'lovers of the simple past will, perhaps, not look kindly on the modern innovations with which the celebrations of "Hallowe'en" at Balmoral seem to have been garnished'.

We will return to these themes in a later chapter, that of the Walking Fire (Chapter 21), but for now, we stick to the more static variety.

15

GUY FAWKES NIGHT GHOSTS

With the previous chapter in mind, it is difficult to see how the establishing of 5th November bonfires from 1606 onwards can possibly be entirely unrelated, even if just experientially, to the older tradition of Hallowmas fires, which in many areas were held in the same place, just a few days earlier. It seems naïve to think that nobody would have felt a connection in practice, even if there are distinctions in principle.

This is not a book about the history of Bonfire Night, so, briefly: in 1605, a group of Catholic terrorists attempted to blow up Parliament and kill the king by filling a cellar beneath the Palace of Westminster with barrels of gunpowder. The plot was discovered and thwarted, with a certain Guy (or Guido) Fawkes being caught red-handed with the barrels. He was taken to the Tower of London and tortured into giving up his accomplices (his signature exists pre- and post-interrogation, and the degradation of it is chilling) before being executed for treason. The following year was the first official, state-sanctioned Guy Fawkes or Bonfire Night, as a piece of propaganda to commemorate the failure of the plot. It continues today and shows no sign of ceasing.

Ever since, sightings of the ghost of Guy have been reported around Halloween and 5th November, especially at the Guy Fawkes Inn in York (supposedly his birthplace) and the Tower of London itself, where the sounds of his tortured screams are also reported. Extensive ghost hunts and paranormal investigations have been carried out at both sites, with little in the way of relevant result, but the stories and associations persist.

The rest of the conspirators had their last stand at a mansion named Holbeche House in Dudley. A bad accident while trying to dry out their gunpowder resulted in burns and related injuries (including blindness) for a couple of them. The militia that found them soon after shot a few others, and the remainder were hanged with Fawkes in London (and drawn and quartered, too).

Holbeche House has been used as a care home in recent years, during which time many sightings, between Bonfire Night and Martlemas, have been reported of the ghosts of those who died there, the phantom sounds of gunshots and explosions, and the smell of gunpowder. At the time of writing, the house is derelict and boarded up, and has been placed on Historic England's 'Heritage at Risk Register'.

Shortly after Guy and the remaining conspirators were executed, Parliament passed the *Observance of 5th November Act*, commonly known as the Thanksgiving Act, on the basis that some official recognition should be given to the apparent divine intervention which had saved the king. Thus, 5th November was established as a day of thanksgiving, with (in theory) mandatory church attendance. A new service was added to the Church of England's *Book of Common Prayer*, town councils provided music, parades and artillery salutes, food and drink was provided for local dignitaries, the church bells were rung, and bonfires and fireworks were lit.

By the 1620s the festival was fully established across all of England, though regional variation was significant. In Whalley, in the Lancashire Pennines (which you may remember from discussion of their 'Teenlay' fire ritual in the previous chapter), Bonfire Night was celebrated on All Hallows Day until 1658. I simply do not believe this is a coincidence.

Bonfire Night was one of the few festivals embraced by the Puritan government during the Interregnum (during which Charles I was beheaded, and Christmas and the theatre were both outlawed), due to its pro-Parliamentary flavour (they ignored the Royalist interpretation). By the 1640s, effigies of Guy Fawkes and the Pope were being burned, money was begged or demanded from passers-by, and the events had grown in wildness and intensity.

By the 1700s, masks and carnival-style costumes had become associated with the festivities, and 'penny for the guy' became common, whereby children or young men would make an effigy of Guy and parade it around the streets for donations of money in a wheelbarrow or cart, before burning it on 5th November. As the connection to Guy Fawkes himself faded, the word 'guy' simply came to mean a strange-looking person, and eventually just a person (as it does today).

This effigy practice still exists among children today, though increasingly rare, and was a notable aspect of my own childhood. Sightings in the wild can be reported to the Penny for the Guy Spotting Project (website: https://pixyledpublications.wordpress.com).

The ubiquitous rhyme for Guy Fawkes Night is, today, as follows. It has an infinity of regional variants and dates (in some form) to at least the 1700s:

Remember, remember, the fifth of November,
Gunpowder, treason and plot.
I see no reason why gunpowder treason
Should ever be forgot.

When extended, it usually continues:

Guy Fawkes, Guy Fawkes, 'twas his intent
To blow up the King and Parliament.
Three-score barrels of powder below
To prove old England's overthrow;
By God's will we did him catch
With a dark lantern and burning match.
Holler boys, Holler boys, let the bells ring.
Holler boys, holler boys, God save the King!

When extended even further:

Guy Fawkes, Guy,
Poke him in the eye,
Shove him up a chimney pot,
And there let him die!
A stick and a stake
For King [insert monarch's name]'s sake!
If you won't give me one,
I'll take two,
The better for me,
And the worse for you.
A rope, a rope, to hang the Pope,
A penn'orth of cheese to choke him,
A pint of beer to wash it down,
And a jolly good fire to burn him.

By the end of the century, the rough carnivalism and riotry of Bonfire Night had gotten out of hand, and come the 1800s, the authorities began to work hard to actively curb the most violent excesses. Anti-Catholic sentiment was no longer considered acceptable, and by the middle of the century, the thanksgiving for 5th November had been removed from the *Book of Common Prayer*. In March 1859, the *Anniversary Days Observance Act* repealed the *Observance of 5th November Act 1605*, and the roaming local gangs who had taken control of the day (called Guys or Bonfire Boyes) were gradually quelled by the authorities – we will speak more of this in the following chapter.

A strange Bonfire Night ghost tradition from the village of Gargrave, in north Yorkshire, acts as a fitting commemoration of the dangers of Guy Fawkes Night revelry (which on more than one occasion resulted in death, and on countless others, disfigurement, injury and damage to property). Reports from the 1920s claim that on more than one Bonfire Night, innocent revellers had heard a gunshot and felt a bullet enter their leg, whereupon they collapsed and screamed in pain, clutching at the limb, only to find that all was well and no such thing had happened. From at least the 1950s there have been sightings of a ghost on or around the village green on the night of 5th November. Both seem related to the following report, from the *Evening Standard* of 11th December 1867:

> Yesterday, at the Leeds Assizes, before Mr. Baron Pigott, Richard Harrison, 21, farm labourer, was arraigned for the wilful murder of Robert Abbotson, at Gargrave, near Skipton-in-Craven, on the 5th of November.
> [...]
>
> It was a remarkable case. No human being saw the shot fired which led to the death of Abbotson, and that shooting took place on the night of the 5th of November, when on the village green Guy Fawkes Day was celebrated by a bonfire and the exploding of guns, crackers, squibs, pistols, and small cannon. Gargrave is a quiet and retired village near the source of the river Aire, and its general tranquillity is such that but one policeman suffices to watch over its affairs. This charge of murder depended entirely on a long string of circumstances.
>
> It was not pretended that the prisoner had any malice against the deceased, but it was known that he owed a grudge to the policeman, James Duckett, and that on bonfire night he had been heard to make

some malicious remarks respecting him. One of these was, 'I'll break his head yet.' On the night in question Duckett went into the house of a person named Birtwhistle, on the village green. Abbotson, the deceased, was the father of Mrs. Birtwhistle. While Duckett was talking to Abbotson he heard a small crack, which seemed to come from the door, and Abbotson cried out, 'Oh, my leg.' He fell on to two chairs, and was sick, while blood came streaming from his legs, and a bullet was picked up.

A pistol was taken from the prisoner, and the lock and barrel were fastened to the stock with a piece of string, and the hammer was entirely without string. The ball, however, which was picked up, was rifled all round, as though it had been discharged from a rifled barrel. It was one of the imputations of the prisoner's council that Duckett had a rifled breech-loading pistol of his own, and that he had said he would never use it until it came to the last gasp, and that the ball could not possibly have been fired from the prisoner's own pistol. Dockett admitted that immediately after the shot he looked out at the door, but saw no one running away.

A factory hand, named William Wilson, said about two years ago the prisoner was charged with rape, but exonerated. After that he said, 'Duckett thought of doing for me at Skipton, but he's let in.' On other occasions he said 'he would mark him,' 'do for him before winter was out,' and 'shoot him.' The witnesses to these threats said they considered the prisoner a great boaster, and did not take much notice of what he said.

The Counsel for the defence argued that the deceased died from a shot fired accidentally at the outside of the house in celebration of Guy Fawkes's Day; and he argued from various facts in the case that it was highly improbable the prisoner had been bent upon vengeance against the policeman. It was entirely consistent that the fatal wound might have been inflicted by some stray bullet innocently fired by some boy in the village green that night. After his lordship had addressed the jury, they acquitted the prisoner.

In the burning of the guy and the sightings of Fawkes's ghost (and others), and, indeed, the remembrance of a dead man in Guido himself, the day retains an indirect association with the dead and the supernatural. Its masks, costumes and revelry likely influenced those of 31st October, as did its fires. When the already discussed Mischief Night is taken into account, it seems uncontroversial to suggest Bonfire Night as a vital part of the development of Halloween – the main reason that it has been left out of discussions of the season thus far is that it remains largely uncelebrated outside of Britain, and so the American focus that has distorted analysis of Hallowmas until now has, by necessity, precluded it.

But now we speak of the Bonfire Boyes.

By the late eighteenth century, in part due to an increase in the number of competing civic spectacles (mainly birthdays of royals, popular politicians or military leaders), the organisation of Bonfire Night was something that the authorities and upper classes were increasingly less interested in. So it was that organisation and fundraising was increasingly taken on by community groups and Bonfire Societies, in lieu of aristocratic or Church patronage.

Though this may sound fairly civilised, in practice, it was anything but.

These gangs of Bonfire Boys were secret associations of youths, usually aged about 20, and mostly comprised of artisans and labourers, though sometimes with young men from wealthier middle-class families in their leadership. They wore masks and costumes, embraced the roughness of old-fashioned revelry, and carried cudgels to fight off anyone who tried to obstruct them. They first appeared in Sussex, and between 1815 and 1830 were being formed in Surrey and Devon also, and in Essex during the 1850s.

The Bonfire Boys' version of Bonfire Night emphasised the traditional values of popular rights, patriotism, a hostility to Catholicism, carnival chaos and extreme drunkenness. Though broadly conservative in their outlooks, they embraced anti-authoritarianism, and would often burn effigies of unpopular politicians or world leaders and local figures of annoyance, alongside the more traditional Pope and Guy Fawkes figures.

This wild vision survives, today, almost exclusively in Sussex.

16

BATTLE, LEWES AND THE SUSSEX SOCIETIES

The oldest of the Bonfire Boy Societies still in existence are the Battel Bonfire Boyes, established by 1646, and possibly earlier. They still, today, organise the festivities at Battle, in East Sussex, and have the distinction of possessing the oldest Guy in the world.

Though Guys are traditionally constructed anew and burned annually, in Battle only the body was burned, with the head kept for the following year. The head, which can be seen at the Battle Bonfire Night, dates to at least 1795 (some place it as much as a century older) and is hand carved from pearwood. Each year, a new body was made for it, most notably in 1897, when an excessively long body made the guy a good 12ft tall.

The tradition of detaching and burning the body stopped around the Second World War, and since then, the effigy is kept as part of the parade but doesn't see the flames of the fire. Throughout the rest of the year, he can be found at Battle Museum.

Though Battle is the oldest, the biggest of the Bonfire Nights is indisputably at Lewes, in East Sussex. Always held on the 5th (unless it falls on a Sunday, when it's moved to the 4th), the event not only marks Guy Fawkes Night, but also commemorates the memory of the seventeen Lewes Martyrs, Protestants who were burned alive at the stake in the High Street between 1555 and 1557, under the Catholic Mary I.

In 1847, after years of intensifying hostility, police forces were drafted in from London to finally quell the Bonfire Boys, and all the major towns of Sussex were visited by the authorities, who read the Riot Act and ensured that no such pyromanic revelry was carried out. Lewes alone defied them

(Battle was, apparently, too small for any police to invest manpower in suppressing, so it was able to continue without issue).

As soon as the lawmen had left, the Lewes Bonfire Boys arrived, with soot-blackened faces and identical uniforms of horizontally striped, black-and-white tops. Indistinguishable from each other, and therefore impossible to identify after the fact, they set to work. This flagrant disregard for authority inspired all of Sussex, and bonfire gangs across the county began to take Lewes's lead in reforming and organising, wearing the same matching outfits as those pioneered by Lewes and organising along a similar, pseudo-militaristic structure.

In 1853, the oldest two of the official Lewes Bonfire Societies formed ('Cliffe' and 'Lewes Town', the latter of which became 'Lewes Borough' in 1859), with another three following in 1855 ('Commercial Square'), 1857 ('Waterloo' – disbanded, but re-formed in 1964), and 1886 ('Southover' – disbanded in 1985, re-formed in 2005). Through the twentieth century more arrived, particularly in 1913 ('South Street' – originally formed for the children of members of 'Cliffe', but now for all ages) and 1967 ('Nevill Juvenile' - specifically for children, they hold their celebrations a week or two early with help from the other societies). These seven now combine to make Lewes the biggest Bonfire Night in the world, putting on separate processions and firework displays throughout Lewes on the night of the 5th. Alongside this, twenty-five to thirty societies from all around Sussex come to Lewes to march the streets alongside them. This can mean up to 5000 people taking part in the celebrations and up to 80,000 spectators attending, in a county market town with a usual population of just over 17,000 – the railway station is now routinely closed for the day to deter as many visitors as possible.

Lewes and Battle, the biggest and the oldest, are the two main Sussex bonfire events (both in the modern county of East Sussex), but many, many more exist, and new ones form regularly. The character of these events tends to be defined by whichever of the two they are closest to, with those in the east of the county having a more gunpowder and flame focus (as pioneered by Battle, due in part to the historic industry of gunpowder manufacture there) and those in the west prioritising fancy dress and carnival (as per Lewes) – there's extensive overlap of course, and all celebrations incorporate the same elements, just in different proportions.

Lewes is the only one of the towns in Sussex to have multiple societies, with all others restricted to just one. These others hold their respective celebrations in the weeks and months leading up to (and sometimes away from) November 5th, and each of the Lewes societies sends out parties to these 'outmeetings' or 'outfires' to march with the local gang.

On the 5th itself, the Lewes societies process separately around their own particular territories, before all except the Cliffe and South Street join together in Western Road to parade down St. Anne's Street, the High Street and School Hill, followed by the other Sussex societies. Seventeen burning crosses are carried through the town, representing the seventeen Lewes Martyrs. A wreath-laying ceremony is held at the War Memorial, and at the start of the evening women's and men's races take place, where flaming tar barrels are dragged along the street in a 'barrel run'. Another flaming barrel is then thrown into the River Ouse, to symbolise the throwing of the magistrates into the river after they read the Riot Act to the bonfire boys in 1847.

Later, each of the participating Lewes societies marches to its own site on the edge of the town, where there is a large bonfire, a firework display, and effigies are burned. The societies then return to their respective headquarters (usually pubs) for Bonfire Prayers. Nearly all members carry flaming torches throughout the day, some light and throw bangers (known as 'rookies', short for 'rook scarers'), and some carry burning crosses, banners, musical instruments or fiery letters spelling out the initials of their society. The floats and effigies are a notable aspect of the Lewes Bonfire Night, usually critically depicting figures relevant to current events (sometimes controversially), always including Guy Fawkes and Pope Paul V (who held the office in 1605).

Both Lewes and Battle kept their bonfires burning despite the Second World War, when the vast majority of Bonfire Societies put them on hold. This was achieved with a single candle under a bucket, and a skeleton crew of non-combatant Bonfire Boys. After the war, many had lost the taste for gunpowder, and it was not until the 1950s that most of the Sussex Societies restarted their events, but Lewes and Battle held strong throughout.

The successful continuity of these two societies really cannot be overstated, and today, Sussex in its entirety has an unparalleled identity where bonfires are concerned, with the season lasting all of October and November – and as much of September as they can get away with. Societies have even begun to cross the borders, cropping up in Kent and Hampshire, operating along the same lines and very much in the same vein.

If you want to do some good in your community, why not think about getting in touch with one for advice on how to go about reviving a society of your own? I'm sure they'd be happy to help. Sussex doesn't hold a monopoly on tar barrels, after all, as we shall see in the next chapter.

17

OTTERY, HATHERLEIGH AND THE BRIDGWATER CARNIVAL

Ottery St Mary, a small town in Devon, is home to the second most famous bonfire celebration in the country, though it should certainly not be thought of as second best. In Ottery alone are flaming tar barrels actually carried on the shoulders of the running men, rather than dragged safely(ish) behind, and the event is of a far wilder and rougher nature than even Lewes or Battle can compete with.

The 'Barrel Rollers' of Ottery wear no specialist fireproof clothing, instead making do with bravery, a towel, and home-made padded gloves of wire and hessian. Burns are to be expected, especially to the hands and the back of the neck.

The evening includes children's, youths' and women's events alongside the climax of the men's run, in which seventeen former sherry or cider barrels coated with tar are lit and 'rolled' (carried), either from outside the pub that sponsored them, or the site of a former one lost to time. Only true 'Ottregians' (those born in the town, owning a business or having lived most of their lives there) are allowed to be Barrel Rollers, and many local families have been passing the tradition on unbroken beyond living memory, with three generations of the same line often running on the same night, across the various events.

Though the late twentieth century has provided a few fanciful origin stories (some say it stems from beacons lit to warn of the Spanish Armada, others that the flames were carried around to fumigate cottages, still more that they ward off evil spirits), all evidence points to the Ottery celebrations as simply being survivals of what was once a very standard Bonfire Night observance, including an informal carnival procession of 50–150 'Guys' in wild costumes, with flames, fireworks, barrels and bands. Ottery's first become notable in 1858, when an over-zealous captain named Dick and a police inspector named Ross tried to stop the event by force. A horde of locals took up cudgels and a fight ensued, after which the eight to twelve officers who remained fled to the safety of the Volunteer Inn, and then out the back windows and on to Tipton St John, over two and a half miles away. The uprising was widely reported in national papers.

The event continued more peaceably thereafter, but with increasing passion. In 1894, an official accompanying carnival was established with proceeds going to the local cottage hospital, and by 1912 newspapers were commenting that Ottery still actively retained that which was dying out elsewhere. By the 1930s the event was overtly referred to as an 'old time tradition', the tar barrels noted as a rare survival of ages past. Alongside the distinctive barrels, the event includes much singing of 'The Ottery Song', a procession of tableaux, and the firing of the 'Rock Cannons' – 10 hand held miniature cannon, ignited by striking a firing cap with a hammer, and once loaded with the same powder used to blast quarry rocks – these are very similar to the 'Fenny Poppers', which I discuss in Chapter 28.

Though the events were paused during the First and Second World Wars (and Covid), they were restarted immediately afterwards. The 1918 tar barrel revival was held on the 16th as an Armistice celebration, with an effigy of Kaiser 'Billy' burned and English, Scottish and Belgian soldiers and sailors taking part in the procession. The 1945 revival included at least two men immediately returned from active service as actual Barrel Rollers: Peter Arbury (Royal Navy) and 'Patchy' Piney (Royal Artillery).

Today the carnival (with its torch lit procession, bonfire and Guy burning – the effigy made by the Young family from 1958–2009, now by local children in a competition) is separated from the barrel rolling, with the former usually held a week or two before the latter, which is held on the 5th itself, or the 4th if a Sunday – historically the barrels were run on both days, and moved to the 6th when a Sunday arose. Though the details vary year to year, the grand finale of the 30kg Midnight Barrel always concludes things in the main square. The town's population of 7000 is more than doubled for the night, with roads in and out closed for safety reasons, and a strict system of buses and diversions enforced.

Inspired by Ottery, in 1903, nearby Hatherleigh decided to revive their own tar barrels and established the Hatherleigh and Meeth Hospital Association Carnival on the first Wednesday in November to raise money for their local hospital (this was before the NHS). The carnival survives, and still donates proceeds to charity. It is now held on a Saturday, with impressive floats, much flame, and health and safety conscious barrel dragging. Despite the marketing, it has no connection to paganism.

Over the county boundary, Bridgwater in Somerset has a Guy Fawkes carnival (sans barrels) of considerable repute. Originating in the standard, raucous celebrations of the English Bonfire Night, this carnival's distinct development dates to 1880. The Bridgwater bonfire festivities were particularly raucous that year, and when at 1am firemen arrived to put out the flames a riot ensued, and much damage was caused. In the aftermath of this it was decided to establish a formalised

Carnival Committee, and from 1881 this was the direction events took – of an illuminated carnival parade of floats, rather than an old-fashioned rustic fire ceremony.

The Bridgwater Guy Fawkes Carnival has run ever since, and where those of Devon and Sussex are recognisable for their focus on historic approaches, Bridgwater's emphasis has always been on modernising. The move away from flaming torches and towards paraffin lamps came early, and the first electric lighting in the procession was introduced in 1903. The bonfire was abolished in 1925 (the new tarmac being too flammable), and the last horse-drawn float took part in 1948. It is now the oldest illuminated carnival in the UK, and possibly the largest in the world.

Just as Sussex has its Bonfire Societies, so Somerset has its Guy Fawkes Carnival Clubs. The four West Country Carnival circuits start annually in August, and last until late November, attracting participants from Britain and beyond. Of the four (the other three being East Devon, Wessex Grand Prix, and South Somerset Federation), the one that concerns us here is the oldest: the Somerset County Guy Fawkes Carnival Association Circuit. Bridgwater Carnival is, to this circuit, what Lewes is to the Sussex Societies, and everyone who is anyone takes part. Thanks to Bridgwater all of the carnivals in this circuit can trace an unbroken lineage back to the events of 1605.

Though there were no parades during the Second World War, as with Lewes and Battle, a local carnival enthusiast, William Henry Edwin Lockyer, also known as 'Nosey', walked the Bridgwater carnival route for six years with a group known as The Kilties, to maintain the living continuity. Due to Covid it was replaced with an online video retrospective in 2020, and a smaller scale procession in 2021, but was back with a vengeance from 2022.

Across the circuit floats are known as 'carts', clubs as gangs (as with most bonfire events), and those who take part as 'masqueraders' or 'features' - as they have been for centuries. A unique element of Bridgwater's event specifically is their trademark firework, the 'Bridgwater Squib' – described by the *Western Daily Press* of November the 6th, 1897, as 'famed for its pyrotechnic effectiveness; it is not the modest, innocent little affair that one observes in the shop windows of other towns; it is of the thickness of a man's arm, some 20 inches or so in length, and sends forth a prolific supply of fiery atoms, and culminates in a cannon-like report.' The crush of modernity has removed the bangs, but the evening still finishes with the annual squibbing display along Bridgwater High Street, when over 140 'squibbers' let them off simultaneously in the air at arms reach, held up on a specially built wooden stick called a cosh, and lit from a line of flammable liquid run along the ground.

Today the carnival welcomes well over 150,000 people annually, with a display of over forty large vehicles up to 100ft long, filled with dancers, costumes, and up to 22,000 lightbulbs, following a 2.5-mile route over two to three hours duration. If you've never been, as with all of the events featured in this book, it is certainly worth the trip.

18

GROATY PUDDING, PARKIN, TOFFEE AND THARF CAKE

Traditional foods are an important aspect of folk culture, and Bonfire Night is no exception. The following delicacies are associated with it.

GROATY PUDDING

A particularly satisfying cold-weather dish from the Black Country, in the West Midlands. It is eaten there most especially (and inherently) at Guy Fawkes Night, with which it has become synonymous. It is very satisfying, and I encourage you to try it. Here's one recipe, from E. Dawson of Castle Eden, submitted to the *Northern Weekly Gazette* on 1st November 1924:

> Ingredients: An ounce of beef dripping, rubbed inside a stew-jar to prevent burning; one teacupful of groats, one quart of water, one teaspoonful of salt, a quarter of a teaspoonful of pepper, one large onion cut in thin slices, one pound of beef or mutton, either raw or left from a roast. Cut the meat small, place all in the jar, and bake in oven slowly for two hours, stirring occasionally. (This is an old Midland dish.)

My mother and hers are both from the Black Country, and grew up with groaty pudding every year. The below recipe is more in line with the version that she is familiar with (though my mother knew it with bacon rather than beef, which apparently worked well due to its saltiness), from the *Birmingham Daily Gazette* of 5th November 1954:

> Take any amount of shin of beef, an equal amount of groats, add onions and leaks and flavouring. You will need to get this on the hob right away – it must simmer for at least 12 hours, preferably 24. When it is good and thick like porridge you are all set to serve your bonfire guests with groaty pudding, the traditional Guy Fawkes night dish of the Black Country. I got the recipe from 69-year-old Mr. Howard Orford, proprietor of the Hagley Court Country Club. It will be served to members tonight at the club's bonfire party. 'It's a tradition that has almost died out,' says Mr. Orford, a Black Country man. 'But for me no firework night is complete without a plate of groaty pudding.'

Groats, for any not in the know, are the hulled kernels of various grains, generally used today as a feed for fowl. As such, they can be bought astonishingly cheaply, and this dish is one of the few peasant foods that really can still be made for pennies, dating to at least the eighteenth century and very probably much older than that.

BONFIRE TOFFEE

A hard treacle delicacy much loved in the north and often accompanied by the tharf cake below, bonfire toffee can still be purchased from shops today, and is referred to from at least the nineteenth century. Here follow three recipes from the *Derbyshire Times*:

> **30th October 1926**
> Put breakfastcupful treacle, ¼lb. brown sugar, half tablespoonful vinegar, and 1oz butter into a pan, stir (till well mixed) over a gentle fire, then boil up without stirring, but watch carefully as treacle very soon burns. Drop a spoonful into cold water, and if it crisps the toffee is done. Add one small teaspoonful bicarbonate of soda, pour into a greased tin, and mark in squares before it is quite cold.

> **3rd November 1928**
> Mix together ¼lb. butter, ½lb. granulated sugar, 1 teacupful cold water, and 1 teaspoonful vanilla essence. Boil up, add 1 tin Swiss milk which has been dissolving by the side of the stove, and boil for three-quarters of an hour, stirring all the time.

> **2nd November 1929**
> Ingredients: 1lb. of brown moist sugar, 1lb. dark treacle, 2ozs. of butter, a pinch of salt, small teacupfull of water, and one tablespoonful of vinegar. Method: Put water, salt and sugar into a clean saucepan and boil until the sugar is melted. Then add treacle and vinegar; when it has boiled ten minutes add your butter. Keep boiling until you find it will go crisp by dropping a few drops into a cup of cold water; then pour into a clean dry tin and put in a cool place to set. For lighter toffee use white sugar and golden syrup.

Try all three, then develop your own.

THARF CAKE AND PARKIN

As touched on earlier, in parts of the north, the soul cake seems to have developed into the tharf cake (a sort of flapjack) and parkin (a sort of gingerbread flapjack), the first of which especially is eaten at Bonfire Night, and both of which are sometimes associated with Halloween and All Souls. The *Miscellanies of the English Dialect Society* for 1876 tell us:

> THARF CAKE is a circular cake made from oatmeal butter and treacle. In Sheffield it is eaten on the 5th of November. As All Souls Day is the second day of November it may be that the custom of eating tharf cakes which obtains in Sheffield on the 5th of November has reference to the soul mass cake formerly eaten on the Feast of All Souls and on that day distributed to the poor [...] A year or two ago I noticed that a shopkeeper in a good street in Sheffield advertised tharf cake for sale by a conspicuous handbill in his window. As a rule I find that people are ashamed of tharf cake. They call it parkin instead of using the old word. Tharf-cake, and tharf-bread meaning unleavened bread are common in early English literature [from Old English *theorf*]. On Caking day, which in Bradfield is the first day of November, boys and young men dress themselves like mummers and go to farm houses collecting money to buy tharf cake with.

Recipes for both follow, from a Mrs Burgess of Burnhope, near Lanchester, contributing to the *Northern Weekly Gazette* of 9th November 1912:

> There are some English recipes in which oatmeal plays a part, and one of them is called tharfe cake in Yorkshire, which is baked for the fifth of November. Here is an old recipe for it:
>
> Take four pounds of fresh oatmeal and rub into one pound of butter, one pound of brown sugar, add a quarter of a pound of candied lemon peel grated, and two ounces of caraway seeds well bruised. Mix the whole with three pounds and a half of treacle. Bake in a slow oven.
>
> Parkin is also a Yorkshire cake, which resembles tharfe cake, but is not so good. The following is a recipe for it:
>
> Rub half a pound of butter into three pounds of fine oatmeal, add one ounce of ginger, and as much stiff treacle as will make it into a stiff paste. Roll it out in cakes of about half an inch thick, lay these on buttered tins, and bake in a slow oven. The tops may be washed over with milk, as it has then a more appetising appearance. All the modern recipes for parkin contain baking powder and sugar, but for the first there is no need at all.

The name parkin is known at least since reports of the court case of *Rex vs Jagger* at the Yorkshire Assizes of 1797, where a husband attempted to poison his wife with 'a cake of parkin laced with arsenic'. An early recipe, from *The English Cookery Book* of 1859 by J.H. Walsh, is as follows:

> Mix three pounds of oatmeal or flour, one pound and a half of treacle, half a pound of butter, half a pound of moist sugar, two ounces of grated ginger, together into a paste and roll it out about an inch thick. Cut it into small cakes any shape you like and bake them. An ounce of carraway seeds may be added if approved.

A form of thin parkin is known as a 'harcake', likely derived from 'hearth cake', and sometimes referred to in the far north as soulmass cake. There are countless recipes available for all three, as each had infinite regional variants. Oft-repeated advice is to leave the parkin/harcake/tharf cake in an airtight container for three to seven days to mature before eating.

Again, try all of the above, tinker with them to form your own preferred versions, then make them for as many people as you can annually. Just remember to write down your recipes.

DEFENCE AGAINST THE DARK ARTS

19

LATING THE WITCHES

Hey-how for Hallow E'en,
When all the witches are to be seen,
Some in black and some in green,
Hey-how for Hallow E'en.

The Denham Tracts, 1846–1849.

While the flame of the bonfire is static, communal and carries out a broad, non-specific social function, it is not the only flame of Halloween. Over the coming chapters, I'm going to attempt to loosen a dense knot of interrelated traditions – though I doubt I'll fully untie them, I hope at least to more clearly show which is connected to what, and how they interweave.

In the context of the candlelit processions of the medieval and continental All Hallows, the West Country custom of giving lit candles to doorstep soulers, and the teenlay fires of the north and the Midlands, a tradition from Longridge Fell in the Lancashire Pennines that more directly relates to protection from witchcraft is worth exploring. To quote from the *London Evening Standard*, 31st October 1878, referencing William Hone's 1829 *Year-book*:

> In Lancashire it was firmly believed that on Hallowe'en the witches assembled together at their general rendezvous in the Forest of Pendle – a ruined and desolate farm-house, termed the Malkin Tower, from the awful purposes to which it was devoted. This superstition led to a curious ceremony called lating, or leeting the witches [from *leoht* – Anglo-Saxon, light]. It was supposed that if a lighted candle were carried about the fells or hills from eleven to twelve o'clock at night, and burned all that time steadily, it had so far triumphed over the evil power of the witches, who,

> as they passed the Malkin Tower, would employ their utmost efforts to extinguish the light, and hence the person whom it represented might safely defy their malice. If, however, the candle by any chance went out, it was deemed highly inauspicious.

Hone's original text informs us, 'It was also deemed inauspicious to cross the threshold of that person until after the return from leeting, and not then unless the candle had preserved its light.' We've already mentioned the Sauin fires of the Isle of Man where, as the article puts it, 'fires were kindled to prevent the baneful influence of witches and fairies. The island was perambulated at night by young men, who stuck up at the door of every dwelling-house a rhyme in Manx, beginning, "This is Hollantide Eve," &c.'

(As a brief aside, the traditional Isle of Man Halloween dish is a mash of butter, potato, parsnip and fish. I am eating it as I type this, and it is surprisingly good. It seems to work especially well with smoked fish. It is generally called Manxen mash, a possible shortening of 'Manx Sauin mash'.)

Witches, witchcraft and the broader supernatural are, of course, a concern of long standing at Halloween, and the lating is just one of several rituals designed to defend against them. Enid Porter's *Cambridgeshire Folklore* tells us:

> The observance of Halloween in Cambridgeshire seems to have been confined to the remoter parts of the Fens, where belief in and fear of witchcraft remained firmly established until well into the present century. Witches were traditionally believed to hold their meetings on this night, so Fen dwellers stayed indoors and took precautions. These included the placing of food on the doorstep to appease any witch who might approach the house; the putting of salt in the keyholes; the safe locking up of all the domestic and farmyard animals; the killing of a cockerel and hanging of its tail feathers on stable doors, and the strewing of osiers [lengths of willow for weaving] on all the exterior thresholds.

Ruth Tongue's *Somerset Folklore* attests similar practices, and P.H. Ditchfield's *Old English Sports* of 1891 confirms that 'All-hallow Even was supposed to be a great night for witches: possibly it was with the intention of guarding against their spells that the farmers used to carry blazing straw around their cornfields and stacks', relating back to the teenlay fires we've already discussed.

Hold on to the concept of this protective walking fire, as we shall return to it after a quick story.

20

THE FAIRBROTHER SUICIDE

In some parts of Staffordshire, particularly around Lichfield and Hanley, a few older people can still be found who remember the local name for mysterious lights in the night, elsewhere called will-o'-the-wisps. Here, so the old folk claim, they were known as fairy brothers, and were particularly active around Halloween. The etymology seems clear.

When Richard Fairbrother died at the age of 23, thirteen days before Halloween of 1807, his family were bereft. None more so than his 18-year-old brother, Henry.

As the nights rolled interminably on, and the days grew darker and colder, and the loneliness weighed ever heavier on Henry, he began to dream of his freshly dead brother. As day passed day, the dreams intensified, and Henry resented waking and losing his brother yet again every morning, the pain growing fresher as the corpse grew more stale.

Thirteen days passed, and All Hallows Eve came. The night of the unquiet dead. Henry sought the ghost of his brother. He avoided the soul-cakers, he stalked the churchyard. He lit a candle, gazed at a mirror. Henry saw nothing. Henry met no one.

A bleak and unhappy Christmas came and passed, and a New Year which held little hope was welcomed in by the Fairbrothers.

Henry grew to hate his work, and grew to hate the tailor to whom he was apprenticed. The tailor grew to realise it. As Henry resented him, so he resented Henry – the arrangement became intolerable. Henry was blamed for anything and everything, from shoddy stitching to stolen food. He begged his father, John, to get back his indentures and free him from the position. John refused – everyone he knew agreed that the boy was lucky to be learning the trade, and all would mend itself in time.

Henry despaired. Still he dreamt. Still he pined for his brother. Still he longed for the happiness he had lost.

When the anniversary came, Henry wept on his knees at his brother's grave. As the light of day went down, Henry vowed to speak with him once more.

Now, had all of this occurred fifty years later, then the course that Henry took would likely have been different. By then, the genteel and scientifically minded religion of Spiritualism would have been established across Britain and accessible even to he, and any efforts to contact the dead would have been conducted in a straightforward, civilised manner, through a medium, round a table, safe and twee. But this was 1808, and Spiritualism had not yet been conceived.

In 1808, the messy business of talking to corpses was a very different thing indeed, and spoken of secretly, in urgent tones, if at all. Half-snatched rumours flitted about; horror stories passed in whispers.

All in all, it was a dangerous game that Henry Fairbrother took to playing, and the sort of game that teenage minds rarely win. As the story goes, Henry went out that All Hallows Eve in search of witches, and witches Henry Fairbrother found. It is said that Henry was used by them for their own ends; that together, they spoke with his brother – of things that the living are not meant to know.

What Henry learned that night weighed heavy on him, and he could not fit it into his skull – the brother he spoke to terrified him, and Henry could not stand it – in a rage, he roared that his brother was dead, and he would not hear the lies they told. So fled he from the graveyard.

The following night, All Souls Eve, Henry lay in bed and heard his woken brother screaming to him. Henry closed his eyes and whispered that he had no brother; tried not to hear the words that scratched his mind.

The following night, All Souls Day, still Henry heard his woken brother's call. Henry closed his eyes and shouted that he had no brother, swore he could not hear the words that scratched his mind. The screaming stopped. The sun rose. Morning came.

But Henry found no peace. That night he heard no sound, but still he could not sleep. He thought of his brother, of other loved ones who lay in ground. He wondered which of them had things to say. He wondered what the witches had done. He wondered many things.

The next night was the same. Then followed Bonfire Night, and Henry had no room for revels. All he had were thoughts of the dead.

The *Staffordshire Advertiser* of 29th December, 1808, tells what happens next more succinctly than any of the versions I heard in pubs:

> On the 6th of November last, Henry went, as usual, to church in the afternoon, but immediately after his return, and never till then, discovered, at his father's house, marks of insanity; he appeared unusually restless, could not sit still, and said to his mother, 'I have never seen my grandmother's tombstone: is there not a verse upon it? I will go and read it.' He went; and there is a report, that after he returned, he said, 'I have seen a ghost.' The same evening he went to the dissenting chapel. The Rev. W. Salt, late of Hoxton College, preached on the recovery of St. Peter; the text Luke, c. xxii, v. 61, 62. The subject was remarkably consolatory.
>
> However, some time after this, the unhappy Henry drank poison, and, during its operation, it is reported that he said to his mother, – 'I am lost, I am damned, and I did it to make me happy.'

He was buried on Martlemas Day at St Chad's in Lichfield – Old Halloween.

Those verses he heard preached on his final day, in case you are unfamiliar, go as follows in the King James Bible:

> And the Lord turned, and looked upon Peter. And Peter remembered the word of the Lord, how he had said unto him, Before the cock crow, thou shalt deny me thrice.
>
> And Peter went out, and wept bitterly.

A common belief is that will-o'-the-wisps are souls in Purgatory, or those doomed to wander the earth without rest. Perhaps, then, the Lichfield Halloween lights of fairy brothers have a different origin than the obvious. Perhaps Richard, Henry's brother, once raised by the witches, was never put back to rest again. Perhaps it is he that some still see at Halloween, though his screams are no longer heard by any. Perhaps Henry himself still wanders in penance.

Fair brothers they make, no doubt.

21

JACK, HOB AND WALKING FIRE

We come now to that most famous and distinctive of Halloween figures: Jack o' Lantern. Bear with me as I loosen the knot.

The *Caledonian Mercury* of 7th January 1784 tells us:

> An *ignis fatuus*, commonly called *Jack of the Lantern*, has for several nights past been seen in St James's Park [London], and a number of nobility and gentry being deluded by the appearance, and following it, have fallen into the *dirt*.

The *Hereford Journal* of 5th December 1821 likewise informs:

> *Singular Effect of a Will-o-the-Wisp.* – On Sunday night [2nd December], about 8 o'clock, as a servant girl was returning from a farm-house not a quarter of a mile from that where she resides, near Frome [Somerset], the boisterous weather extinguished the candle in her lantern, and she was left in total darkness in the midst of a large field. At this moment a *jack-o'-the-lantern* appeared; and the poor girl, with every expectation of meeting a neighbour, proceeded towards it; on which the *ignis fatuus* retreated, and led her over several hedges completely in the dark, and in weather the most dreary. Here *two* of these mysterious visitants appeared, and by their delusive attraction the poor creature was led (and frequently at the imminent hazard of her life) many miles through marshes and brakes, until seven o'clock the next morning! When she found herself at a considerable distance from home nearly exhausted.

The *Worcestershire Chronicle* of 10th July 1839 writes:

> Every old rustic one meets with, is still full of fearful tales of that 'Hobbimy's Lantern,' or *Ignis Fatuus*, which in his youthful days was such a fertile source of terror and annoyance, leading the bewildered and benighted wanderer far away from his known course, and at last, perhaps, after a long chase, plunging him knee-deep in water, comfortably fixed in palpable darkness in some muddy morass.

The 14th February 1880 edition of the *Framlingham Weekly News* contains a poem called 'A Story of the Parham Fens', which I include part of here:

> The Fens of Parham soon are reached;
> When suddenly they spy
> Amidst the dark'ning gloom a light!
> 'Tis not in earth nor sky!
>
> With eyes wide open they did look,
> And stood most like a post.
> What is it? What is it we do see?
> O dear, is it a ghost?
>
> But soon they hit on what to them
> Appeared to be quite true:
> A hobby lantern, I think it is!
> I'll go old boy, will you?
>
> An *Ignis-fatuus, Will o' the Wisp*,
> We will give it chase to-night.
> For once we have a chance to see
> This strange and wondrous light!

In the *Eastern Evening News* on 5th September 1908, the following letter was published:

> Sir – Last evening, about eleven o'clock, ten of us were witnesses of a sight which to us was very puzzling. On the marshes near Reedham, midway between the river and the uplands, a series of lights were seen. They appeared to ascend to a height of between 20 and 40 feet, and in falling

> to be extinguished. At first we attributed this uncanny spectacle to the explosion of marsh gas, but on consideration we found several objections to this. These lights were bright red and globular, in some cases appearing to be fully three feet broad; they travelled for some distance at a considerable pace, returning again to their original position before being extinguished. Is it possible for C.H.[4] [methane] to behave thus in combustion?
>
> We should have expected a scarcely visible blue flame to have risen slowly and vanished. What then could have caused this phenomenon? The lights appeared from different places, sometimes two or three at once. Are these what local folk call 'Hobby Lanterns,' if so, could any reader offer an explanation for the enlightenment of marsh dwellers?

The *Cornish Guardian* of 21st July 1966 includes a letter from Judith Cobbledick of Miniver, responding to reports of a ghost sighting:

> Sir, – With reference to the recent article on the 'Ghost at Trewornan Bridge,' this is probably ignis fatuus – a flickering flame due to marsh gas, sometimes seen floating over marshes and in places where there is decaying animal matter. This phenomenon is often seen in Cornwall where it is known as 'Will-o-the-Wisp' and 'Jack-o-Lantern.'

Another was sent in by E. Strutt of Sherwood to the *Nottingham Recorder* on 8th January 1987:

> Mr Peter Jackson, interviewed by Scott Fisher in the *Recorder* of January 1, describes his encounter with a supposed UFO at Oxton and refers to lights floating around at hedge height. I would surmise Mr Jackson's experience was physiographical rather than interplanetarial, as I imagine he saw the Will o' the wisp or ignis-fatuus – a spontaneous combustion of marsh gases. Although I have never witnessed these emanations, I can confirm that the description is exactly as related to me by my grandfather who lived in Oxton many years ago.

Ignis fatuus (meaning 'foolish fire'), Fairy Brother, Jack of the Lantern, will-o'-the-wisp, Will of the Wykes, Hob of the Lantern, Joan of the Wad, Friar Rush, corpse candle, dead candle, Jenny Burnt Tail, Gyl Burnt Tail, Kit in the Candlestick, Peg a Lantern, the Lantern Man, Pinket, Punkie, Spunkie, Hunky Punk, walking fire, and many alternatives, contractions and corruptions besides, are all names for this singular phenomenon. It is an old observance, and Shakespeare's descriptions of Puck see him taking on a similar role back in the 1500s.

The *Oxford English Dictionary* records the use of Jack o' Lantern in Britain from 1658, in reference to ignis fatuus, and from 1663 to 1704 in reference to a man with a lantern, or a night-watchman. It likewise gives 1837 as the earliest date for when the term was used to refer to a lantern carved from a pumpkin, though they would not become synonymous until the mid to late twentieth century.

A standard naming formula seems to be:

- First name (monosyllabic, simple, common)
- 'of the' (or some provincial slang to the same effect)
- fire (usually some local word for torch – rush, wad, lantern, etc.)

Sometimes (usually, in fact) it is a tricksy fairy or boggart, at other times it's ghostly, a soul who could not rest for some sin – supposedly, a man who moved his neighbour's landmarks would be doomed to haunt the patch as just such a light, for instance.

An early Victorian short story from Dublin called *Stingy Jack* is often cited as being some sort of folkloric origin, but it is not, and was written as literature. The term 'Stingy Jack' was an old one that simply denoted a miser, and the plot is appropriated from a genuine folktale from Shropshire. It is no more 'an old Irish legend' than Dickens's *Christmas Carol* is an old English one.

The more scientifically minded, consider it to be the combustion of natural gases along the ground from decaying matter, and in this context, the teenlay custom of taking flame in procession around a field may have actually burned such gases away before they ignited naturally, as Brand described in 1777, thus effectively keeping the fairies at bay.

In Cornwall, the fairy could sometimes be invoked for guidance in storms, as a rhyme recorded from Polperro by Jonathan Couch shows:

Jack o' the lantern! Joan the wad,
Who tickled the maid and made her mad
Light me home, the weather's bad.

In Shropshire, as mentioned, there is a story that it is Will the Smith, who was given a second chance at life by St Peter but spent it so poorly that neither Heaven nor Hell would take him thereafter, though the Devil gave him some burning pit coal to warm himself with, and he uses it still to lure travellers to their deaths. Another version has Will tricking the Devil into a steel purse and beating it so hard that the Devil dare not take him to Hell, but in this variant he gains access to Heaven instead.

Ruth Tongue's *Somerset Folklore* confirms:

> Will o' the Wisps in Somerset are called *Spunkies* and are believed to be the souls of unbaptised children, doomed to wander until Judgement Day. These are sometimes supposed to perform the same warning office as the corpse candles.
>
> Stoke Pero Church is one of the places where 'they spunkies do come from all around' to guide this year's ghosts to their funeral service on Hallowe'en (though another tradition has this as Midsummer Eve). One St John's Eve, an old carter called me to watch from Ley Hill. The marsh lights were moving over by Stoke Pero and Dunkery. 'They'm away to church gate, zo they are. They'm gwaine to watch 'tis certain, they dead cannles be.'

These fiery fairies became gradually interwoven with the season, just as flaming torches became more and more commonplace among the darkening nights and spreading evenings. Halloween's association with both the supernatural and the purgatorial dead makes this a seeming inevitability.

So it was that people began to lean into this folklore, carving special lanterns with grotesque faces in likeness of such a creature – the motivation here is debated; it may have been simply to scare people, as we've seen already at Mischief Night, though as with the lating of the witches, it could also be designed to ward off the evil spirits, as many believe, or to trick them into thinking such a fairy was already present with its bearer. Others think that it was designed to lure and trap the fairy into the controlled flame of the torch, where they would be safely imprisoned until the light went out.

Whichever of the theories holds true (and I see no reason they all can't), of our various fire sprites, it was Jack who became permanently trapped in the lantern, the others remaining free to do as they please all year round. Jack now comes out only at Hallowmas, and his power gutters into nothing throughout the rest of the year. Debilitated and incapable of travelling of his own accord, Jack must now be carried in a carved cage; for Jack is not the grotesque face that carries the flame, but rather the flame itself.

22

TURNIPS, PUMPKINS AND PUNKIE NIGHT

As I say, Jack is the flame and not the face, but the face is an intrinsic part of his summoning. Any receptacle over Hallowmas, carved into a grotesque and with candle inserted, will conjure the flame of Jack into it, trapped for as long as the candle burns, before harmlessly returning to his dormancy. Whether Jack is a willing servant against the night, or a defeated prisoner on humiliating parade, is up for debate.

The history of his hollowed vegetation is likewise obscure, and though today the pumpkin is ubiquitous, this was not always true, and alternatives include turnips (generally referring to what we call swedes, short for 'Swedish turnip'), mangold-wurzels (a large, red or pale root vegetable generally used for cattle feed), and even potatoes or marrows in a pinch. Such lanterns were considered extremely old hat by the early 1800s, and so it can be taken for granted that the tradition dates to at least the 1700s and very plausibly from earlier. A common misconception (as we so often see) is that this was an exclusively Irish practice. The earliest evidence is all English, as are the many examples I will now explore, which thoroughly encompass the entirety of the past two centuries.

The *Examiner* of 19th July 1818 compares a pointless endeavour to attempting to 'frighten the daylight with a candle in a hollow turnip'. *Johnson's Sunday Monitor* of 4th December 1825 writes, 'a hollowed turnip containing a burning rush-light, whose rays dart through four apertures which form eyes, nose and mouth, is a creation to conjure up the most awful, yet no less pleasurable feelings'.

The *Morning Post* of 27th December 1825 refers to a false head prop in a play being 'composed of a hollow turnip, cut out and lighted up after the most orthodox schoolboy fashion', and the *London News* of 11th April 1831 again criticises a play at the Theatre Royal, Drury Lane (*Nettlewig Hall*) for using such an old-fashioned, basic costume as 'a white sheet, surmounted with a couple of hollow turnips and a pair of rush-lights ... preposterous'.

George Cruickshank, in his *Omnibus No.VI* of 1841, includes an essay on 'Frights', referring to 'the hollow turnip of the schoolboy'. The *Chester Chronicle* of 31st December in the same year states, 'A hollow turnip curiously cut into the resemblance of the human face divine, with a farthing rushlight, a pole and winding sheet, will frighten any one, who is not aware of its harmless reality.'

The association of the lantern with schoolchildren is one that has clearly been a constant, as we've seen in the Mischief Night celebrations. Indeed, the lantern did not have an exclusively All Hallows association until relatively recently.

The *London Sun*, 9th November 1831, describes the burning of the effigy of a locally disliked bishop at the Plymouth Bonfire Night, 'The head was composed of a hollow turnip, with a candle in the centre, in which were cut the nose and mouth, but no eyes – showing, that though the head possessed light, the Bishop was blind to the past and present scenes around him'. The *Melton Mowbray Times* of 8th November 1907:

> The Fifth of November was celebrated with a prodigal waste of fireworks, while a number of the youngsters visited the various residences with 'Guy Fawkes lanterns' – ingeniously hollowed mangold wurzels with illuminated interiors – begging coppers.

Iona and Peter Opie's 1959 *Lore and Language of Children* further testifies to this:

> A boy at Castleford in the West Riding [Yorkshire], where the lanterns are similarly carried, shows how in some places Hallowe'en and Guy Fawkes celebrations have become entangled. He says that the faces on the turnip lanterns 'represent the men who plotted to blow up the Houses of Parliament', and that after they have been carried about the streets, the heads are 'thrown on the Guy Fawkes fire'.

Recalling Christmas of 1880 in Camborne, Cornwall, in *Christmas 70 Years Ago*, T.C. Quintrell could be describing any of the Mischief Nights we've already discussed, in the *Cornishman* of 14th December 1950:

> I can recall Christmas scenes of seventy years ago in the Victorian Days, long before the first of the two Great Wars. I have spent Christmas in Camborne every year since my birth [...] Some of the young girls or women dressed themselves in men's attire, and the men posed as women. This caused great amusement among the household, and then the dress-ups moved into the street and called at friends' houses, to see if they could be recognised. Children would accompany them carrying a lantern made out of a mangold or turnip. Two eyes, a nose, and a mouth were cut in the hollowed mangold, and a lighted candle placed inside.

The final stage in the development of our current Jack is, of course, his hermit-crab rehoming from turnip to pumpkin, but there's no reason to assume that the pumpkin lantern tradition is American in origin just because the pumpkin is. Pumpkins (or pumpions) were introduced to Britain in the sixteenth century, and have been grown here ever since (the earliest pumpkin pie recipe is English). Today, England, and specifically David Bowman, near Spalding in Lincolnshire, is the largest supplier of pumpkins in Europe, exporting them annually in their hundreds of thousands since the late 1990s, and supporting the Spalding Pumpkin Festival since 2002.

The *Berkshire Chronicle* of 19th May 1832 describes a superstition among Greek sailors in the Black Sea, where to disperse a bad fog they lit candles and prayed to an icon of St Nicholas, then placed a special candle that had been blessed at Easter inside the bottom half of 'a large hollowed pumpkin; a few holes were then made in the upper part of the pumpkin, which was put on and fastened to the lower part, enclosing the candle as in a lantern'. The pumpkin lantern was then lowered down into the water to disperse the fog (it failed). The *South London Press* of 26th December 1885 tells us that when the explorer William Winwood Reade (1838–75) was in Africa, spending 'Christmastide in Christian company at Sedha', 'hollowed pumpkins' were 'lighted up for the occasion [...] and illuminated within'. Certainly by 1873, the image was familiar enough that the *Burton Chronicle* of 20th February could use the phrase 'holding the candle behind the carved pumpkin', confident that its readers would understand the allusion.

Pumpkin lanterns are recorded in America from the mid-1800s, but are not associated with Halloween until later, and even then, not exclusively. Prior to the twentieth century, they were most often connected with harvest and thanksgiving celebrations.

Though today in Britain pumpkins are more common at Halloween than turnips or mangolds, even this is a surprisingly recent development.

The *Hampshire Telegraph* of 18th November 1938 tells us that, within the Meonstoke Women's Institute, a 'competition for carved mangold heads will be the attraction for next month', presumably as a Christmas festivity. The *Western Gazette* of 10th November 1950 describes the Iwerne and Fontmell Young Farmers' Club's first harvest supper in Fontmell Village Hall on 3rd November as 'lit by candles in hollowed mangolds'.

The *Lynn Advertiser* of 4th November 1960 describes the Halloween party at the Swaffham Assembly Rooms as being decorated with 'witches on broomsticks, skeletons and lighted carved mangolds'. The *Sheerness Times Guardian* of 4th November 1966 speaks of the Borough Hall's Halloween party, where lighting was restricted to candlelight, and 'on the windowsills around the hall gruesome faces made by cutting faces into hollow mangold-wurzels and lit from inside grinned at the dancers'. The *Lichfield Mercury* on 12th November 1992 informs us of the '1st Hopwas Beavers' Hallowe'en Party', where 'Dean Smith's carved swede' won 'Best Lantern'.

The most prominent anti-pumpkin Halloween tradition today is that of the Somerset Punkie Night. I will quote the description given in one of the earliest references to it, in the *Taunton Courier* of 11th November 1931:

> An interesting parade and competition organised by the Women's Institute at Hinton St. George on the last Thursday in October, which is known in that neighbourhood as 'Punkie night.' A 'Punkie' is a mangold scooped out and filled with candle ends, and these primitive lanterns are carried through the streets [...] The custom is a century old, and appears to be peculiar to the parishes of Hinton St George and Lopen.
>
> Tradition, which is somewhat vague, has it that some hundred years ago a party of Hinton and Lopen men visited Chiselborough Fair [29th October], and as they did not arrive home their good wives formed a party to fetch them home. It is a moot point whether the lady folk found the fascination of the fair too much for them, but they seem to have become as merry as their men folk, and like the foolish virgins ran out of oil for their lanterns. Legend has it that on their return journey they improvised lanterns from mangold wurzels from the wayside fields.
>
> This year the Women's Institute determined to foster the custom, with the result that on Thursday evening some 50 'Punkies' appeared at the cross – mostly in fancy dress – singing the old doggerel lines.

The song referred to is still sung, and its lyrics are recorded in the 1959 *Lore and Language of Children*:

It's Punkie Night tonight,
It's Punkie Night tonight,
Give us a candle, give us a light,
If you don't you'll get a fright.

It's Punkie Night tonight,
It's Punkie Night tonight,
Adam and Eve wouldn't believe,
It's Punkie Night tonight.

In the early 1930s descriptions, only the second verse is used, and today the last line of the first verse usually repeats 'It's Punkie Night tonight'.

Kingsley Palmer's 1973 *Oral Folk-Tales of Wessex* gives the best account of the custom, and he specifies that though both Lopen and Hinton St George provided similar Punkie Nights, each claims themselves the true originator. He records several conflicting traditions – sometimes it is 28th October, sometimes the 29th, sometimes in early November (Chiselborough Fair is 29th October). Sometimes the men carve the lanterns on their own and the women don't go looking for them, sometimes they do, but in scarlet cloaks. Sometimes they take their children, and it is the children who make the lanterns. Sometimes it is not mangolds they carve, but softer vegetable marrows (more akin to pumpkins).

The tradition has also been found at Langport and Long Sutton, though today it is Hinton St George that's most associated with it, where the last Thursday in October is maintained. The Lopen tradition is more haphazard, and often muddled with Halloween and Bonfire Night. It is unclear whether any village other than Hinton still holds the event annually.

The true origins are unknown, and the 1931 article implies that it might be an invention of the Women's Institute inspired by broader traditional mangold lantern activities. Though the idea of it being 100 years old could have some merit (and is more likely than if older origins were claimed), if it does commemorate a real event it seems unlikely that tough wurzels would have been used, as they'd take far longer to hollow by hand than would be practical.

Elsewhere in Somerset, the ignis fatuus spunkie traditions we have already discussed are rife, and worth considering in context – many in Hinton consider the punkies as wards against evil, as discussed in the previous chapter.

In Exmoor and on the Brendon Hills in north Somerset, a tradition exists of placing such lanterns on gateposts and entrance ways 'to keep evil spirits away'.

Punkie Night is still ongoing and well attended. Though it was almost cancelled in 2018 due to difficulty in finding organisers, the deprivations of Covid (and the forced cancellations of 2020 and 2021) have reminded people of the value of such things, and enthusiasm remains strong. The current order of events is for everyone to meet at St George's Hall, Hinton, for 6pm, with the procession starting at 6.20 (often led by morris dancers, with a newly crowned Punkie King and Queen), then back to the hall afterwards for mulled cider, refreshments, music, games and sometimes a raffle, with the judging and prize-giving at 7.30.

Many of the carvings are intricate and are not restricted to faces. Mangolds can be obtained from the shop in Hinton St George throughout October (with a donation encouraged), and whilst pumpkins can take part, they are eligible only for runners-up prizes. There is a cup for best Hinton Children's Punkie and another for Best Overall Punkie, with the recent addition of an adults' category. Though in the past props such as pipes or spectacles were allowed, today they are strictly disbarred.

I quote now from the official handout, *How to Prepare a Punkie Lantern*, 'By Brian Cornelius who took over from the late Douglas Gillard in keeping the Punkie Night tradition alive in Hinton St George':

> Firstly, the mangold has to be washed. Then the top or the bottom is cut off to make a lid, (which is removed to fit a candle when necessary). A hole about the size of a finger is made in the lid for air to keep the candle alight.
>
> The mangold or similar vegetable is then hollowed out using items of kitchen cutlery, (knives, spoons, etc. and plenty of patience) [an electric drill also works] to form a bowl, leaving the outer wall thin enough to let the light shine through but thick enough to stop the mangold collapsing.
>
> The outer coloured skin of the mangold is then marked out with a suitable face, pattern or image where the candlelight is to shine through.
>
> The outer skin is then gradually removed to form the pattern with the only hole on the lid. If other holes are made then the candle may blow out much easier and on a windy night it is not easy to light matches to relight the candle. [This distinguishes punkies from the more standard, static pumpkin Jack o' Lantern, and from some descriptions of earlier turnip lanterns, whereby full holes for eyes and mouth are carved, and no external skin membrane preserved.]

> The final stage is to make a handle (using wire or string), to carry the lantern without burning yourself with heat from the candle but with enough heat to keep your hands warm on a cold evening!
>
> Mangolds are becoming increasingly difficult to come by and punkie lanterns are often made using pumpkins.

As we have seen, then, the British folklore of a mysterious flame fairy/sprite that leads people astray (called, amongst many other names, Jack o' Lantern since at least the 1700s) was combined during the twentieth century with the unrelated British tradition of carving faces in vegetables, and then using a candle to create a fake ghost, likewise dating to at least the 1700s. This custom was already heavily associated with Bonfire Night and Mischief Nights (and less so with Christmas) in England, and later with harvest festivals in America. As the two separate traditions melded, the association shifted slightly to Halloween. Both of the traditions were consistently widespread throughout England over the eighteenth, nineteenth and twentieth centuries, and the earliest evidence for both is English.

This is as loose as I can get the knot, and I hope it's been helpful. The specific process by which the traditions melded is the element that remains obscure, but the associations of the season make such a development seem perfectly natural and organic. Though many commentators have assumed it to be an American elision of customs, the evidence I have presented makes it more likely that this process began with the back-influence of Bonfire Night on Halloween that started in Britain over the latter half of the nineteenth century.

23

RING BELL, TURN STONE

Prior to the Reformation, one of the most recognisable elements of All Hallows was the intensity of the church bells, which rang avidly between the eve and the day, from the end of the liturgy until midnight. In some quarters, the ringing was believed to help souls in Purgatory; in others, to protect against witchcraft and ghosts (the ringing of church bells can be found often in fairy lore to protect against the pixies).

The intense ringing of All Hallows survived Henry VIII, who refused to sign an abolition drafted by Archbishop Cranmer in January 1546, but suppression began under Edward VI. There was a widespread revival under Mary, but it was finally dropped from the new liturgy in 1559 under Elizabeth I. This did not kill the custom, however, and under cover of dark it was continued, illegally, across the breadth of the country over the next three decades, as detailed in various church court documents and bishops' visitations. An indicative case was at All Hallows of 1587 in Hickling, Nottinghamshire, when the assembled ringers 'used violence against the parson at that time to maintain their ringing'.

Less than twenty years later, the establishing of Bonfire Night reinvigorated the ringing, with the compromise of simply having it a few days later. As has already been mentioned, these dates are mutable, and at least one church (the Parish of Whalley in Lancashire) simply conducted its Guy Fawkes Day bellringing at All Hallows instead – continuing to do so until 1658, a full century after it had officially been outlawed.

This Guy Fawkes ringing continued, on or around the night of the 4th, to the extent that in some areas (especially Cornwall and the south-west), it became known as Ringing Night and twined with the Mischief Nights of the same date, which we have already discussed. Jonathan Couch, in his 1871 *History of Polperro*, describes the custom there thus:

> 'Ringing-Night' is on the fourth of November [...] The usual belfry rules, imposing fines on those who in a drunken or 'choleric' mood, should overturn a bell or 'by unskilful handling' mar a peal are, for the time, not rigidly enforced, and I fear that many cracked bells can date their ruin from this night.

John Camp, in his 1988 book *In Praise of Bells*, tells us:

> In some areas the custom of 'firing' the bells (the old method of alarm) is still used on Guy Fawkes Day and is known as 'shooting old Guy'. This also happens at Harlington, Bedfordshire, where the ringers are rewarded with pork pies and beer.

In more recent times, the practice has lost any pretence of Guy Fawksery and has simply been engaged with on 30th or 31st October as All Hallows ringing again, and so in some areas, this too is known as Ringing Night. The longevity of Church anxieties is attested in the *Beccles and Bungay Journal* of 24th October, 2008, which announced, after much local debate:

> Church bells WILL ring out in Bungay [Suffolk] at Halloween, despite opposition from Church leaders who say it should not be done to mark a pagan festival. A snap decision was made to allow the bells of St Mary's Church to ring during the Pumpkin Night festival, after the bell-ringers pressed for an answer, saying they needed preparation time.

The most interesting of all the bell-ringing traditions, however, barely features bells at all.

On the small green in the village of Shebbear in Devon, sat between the pub and the church, beneath a centuries-old oak lies a large stone, about 6ft by 4ft and supposedly a ton in weight. It has a number of names, including the Devil's Boulder, the Shebbear Stone, and many other variations between the two. The pub opposite is called the Devil's Stone Inn, but has only been known as such in recent decades (the change occurred some time since the 1960s, before which it was the New Inn).

Every year, on 5th November, the bell-ringers (usually extra bell-ringers are drafted in from surrounding parishes) gather in the church to ring the bells, concluding with a brief but raucous discordant cacophony sometime between about 7.30 and 8pm. They then collect up their long crowbars and depart from the church to the stone, where a large group of people with flaming torches and lanterns will have gathered (usually morris dancers, too). The vicar gives a short prayer and sermon, telling the story of the stone and the importance of turning it, whereupon, to chants of 'turn the stone', the bell-ringers (generally consisting of six men) set to work. The boulder is levered up and turned completely over, to exultant cheers from all. The bell-ringers return to the church and ring the bells again, but tunefully this time, then everyone repairs to the pub for drinks and a hog roast.

The *Western Times* of 9th November 1934 quotes the vicar of the time, Reverend A.H. Evans:

> 'The ceremony has been performed every year within living memory [...] some of the old folk in the village fear that something terrible would happen if the stone was not turned. No one knows how the custom originated. It is significant that the oak and the stone are both to the south of the church, and that the stone is due east of the tree [...] certain of the old folk in the village tell me that the oak used to be hollow, and that they played inside it, but now in some mysterious way the tree has healed up [...] there is a tree of similar age at Newton St. Petrock, three miles away.'

If we take a conservative view of 'living memory', this probably puts the ritual as far back as at least the 1850s. The same paper, of 11th November 1949, records an 84-year-old villager named Mr W. Ayre as attesting to the ceremony having been performed for as long as his parents and grandparents could remember. Though the earliest documentary evidence dates only to the early twentieth century, I think it unlikely the entire village and its vicar were lying.

The 12th November 1937 edition quotes an elderly resident as saying, 'If we didn't do this we should lose all we have, and be dead in a fortnight'. In 1939, according to the paper's panicked 10th November headlines, 'THE DEVIL'S BOULDER WAS NOT TURNED ON THE 5th'. The article confirms that though 'throughout the hostilities of 1914–18 with due ceremonial the rite had been observed', the wartime 'black-out put a stop to the womenfolk with torches, candles and lanterns forming a lighted bodyguard [...] they came to the conclusion that their efforts, especially in the dark, would be insufficient to turn the stone [...] Shebbear is not happy'.

It then assures the reader that certain individuals have vowed to turn the stone anyway, in secret, as late is presumably better than not at all. 'Whether tradition will agree, under the exceptional circumstance, to granting a period of grace is a situation the super-superstitious view with some feeling of misgiving.' The general opinion is that it was not, and the Battle of Britain, which started about eight months later, was considered the bitter consequence of Shebbear's failure. They have not repeated the mistake.

There are a number of brief stories to explain the nature of the stone, which is geologically distinct from any in the area, but none are unique to Shebbear. Some claim the stone fell from the Devil's pocket as he was cast into Hell, others that he threw it there for some reason. Another theory is that he dropped it from his numbed hands before perishing from the cold at Northlew, and yet another is that he was buried beneath it and is digging his way out – the turning blocks his escape and foils his plan for another year. A completely different tradition states it was intended to be the foundation stone for nearby Henscott Church, but every night during construction it was inexplicably moved back to the spot in Shebbear until it was agreed just to leave it.

The custom continues to be carried out, even during covid, pretty much unchanged. The *Express and Echo* of 6th November 1963 tells us of an accompanying 'barbecue and fun fair arranged by Shebbear football club', and one P.H.T. Evans, in a letter to the *Illustrated Sporting and Dramatic News* of 23rd October the same year, tells us that 'at one time [...] a gallon or two of beer was provided for the ringers, after they had performed their task'.

The giving of beer and refreshments to bell-ringers at All Hallows and Bonfire Night is a long-standing practice, attested by numerous churchwardens' accounts, such as those at Sennen in Cornwall, where eighteenth-century 'payments made for beer on ringing night' are documented. Roud's *English Year* tells us of another distinctive example from elsewhere in Devon, recorded at East Budleigh in 1885:

> A very curious custom prevails here on the night of Nov. 4. The children are allowed to 'holloa for biscuits', as they call it. Seventeen shillings and sixpence is allowed by the parish for bell-ringing. Two and sixpence of this is spent in biscuits (i.e. farthing cakes). One shilling's worth of these are retained by the ringers; the remaining ones are given to the children, who formerly came into the churchyard and shouted, the biscuits being distributed from the porch. A few years since the people awoke to the fact that a churchyard was hardly a suitable place for holloaing, and the biscuits were distributed from the church gate. For the last two years the biscuits have been given away at some distance from the sacred edifice. No one appears to know the origin of this custom.

A connection to soul cakes is certainly plausible.

DIVINATION

24

PRYING INTO FUTURITY

A key element of the traditional Halloween, often obscured today, is that which Burns terms 'prying into futurity' – foretelling the future. As Volume III of the Folk-Lore Society's 1940 *British Calendar Customs: England* puts it:

> Of all festival days offering opportunities for looking into the future in respect of love, marriage, health, wealth, sickness and death, none is more famous than Hallow-E'en, the 31st of October [...] St. Agnes is famous for her reputed solicitude for the love affairs of young girls; St. Mark for the dread proceedings in the porch of the village church; Midsummer for testing the fidelity of lovers, but the divinations of Hallow E'en extend over the whole range of events in human existence. There was also a serious and weird feeling, on Hallow E'en night, not felt so much on any other night; witches and evil spirits were believed to be more numerous than usual; fairies were believed to be unusually active; ghosts were supposed to make their appearance on this night; and a full-dress performance of the watch in the church porch on that night was capable of teaching the watchers that the Angel of Death is sometimes nearer than they imagine.

For the most part, these divinatory rituals take the form of simple party games involving other well-established Hallowtide symbols – apples, nuts, flame, etc. So popular were these customs that in many parts of England Halloween was referred to as Nut-Crack (the north) or Snap-Apple (the south) Night, alongside other, similar variations.

Halloween fortune telling was overwhelmingly female and often conducted in groups, though some examples of men engaging in it exist also, as do solo rituals. The bulk are preoccupied with the practitioner's love life and future prospects of marriage, and to this day, it is considered that 'Cuffing Season', when single people search for wintry romance, begins in October.

This tradition of foresight may seem out of step with the core Halloween element of death, but it is not so – a thinning veil between the living and the dead is merely a thinning veil between the present and the past; when those two begin to blur, so too must the barrier with the future. The dead have a long-established association with hidden knowledge of what is yet to come, and historically were often consulted on such matters.

I'll go through the various surviving spells of Halloween in due course, but these active rituals were not the only form of seasonal precognition, and passive forms existed too – usually focused explicitly on foretelling deaths. The most significant was church porch watching, whereby should you watch at the parish church as the clock strikes midnight, you'll see those who are feted to marry over the coming year enter the church, hand in hand, and then those doomed to die exit in single file, parading about the churchyard.

Probably rather than seeing all who would die in the parish, it's merely all whose funerals will be held at that church. Likewise, it would make more sense if the married couples were those who are to get married in that specific church, rather than all those currently living in the parish who were to marry.

These customs are found throughout Britain and are testified in many sources with many subtle variations (sometimes just death, sometimes just marriage). In some places, those who were to die in the coming year were the only ones who did not exit the church, with the forms of all in the parish who would live out the year visible in procession. In Chirbury, at Halloween of 1788, Charlotte Burne's *Shropshire Folk-Lore* tells of two men who went to *hear the names* of the doomed (in the hopes of then borrowing money), only to hear the names of their loved ones, who died shortly after.

The most striking version of the English church porch customs comes from Dorstone in Herefordshire where, according to the 1901 *Celtic Folklore: Welsh and Manx* (by J. Rhys), there was a belief that on All Hallows Eve at midnight those who were bold enough to look through the windows would see the church lit with an unearthly glow, and Satan in monk's habit at the pulpit, calling out the names of those who were to render up their souls.

It is hard to say whether variations in the result are down to differences between churches, localities, rituals or the individual watchers. Give it a go and let me know how you fare.

25

THE SPALDING STORY

Spalding has a far darker Halloween association than mere pumpkins.

I was first given the tale of Tyler and Ives some years ago in Ye Old White Horse, a picturesque, thatched pub that has spent recent years tragically closed and empty. The building itself is from the sixteenth century, and it has been run as a tavern since the early eighteenth. It was in this pub, so I was told, that every Halloween is seen the melancholy figure of Tom Tyler, long-since deceased. From Halloween until Martinmas Eve, Tyler's skeletal, decomposing spirit could be seen, melancholy at the bar, in glimpses snatched from the corner of your eye; heard sighing into the void that hasn't held a drink for him in almost three centuries.

As the table of elderly Lincolnshire locals told me, over the sound of the White Horse Cribbage team playing a particularly lively set, it was on 31st October, 1741, that Tom Tyler took part in the old games, and pried into futurity to find his love. Much drinking and revelry there'd been that night at the Horse, when the midnight hour came and passed, and the spirits of All Hallows rose. It was then that Tyler, his companions paired off with drunken conquests, felt the full weight of his loneliness, and came to dwell on solitude.

But it was Halloween – what better time to divine his tomorrows and spy on the secrets of the heart? So Tyler took himself to the fire, found himself a looking glass, and spoke the words that he had only before heard whispered.

There, in the flickering of the fire reflected in the glass, he saw the form of a girl he knew well – a wild girl, known for her black hair, brazen ways and stubborn beauty. How could a man such as he tame a woman such as she? But as he stared at her form, she stared right back, and from the mirror she stepped, and filled his heart with something he had never before known that he lacked.

But Tom was not the only one in Spalding to pry into futurity that night. For in the fine home of the widow Mrs Ives, the loneliness likewise weighed heavy. For some years had her husband been dead, and though she now was a wealthy woman, that wealth brought little comfort. Though well into her 60s (not quite the same in the 1700s as today), she longed once again for the warmth of another, to feel the embrace of a man once more.

So it was that, in her empty home, while the servants were out at the revelry, old Mrs Ives likewise pried, and she flung nuts to the fire and heard them crack, and by dancing candlelight, through her looking glass, she saw a fine young man (for youth is the greatest cosmetic, and hunger the finest seasoning), and she watched as he rapped at her door, and she watched as she flung it open, and she watched as he held her in embrace, and as she watched she wept tears of joy.

Both, in turn, become obsessed with their foretold lovers; she waiting for her love at the door, night by night, he whispering with the future shade of his dark lady, who giggled and encouraged him to woo her in the flesh, and bring the future to pass.

'But how?' he asked.

'You'll need money,' she replied.

And so it was that dark seeds were planted in the mind of that Tom Tyler, and dark plans began to form and dark deeds began to fruit, achieving full ripeness at Martlemas Eve, when Tom Tyler, with cudgel in hand, knocked three times at the door of old and wealthy Mrs Ives.

Mrs Ives had likewise spent her days in dreaming, and when three times the knocks came hard, she ran like a schoolgirl to open up and be held once more. As reported in the *Ipswich Journal*, of 5th December 1741:

> We hear from Spalding in Lincolnshire, that on Tuesday the 10th Instant, between seven and eight in the Evening, Mrs. Ives, a Widow Gentle-woman of that Place, about 64 Years of Age, was barbarously murdered in her own House, her Skull being broke and her Throat cut in three or four Places besides a mortal Wound under her Ear: The House was robb'd of Money, Plate, Linnen, etc. to a considerable Value. One Tyler, a Thatcher, is taken up for the said Murder and he has confess'd that an infamous Woman of Spalding was concern'd with him; but the Circumstances not appearing clear against her, the Jury acquitted her; yet he continuing to aver she was concern'd with him, she was secur'd in Spalding Gaol, and he on Monday last sent to Lincoln Gaol.

Tom spent his Christmas jailed; his New Year too. Valentine's Day was spent alone. The ending of his story is given, glibly, in the *Derby Mercury* of 25th March 1742:

> We hear from Lincoln, that at the Assizes there six Persons received Sentence of Death, only two of which were ordered for Execution viz. One for the Murder of an ancient Gentle woman at Spalding, and the other for a Robbery on the Highway; the former is to be hung in Chains, near the Place where the Fact was committed.

Now, every day between Halloween and Martinmas, the rotting corpse of Tyler drinks at Ye Old White Horse, ever alone. Come Martlemas, he dwells elsewhere, hung skeletal in chains, in view of the site of his crime. Screaming unheard, writhing unseen, his bones desperate to pry into the past.

Old Mr and Mrs Ives rest easy, meanwhile, reunited in eternal embrace.

26

THE MAGIC SPELLS OF HALLOWMAS

I will begin with the divinations surrounding apples, which are numerous – we have already heard how, in Cornwall, it was common practice to receive an Allan apple and to dream of your future love if you slept with it under your pillow. Apples are not the only fruit for divination, however. If you have none to hand, get the unbroken peels of two lemons, wear them all day, one in each pocket. At night, rub the four posts of the bed with them. If successful, in dreams your future love will appear and hand you a pair of lemons. If no such figure appears, then no such figure will appear (Macclesfield – *Macclesfield Courier & Herald*, 30th January 1858).

This practice may also have been carried out with apple peels, and it is similar to another recorded from Nottinghamshire – after the apples have been roasted, the skin is to be thrown over the left shoulder. 'Notice is taken of the shapes which the parings assume when they fall to the ground. Whatever letter a paring resembles will be the initial letter of the Christian name of the man or woman whom you will marry' (Nottinghamshire – S.O. Addy, *Household Tales, with other Traditional Remains. Collected in the Counties of Lincoln, Derby, and Nottingham*, 1895, p. 82).

Similar can be performed a couple of days earlier, on 28th October, the Saints Day of Simon and Jude. Here, the apple must be skinned in a single, unbroken length. Then take the paring in the right hand, stand in the centre of the room and, while waving the paring gently round your head, say:

Saint Simon and Saint Jude, on you I intrude,
By this paring I hold to discover,

Without delay, tell me I pray,
The first letter of my own true lover.

Drop the paring over your left shoulder to form the initial letter of your future spouse's name - whether surname or Christian name is unclear - and should the paring break, the implication is that you remain alone (Sarah Hewett, *Nummits and Crummits*, 1900, p. 70).

Even the roasting of the apples can be a source of divination. Assign an apple to all present and hang them over a fire on the end of a length of string. The owner of the apple that falls first will be the first to marry, with the remainder falling in the order their owners will marry. The owner of the final apple will be doomed to spinsterism (Sussex - *Folk-Lore Record*, Mrs Latham, Vol. I, 1878, pp. 30–31).

To see the face of your future spouse, creep upstairs on All Hallows Eve with a candle in one hand, an apple in the other. Go alone to the looking glass, holding eye contact with yourself by the candlelight while eating the apple and combing your hair. Behind you they will appear, but you must not look directly at them, and you must be alone. Many variations on this exist in many places, all involving staring at yourself in the mirror by candlelight, sometimes repeating words or names three times, sometimes with or without the apple, sometimes with or without the hair combing, sometimes with the washing of one's face (Derbyshire - *Westminster Gazette*, 30th October 1926, p. 4).

If a girl has two lovers and is curious as to which is the most faithful, she can take two brown apple pips, name each after one of the lovers, and press one onto each of her cheeks. She should say, 'Pippin, pippin, I stick thee there, that that is true thou mayst declare.' The first to fall is the least worthy of the two (Nottinghamshire - *Journal of the British Archaeological Society*, Vol. 8, 1853, pp. 236–37)

Alternatively, another use for apple pips is to take a single one, name it after a lover or prospective lover, then place it in the fire. If, in burning, the pip bursts and makes a noise then the love is passionate, true and good. If the pip burns without crackling, no real regard is felt (Suffolk, etc. - *Bye Gones relating to Wales and the Border Counties: Oswestry and Wrexham*, 1886–87, pp. 317–18).

This same divination is also (and more often) practised with nuts, whereby two nuts are placed in a bright fire, side by side - one belonging to the placer, the other to the prospective lover. With the name of the person in question in mind, the following must be said:

If s/he loves me, pop and fly,
If s/he hates me, lie and die

Whereupon the nuts that pop wildly indicate that the pairing is filled with passionate romance, and the ones that lay still mean the match would be insipid and loveless (Sussex – *Folk-Lore Record*, Mrs Latham, Vol. I, 1878, pp. 30–31).

In the north of England (and likewise in Scotland), however, the opposite of the above is true – if nuts burn quietly together then a stable and faithful married life is in store, if they fly apart tempestuously, so too will the couple (northern England – *A Glossary of Words used in Northumberland Vol. II*, Richard Oliver Heslop, 1894, p. 507).

Take a lighted brand, stick or similar from the fire and whirl it before your face while singing out, 'Dingle, dingle, dowsie, the cat's in the well; The dog's awa' to Berwick, to buy a new bell'. The last sparks of the fire are then observed. Many sparks mean prosperity, money and so on, while a fast extinction means penury, loss of property, etc. (northern England – *Notes on the Folk-Lore of the Northern Counties of England and the Borders*, William Henderson, 1879, p. 97).

Light a candle on Halloween and stick pins down its length for each eligible suitor. The candle, burning down from pin to pin, will go out when it reaches the right one. This would seem enough for any divination, but apparently it goes further, as the door will then open, and your future bridegroom will appear (Lincolnshire – *Grimsby Daily Telegraph*, 20th January 1949).

Another candle practice, perhaps more prosaic, was found amongst Derbyshire farmers, who would carry a lit one down the garden to ascertain which way the wind blew. Supposedly, the wind that blew that night would be the prevailing one for the next three months (Derbyshire – *Household Tales*, Sidney Oldall Addy, 1895, p. 118).

A number of rituals involve the garden. One is to go outside at the approach to midnight on All Hallows Eve and find sage growing healthily. Pluck one leaf at each stroke of the clock, up to a total of nine. If done correctly, during the remaining three strokes, the face of one's future husband will appear. Should one see a coffin, then it means you will die alone (Shropshire – *Shropshire Folk-Lore*, Charlotte Sophia Burne, 1883, p. 177; Standon, Staffordshire – *Notes on the Folk-Lore of North Staffordshire*, W. Wells Bladen, North Staffordshire Field Club XXXV, 1900–01).

To dream of your future husband, place a sprig of rosemary and a crooked sixpence under your pillow. A crooked sixpence was known as a 'bender' and was often used as a love token – it denotes a high silver content, which makes it softer and thus easier to bend (Derbyshire – *Household Tales*, Oldall Addy, 1895, p. 80). For those interested, the Royal Mint still produces silver sixpences annually, and has done so since 2016.

We're all familiar with the magical properties of four-leaf clovers, but in English tradition similar is true of the two-leaved variety. If found:

Put it in your right shoe;
The first young man you meet,
In field, street, or lane,
You'll have him or one of his name.

(Cambridgeshire, Norfolk, Suffolk – *Notes and Queries*, i, 6, 1852, p. 600.)

If a girl goes into a garden and cuts a cabbage as the clock strikes midnight on Halloween, a vision of her future husband will appear. The Scots have similar cabbage and kale-related traditions, and another involving the sowing of hemp seed, with significance in the way that it then grows (Herefordshire –*The Folklore of Herefordshire*, Ella Mary Leather, 1912, pp. 64–65).

Take a sprig of yew from a tree at Halloween, in a churchyard where you have never been before, and sleep with it under your pillow to dream of a future husband (Herefordshire – *The Folklore of Herefordshire*, Ella Mary Leather, 1912, pp. 64–65). Charlotte Burne's 1883 *Shropshire Folk-Lore* tells us that this was also done with a half-brick found in a darkened graveyard.

Give a leaf of ivy for each person present and place them in a bowl of water overnight at Halloween (mark or separate the leaves so that they do not become muddled, and each person knows which is theirs). Should any show the shape of a coffin by morning, the bearer of that leaf will soon die (Herefordshire –*The Folklore of Herefordshire*, Ella Mary Leather, 1912, pp. 64–65).

Take three dishes, fill one with clear water, one with cloudy water and leave one empty. Blindfolded young men and maidens take turns to pick a dish to dip their fingers into. If the clear water is touched, they'll wed a maiden or a bachelor, if the cloudy is touched then they'll marry someone with more worldliness under their belt, and if the dish is empty, they'll marry no one at all (various – *Westminster Gazette*, 30th October 1926, p. 4).

Take a front door key and pour molten lead through the hole in the handle into cold water. The shapes made by the cooling lead will foretell the trade or profession of the future husband (Cornwall – *Folk-Lore Journal*, Vol. 4, 1886, p. 111).

Thread a wedding ring through a piece of cotton, then suspend it between forefinger and thumb, saying, 'If my husband's name is to be [insert the relevant name here] let this ring swing'. When the correct name or names are asked, the ring will move – a slight movement may indicate a brief dalliance, and significant movement, a stronger, more lasting affair (Cornwall – *Folk-Lore Journal*, Vol. 4, 1886, p. 111).

'On All Hallowe'en or New Year's Eve,' says Mr W. Henderson:

> ... a Border maiden may wash her sark [a shift, or underskirt], and hang it over a chair to dry, taking care to tell no one what she is about. If she lie awake long enough, she will see the form of her future spouse enter the room and turn the sark. We are told of one young girl who, after fulfilling this rite, looked out of bed and saw a coffin behind the sark; it remained visible for some time and then disappeared. The girl rose up in agony and told her family what had occurred, and the next morning she heard of her lover's death.

Variations on this are widespread across Britain (W. Henderson, *Folk Lore of the Northern Counties of England and the Borders*, 1879, p. 101).

I have mentioned already that there is some evidence that men also engaged in these predominantly female rituals, and one such testament is given as follows:

> Mr. George Wood, in possession of one of the largest farms on the Raynham estate, at Morston, told me of a ceremony which he witnessed. Returning home late on All Hallows' Eve, he saw a light shining in the window of the huge cart stable. Dismounting from his pony, he stole softly to the window and saw five men sitting round a pitchfork, placed upright, upon which was a clean white shirt. They believed firmly that the sweetheart of one of them, were she true to him, would enter and take away the shirt, in solemn silence, before twelve o'clock; and there they sat, silent, waiting for her appearance. The clock struck the midnight hour, but no one appeared, and the men concluded that not one of them had a faithful lover. [Norfolk – Major Charles Loftus, *My Life from 1815–49*, 1877, Vol. I, pp. 302–03.]

Clothing seems to be a running theme. It is said that a girl at Halloween may cross her shoes upon her bedroom floor in the shape of a T, and proclaim: 'I cross my shoes in the shape of a T, Hoping this night my true love to see,

Not in his best or worst array, But in the clothes of every day'. She must then get into bed backwards, without speaking any more that night, to dream of her future husband (The North – S.O. Addy, *Household Tales, with other Traditional Remains. Collected in the Counties of Lincoln, Derby, and Nottingham*, 1895, p. 85).

An even more involved ritual to the same end can be carried out a couple of weeks beforehand, on St Luke's Day (18th October) – take marigold flowers, a sprig of marjoram, thyme and a little wormwood. Dry all before a fire and rub to a powder. The instructions then call one to 'sift this through a fine piece of lawn and simmer the powder over a slow fire', which I can only guess at the specific meaning of, before adding a small quantity of virgin honey and vinegar. Anoint yourself with this preparation, then go to bed repeating, 'St Luke, St Luke, be kind to me, in dreams let me my true love see' (James Orchard Halliwell, *Popular Rhymes and Nursery Tales*, 1849, pp. 217–18).

Do try these yourselves, and please let me know the results.

In every case, these customs predate considerably the year in which they were written down, being described as older than memory in all instances. Many also have parallels mentioned in Robert Burns's 1785 Halloween poem, and so we can likely date them to at least the 1700s, and plausibly earlier still. Some are clearly party games, whilst others are more committed, genuine examples of folk magic - it is often hard to draw a definitive line between the two, and much relies on context and intent. I believe this to be the most complete collection of English examples yet compiled (there are variants I have not included from Scottish, Welsh and Irish sources, in the interests of space), but there are certainly many, many more fragments out there, and should you come across any then please do write them down and send them over.

Though it hasn't been given proper focus, the most prevalent of all forms of Hallowmas divination spell is that which involves candlelight and the mirror. As mentioned already, there are countless iterations of this ritual (again, far too many to include here), and it is certainly still widely practised today - there are many modern accounts of children dabbling in just this sort of thing, and many different approaches and interpretations. Both flame and reflection have been elements of mysticism and mystery for as long back as records go, and we will explore one such tradition in the chapter that follows.

27

FREEMAN, HAMBIDGE, OLD DEVIL

A curious Halloween custom exists among children in the Cotswolds. The tradition goes that if, at midnight on Halloween, you make eye contact with yourself in a mirror, your face lit by candlelight, and say, 'Freeman, Freeman, Freeman; Hambidge, Hambidge, Hambidge; Old Devil, Old Devil, Old Devil', in some form or another, a dark being will appear. Whoever appears, and whatever the form they take, so long as you do not look directly at them (achieved either by maintaining eye contact with your own reflection or by keeping them in your peripheral), they will offer you a deal. The trade is of the classic Faustian variety, and interestingly, we see this basic narrative trope arise more than once in stories set during the season (the Irish *Stingy Jack* short story, and the Shropshire folklore it's based on, both utilise it – as do various other Halloween playlets from the nineteenth and early twentieth centuries).

In Stow-on-the-Wold, however, it is not your own soul you're bartering with, per se – rather, the trade is that somebody else will die (though if this counts as murder on your part then perhaps you're damned all the same). You cannot know who, and you cannot know how, but the death will occur on All Souls Day – usually the one which has just begun, but perhaps years later, to lull you into a false sense of security. It could be a stranger or a loved one, near or far, but the deal will protect you from ever being seriously punished in any official, judicial sense.

This tradition was testified by several people of varying ages, all local to the area, and is a regional variation of the widespread custom of repeating a name or incantation three times, often at midnight and in front of a mirror with a candle (Bloody Mary, Candyman and Beetlejuice are other examples). In this instance, the triple repetition is, itself, repeated three times (making the total nine), and it seems likely to derive from a well-documented historical event that anchors it to the very middle of the 1800s, in the tiny hamlet of Icomb.

What follows is a combination of objective historical fact, as attested in the papers of the time, and folkloric tradition, as passed on orally over the last century and a half. It is far more of the former than you would think.

George Hambidge was a well-to-do and well-respected farmer with 100 acres at Icomb, near Stow-on-the-Wold. His son, John, had been born out of wedlock, and so used both the Hambidge name and that of his mother, Hannah Freeman, as and when his mood demanded. Though legally illegitimate, John was not unacknowledged by his father – on the contrary, he was doted on, spoiled and given every privilege and opportunity that it was in old George's power to give, despite John's idle, drunken, dissolute ways.

But his ways were not just dissolute.

Often it is the way that those who are doted on come to disdain their doter. What begins as a gift, gratefully received, soon becomes an entitlement, impatiently taken. The receiver adjusts their life and comes to rely on the giver – and comes to resent them for it. This resentment soon presents in hate and in cruelty, and when the giver is tied by bonds of love, and perhaps by a sense of guilt, then that cruelty is given freedom to grow unfettered.

So it was for poor George Hambidge.

Young John had always nursed a resentment towards the world, and always felt that he was owed more than he got; that he counted for more than the common herd. John did both love and resent his father, and looked up to and down on him, admiring the man who had built and made and given so much. The man who was everything that John was not, but all he wanted to be.

In time, John came to live with his father, and as he grew in strength and age, but not maturity, so too he grew in anger and love, and in sentiment and cruelty. Young John learned to drink, and this was the path to his undoing.

When sober, John was kind and considerate, good fun and hearty company for his old and increasingly infirm father (for whom age brought only weakness). But he was sober less and less. Regularly, when drunk, he demanded money from old George, and regularly when drunk, he used violence to get it. Often he would grab him by the throat or clutch at the nearest stick and lash out. As John grew, so did his thirst, and deeper and deeper he fell, dragging his father with him.

Time and again the parish constable was called, at which threat of authority John became humbled and contrite, though as soon as said authority departed his rage was unleashed once more, and he took to throttling the concerned housekeeper just as he did his father. It was no surprise that the Hambidges found it hard to keep anyone in service for long.

When John turned 19, George knew that it was past time to stop, and he refused to fund his bad habits any longer. John took him by the throat, and still he refused. John hit his head against the back of his chair, and still he refused. John took him by the leg and dragged him out, dashing his skull against the stone of the floor, still he refused. Roaring with rage, John left the house while the housekeeper tended to George's wounds.

When John returned, it was with a gun. As the clock struck midnight, he kicked in the door of his father's bedroom, pulled him out of bed by the hair, shoved the firearm in his face and threatened to 'blow his bloody old brains out'. When the terrified housekeeper screamed at him to stop, he threatened to do the same to her. It was December. By Christmas John was in jail, where he remained a twelvemonth.

When John was released, the housekeeper, like so many before her, left George's service. John returned to his old ways soon after, demanding money and, when refused, threatening to 'kill the old devil, damn him'. George decided to do all he could think to, and set John up with a farm of his own in nearby Oddington. John found a wife, Mary Ann Campin, and the hopes were that he would reform.

But John did not.

Still he drank, still he lazed, still he demanded more money from his father, still he was refused. 'Miserable old devil, if I want money I shall have money, or there will be murder in this house. It's no matter to me when you're shoulder high.'

George was not a strong man, and his health was poor. He was tired and he wanted peace. He gave in. When John turned 24, George gave him the money he demanded, called his solicitor, made up a will that left his son with the bulk of his estate, and had it read to John and his wife. 'Let that be an end to it and let me rest.'

But that was not an end to it.

John became paranoid, convinced that his father's openness was a ruse. He started to call at the solicitors, demanding to know if the will had been changed; became obsessed by it.

Months passed, years passed. Mary Ann fell pregnant, and John had a son. George allowed them all to live with him in the larger house. As George's charity increased, so John's paranoia intensified, until mere drink could not nullify it, and no remedy of the natural world would suffice.

So it was that at the age of 26, when All Hallows Eve rolled around, drunken John went to a churchyard that he had never before been to. He tore a dead branch from the yew, and took this branch home to his fire and lit it as the clock came up to midnight, and ran he to his mirror with the flaming branch, which he whipped about his face.

John stared into his own eyes by the light of the flaming yew as the clock started to strike twelve times. He repeated his father's name three times, and his mother's name three times, and he called on the devil three times, and he stared, unblinking, into his own eyes. The clock stopped at the ninth stroke, and all was silent and still, and the room about him seemed to change into another place. Hambidge-Freeman held resolutely his own eye contact, and Hambidge-Freeman dared not breath.

'What wouldst thou?'

The voice was all about and inside of him. John stared into his own eyes, unblinking.

'I would have respect and good will. I would have prosperity and long life. I would have the means to build all that my father has. I would have that which I desire.'

'And so thou wilt.'

The silence became less still, and John blinked. The clock struck three more times, and midnight came, and the light of his branch went out.

John dreamt such dreams that night. And when he woke, he was ecstatic from the rest, despite the few hours sleeping.

His future was assured. He soon would be the man he'd always wanted to be. He soon would show his father that he too could build. He kissed his still-sleeping wife and went to greet the day. Celebration was in order.

So John did drink, and John did quaff, and John, he did imbibe. John turned dark and John turned nasty. And drunken John decided he and Mary Ann would spend the day in Bourton, and would make merry. And drunken John went about his father's tenants and collected up late rents, and drunken John sought out Elizabeth Watts, a neighbour girl, and paid her to act for the day as babysitter. Merry he was as he handed over the rent to his father, and merry as he demanded half back to spend in Bourton.

George Hambidge refused.

'No matter!' bellowed John, as he disappeared down a corridor, returning with his empty shotgun held aloft. 'I'll get what's mine alright, sooner or later', and collapsed into further laughter, dropping the gun onto the table.

'What are you to do with that?' asked Mary Ann.

'Cheer up, old girl, 'tis for the trip to Bourton.' Further laughter.

She went upstairs to dress for travel, and young Elizabeth Watts went too to hold the baby. George sunk down into his chair.

'Won't help a poor couple to have a fine time, is it, Father? Ah, go along you old rascal! Here's my wife in the family way – I don't care a damn for any of the Hambidges. A Freeman I was born and a Freeman I will stay.'

And John looked down on his foolish old father and he laughed. He picked up the empty gun and raised it to his breast, to watch him flinch as he pulled the trigger.

Click. The old man jumped, and John cackled at how small he was, and pulled the trigger again.

Click. The old man bowed his head and shut his eyes, started whispering his prayers.

John was in hysterics. He cocked the gun a third time. Pressed it against his father's breast a third time. Pulled the trigger a third time.

Bang. The clock struck one.

The *London Sun* of 7th November 1851 continues the narrative:

> They had scarcely been up stairs ten minutes when they heard the report of a gun in the kitchen, and Mrs. Fisher [John's wife], fearing some catastrophe, ran down stairs, and there to her horror beheld her husband standing in the room with a gun in his hand, and his father lying a mangled corpse in his chair. She screamed out for help, and on Mrs. Watts going down she found the prisoner supporting his father in the chair, but he was quite dead. Others of the neighbours rushed in, and found the poor old man in the state described, with his blood flowing on the floor of the room, and his daughter [in law] in a violent fit, from which it was some time 'ere she recovered.
>
> [John], who had been drinking, but was described as in a state to know what he was about, repeatedly exclaimed that he 'had killed his father,' and he added, in an apparently cool and collected manner, 'I nicked the gun twice, and it didn't go off, but it went off the third time.'
>
> The police shortly afterwards arrived, and took the prisoner into custody, and while in the house he went to a cupboard in one of the rooms, and took from it a paper. The policeman immediately took it from him, and replaced it. It proved to be the deceased father's will.
>
> When in custody of the policeman [John] said, 'I have shot him, and must take the consequences. I shall be tried for my life. It was a good thing my wife was up stairs, for it was as likely to be her as him. If Mary Ann had not snatched the gun out of my hand I should have shot myself'.

On 31st March, 1852, with his best velveteen jacket not distracting from the drawn and shabby look he now wore, the jury declared John guilty of manslaughter. The newspapers of the time recorded the judge's sentencing as follows:

> Prisoner at the bar, the jury have taken a very merciful view of your case. I should not have been surprised if they had found you guilty of murder. But they are the proper judges of the facts of the case before them, and they have brought their intelligence and experience to bear on those facts; and I cannot bring myself to think but that they have arrived at a proper and just conclusion. The conclusion at which they have arrived is, that you, by gross negligence in the handling of that gun, sacrificed your father's life without having intended to do so. It is not, therefore, a case for severity of punishment, as they have found that it was not a deliberate act on your part. Your own feelings in this case must always present to your mind this sad event. The blood upon your hands can never be washed out. In the hope, therefore, of your repenting of your past life – of your taking this opportunity of reviewing and abandoning the career you have hitherto pursued. The sentence of the Court is –

The judge handed down a sentence of just thirteen nights in jail – solitary confinement. John left the dock with a smile on his face.

After the fourteenth day, he was free not only to go but to enjoy his inheritance. Outrage reigned.

John was hated. John was despised. John was outcast. Not one person in the Wold thought him anything but guilty, and not one person believed that he should not have swung.

John had always liked to think himself a stain on the community, but he had never experienced anything before like this. It near destroyed him. No friends would speak to sordid John, no women would laugh. Soon, all that he could do was drink, and hate.

Two weeks after his release, in a drunken rage he burst into the police station and demanded the return of his gun. He was refused and ejected into the street, where he demanded passers-by fight him until he collapsed.

He was taken in by his wife's family, the Campins, but as had always been the way with John, the more charity he received, the greater his hatred grew. His loathing reached new heights – he had gained his land and his money at the cost of his father. Freedom from official punishment just made the social one all the greater.

In a trough of drunken rage, on 7th May, he grabbed Mary Ann by the throat and hit her with the back of his hand. Her mother Elizabeth screamed, picked up a birch broom and hit him in the back. John seized her by the throat, thrust her to the ground and hit her. Again and again and again. Henry and Charles, his father and brother-in-law, soon arrived, wrestled him off and kicked him out of the house. John threatened to 'have your blood at the first opportunity'. Nevertheless, away he skulked.

He was arrested once more, and on 10th May 1852, having been free for less than a month, he was sentenced by the magistrate, Reverend F.E. Witts, to a full year in jail.

John descended, and his rage became bottomless, and his mind was broken by his hate. As midnight came that Halloween, he closed his eyes in his dank cell and heard again that voice.

'What wouldst thou?' The voice was all about and inside of him.

'I would have respect and good will. I would have prosperity and long life. I would have the means to build all that my father had. I would have that which I desire.'

'And so thou wilt.'

John's year concluded, but John had not behaved well. He was not subtle in his hate, and he brawled and he argued and he held onto any opportunity to damn the Reverend Witts, who'd sent him down. He promised to any who'd listen that as soon as he was free, the first thing he'd do was march his way to Witts's house and 'shoot the bastard dead'.

In June of 1854, he was, instead of being released, tried for these threats and abuses and sentenced to another two years. John left the bar with the greatest nonchalance and returned in silence to his cell.

When Hallowmas rolled back around, again he closed his eyes in bed, again he heard that voice. 'What wouldst thou?' The voice was all about and inside of him.

John was numb and whispered back, 'I would have respect and good will. I would have prosperity and long life. I would have the means to build all that my father had. I would have that which I desire.'

'And so thou wilt.'

John's behaviour did not change. He continued to fight with other convicts. He kicked the prison chaplain in the chest. A man of ungovernable temper, with every rage his world grew tighter, and his life grew smaller. Whenever an appeal came up to end his sentence early, violence took full reign and the sentence was let stand.

On Halloween of 1855, as the clock struck midnight, John held the lit, waxen match to his face and stared into his eyes in the reflection of the shaving mirror. He whispered his father's name three times as he wept, and his mother's name three times as he begged forgiveness, and he called on the Devil three times as he gave up his evil soul. He stared, unblinking, as the clock stopped at the ninth stroke, and all was silent and still, and the cell about him changed into another place. Hambidge-Freeman held eye contact, and Hambidge-Freeman dared not breathe.

And the silence became less still, and John blinked. There was no shadow in the corner of his eye, and the clock struck three more times. Midnight came, and the light of his match went out.

John dreamt such dreams that night. Dreams of a farm, of seven happy children and a single happy wife, and all loving him and needing him and forgiving him his faults, and he a good and loving, caring father to them all. He dreamt of walking down a street and being known by all he passed, of being spoken to with deference and with respect. Of people being pleased when he entered the door of the inn, and people who would not turn away. John dreamt of this and saw the path to it.

Come summer, John was freed from jail.

No leopard fully rids itself of spots, and yes, John still did drink and still he would be drunk. But never again was John in serious trouble, and soon enough he disappears from the historical record – and we are left to guess at why.

We cannot know what John thought. All the archives retain are his misdeeds, which were manifold, and by the end of his 30s these seem to run out. All is silence.

Almost forty years later, a final word on old John Hambidge is given in the *Banbury Guardian* of Thursday, 2nd June 1892:

> DEATH OF MR. J. HAMBIDGE. – With deep regret we record the death of Mr. John Hambidge, of this village. For over 30 years deceased farmed The Downs, Chadlington, earning for himself, throughout a long career as a tiller of the soil, high esteem by a large circle of acquaintances. He relinquished his occupation in 1882 in favour of his eldest son, retiring to The Lands, Swerford. The climate there never suited him, Mr. Hambidge was seized with bronchitis, expiring on Thursday morning last, after a week's illness, despite every medical attention, at the advanced age of 77, leaving behind him a sorrowing widow, two daughters, and five sons to mourn their irreparable loss. The funeral took place on Monday at the Parish Church amidst universal signs of respect, the sons alone (four in number) following the mortal remains of their beloved father to his last resting place. The coffin was covered with a number of lovely wreaths and other floral tributes.

So thou wilt. So he did.

BLOODMONTH

28

MARTLEMAS GOOSE AND REMEMBRANCE

You may remember that the Heathen Anglo-Saxons called November Bloodmonth, due to the animal sacrifices they made then to England's old gods. Long after such ritual intention had ceased, the start of November remained a time for mass slaughter – thinning down the herd in advance of the harshness of winter, when the cost of keeping livestock would rise, and their weight would inevitably wane.

Martlemas, also known as Martinmas and Martinalia, is the feast day of St Martin of Tours, on 11th November. For many centuries, it was one of the most important days of the calendar, on which various rents were paid and tenancies terminated, until the ascendancy of Christmas as the main winter festival. It is still widely celebrated on the Continent, far more so than here, and relatively few observances survived in England long enough to be culturally integrated into our secular Hallowmas season.

The main tradition of Martlemas that has survived in the English calendar, thanks in no small part to the retained practice of November cattle slaughter, is that Martlemas is the time to feast, to drink and to glut – thus, a particularly descriptive name for the nearest Sunday to Martlemas is the wonderful 'Tear-Stomach' Sunday, and the season retains various heritage food customs. William Hone, in his *Every Day Book* of 1826, explains to us that 'Martlemas beef was beef dried in the chimney, as bacon, and is so called, because it was usual to kill the beef for this provision about the feast of St. Martin'. Martlemas beef, then, is a sort of beef bacon, or (more likely) an English alternative to the American beef jerky or the South African biltong. For the likely related St Brice's Day beef, see Chapter 30.

Hone also tells us that Martlemas saw rustic families in Northumberland club together into groups known as 'marts' to purchase a cow (or other animal). 'After the animal was killed, they filled the entrails with a kind of pudding meat, consisting of blood, suet, groats, &c. which being formed into little sausage links, were boiled and sent back as presents. These are called "black-puddings" from their colour.'

A Martlemas goose roast, of course, has always been the great traditional observance of the day, both across the country and abroad, and so a true Martlemas should include both black pudding and a grand roast goose (the Martlemas beef, of course, won't be ready yet; traditionally, cured beef or jerky was not enjoyed until deeper winter). Furthermore, much ale should be drunk – Dr William Stukeley, writing in 1724 in the first volume of his *Itinerarium Curiosum*, explains the name of Martinsell Hill, an Iron Age hillfort near Oare and north of Pewsey, in Wiltshire, thus:

> I take the name of Martinsal Hill to come from the merriments among the northern [Germanic] people, called Martinalia or drinking healths to the memory of St. Martin. There is no doubt about the young people of the neighbourhood assembling here, as they do now upon the adjacent St. Ann's Hill, upon St. Ann's day. At a later time, the people being unwilling to lose a day devoted to pagan rites, such rites were blended with Christian ceremonies.

There is a ballad to be sung at Martlemas, recorded in the sixteenth century, which testifies to bonfires, feasting and revelry. As follows:

> It is the day of Martilmasse,
> Cuppes of ale should freelie passe;
> What though Wynter has begunne
> To push downe the Summer sunne,
> To our fire we can betake,
> And enjoy the crackling brake,
> Never heedinge Wynter's face
> On the day of Martilmasse.
>
> Some do the citie now frequent,
> Where costlie shows and merriment
> Do weare the vaporish eveninge out
> With interlude and revellinge rout;
> Such as did pleasure Englande's queene

When here her Royal Grace was seen
Yet will they not this day let passe,
The merrie day of Martilmasse.

When the dailie sports be done,
Round the market crosse they runne,
Prentis laddes and gallant blades
Dancing with their gamesome maids,
Till the Beadel, stout and sowre,
Shakes his bell, and calls the houre;
Then farewell ladde and farewell lasse
To the merry night of Martilmasse.

Martilmasse shall come againe,
Spite of wind, and snow, and raine;
But many a strange thing must be done,
Many a cause be lost and won,
Many a fool must leave his pelfe,
Many a worldlinge cheat himselfe,
And many a marvel come to passe,
Before return of Martilmasse.

Though the observance of Martlemas had faded in many parts of Britain by the nineteenth century, it was maintained in a number of regions well into the twentieth century and survives still in localised custom across the country. One such example is at Fenny Stratford, near Bletchley, on which St Martin's Day has been heralded since 1730 by the firing of an array of small (very small) cannon known as Fenny Poppers, alongside a church service and a good dinner.

This curious tradition was established by politician, antiquary and Lord of the Manor, Browne Willis (1682–1760), who built Fenny Stratford's church (St Martin's) between 1724 and 1730 as a memorial to his grandfather, Dr Thomas Willis, a famous physician who had lived in St Martin's Lane in the parish of St Martin-in-the-Fields, London, and who had likewise died on St Martin's Day, 1675. After construction was complete, he arranged for a sermon to be preached at the church every Martlemas and celebrated the occasion with a grand dinner attended by the local clergy and gentry. The Fenny Poppers developed as part of these festivities some time prior to 1830 (the exact year of their first use is unknown), and in 1740, Willis purchased a dilapidated thatched house and grounds 'fronting the common street of Fenny Stratford', rebuilt the front wall, and gifted the property to the town on the proviso that its rental income was specifically set aside to pay for the sermon, as well as annual relief to the poor, and later also the cost of gunpowder for the poppers – it was this that enabled the custom to continue after his death, twenty years later (by 1839 the premises had been divided into two dwellings, St Martin's Cottages, at 25 and 27 Aylesbury Street. By 1914 they were in such poor condition that they were condemned, and demolished 12th January the following year. The site was then taken on by a firm of wheelwrights named Manyweathers, and today appears to hold a car dealership).

The Fenny Poppers, similar to the Ottery Rock Cannons previously mentioned, continue healthily today, with the original poppers still in use (though original in a material sense, they were actually all recast in 1859 by Barwell and Co, at Northampton's Eagle Foundry, after one developed a crack and exploded, partly demolishing the roof of the Bull and Butcher pub. They are now well maintained and regularly tested for faults).

The six poppers weigh about 19lb (8.5kg) each. The bore is 6in by 1.75in and they are charged with Pyrodex (a modern alternative to black powder), which is then plugged with well-rammed newspaper and ignited by means of a long poker whose tip has been made red hot in a brazier. At time of writing, the poppers are fired thrice (at noon, 2pm and 4pm) every Martlemas in Leon Recreation (they originally took place at the church, until the 1949 event damaged the clockface. In 1950 they were held at the Watling Street entrance of Manor Fields, but due to general dissatisfaction they then moved to the current site), and since 2008 also in August as part of the summer 'Fenny Poppers Festival', as well as on select special occasions.

In Warwickshire, a far older Martlemas tradition is observed, in the customary collection of Wroth Silver. Before dawn on 11th November, at Knightlow Hill off Holyhead Road, near Dunchurch, officials from the twenty-five parishes in the Hundred of Knightlow (including Ryton and Bubbenhall) gather at the surviving stub-base of a long since lost, old stone cross, alongside anyone else who wishes to attend (and many do, often annually, as a family event).

When the light has just about risen enough to read the Charter of Assembly (generally around 6.45am), the Agent to the Duke of Buccleuch steps forward and does so, reading out the names of the parishes and the sums owed, 'as an acknowledgement of certain concessions made by his ancestors' – what these concessions were, or which ancestors made them, has long since been forgotten.

The rates owed vary, and before decimalisation totalled 9*s* 4*d*. Today, the full sum is 46p. Should the Wroth Silver not be paid, the parish must pay a forfeit of 20 shillings for every penny, or a 'white bull with red nose and red ears' – an interesting detail, as such cattle have long had an association with fairies and the supernatural.

As each parish is named, the appropriate representative steps up, throws coin into the hole in the centre of the stone and exclaims, 'Wroth Silver!' The ceremony itself takes only about four and a half minutes, at which point those gathered repair to the Half Moon Pub in Wolston for the official Wroth Silver Breakfast (a ticketed meal, previously held at the Queen's Head, Bretford), which has been open since 6am serving the traditional rum and hot milk to attendees.

The breakfast starts with a toast from the host to His Grace, the Duke of Buccleuch and Queensberry (currently Richard Walter John Montagu Douglas Scott, the 10th Duke of Buccleuch and 12th Duke of Queensberry) with further rum and hot milk, alongside an update on the duke's local Boughton Estate by his agent, a speech from the Mayor of Rugby, a brief history of the ceremony (previously given by David Eadon, since by William Waddilove) and, for the past decade, also a poem by the official Wroth Silver poet, Barry Patterson.

As part of the breakfast, attendees are provided with a clay churchwarden's pipe (previously 15in, currently 9in), which is smoked in the usual way outside in the smoking shelter (previously in the pub itself, before this was banned) and retained as souvenirs. Tobacco and matches are provided.

Special note should be made of the aforementioned Mr David Eadon, author of the definitive book on the subject (*Wroth Silver Today*) and the main organiser of the event for a huge chunk of the twentieth century. The ceremony of 2023 was the first he had not attended for eighty-five years, due to advancing age and declining health – he single-handedly kept the ritual alive during the Second World War, repeatedly attending alone to carry it out, and deserves permanent acknowledgement for his service.

The ceremony likely dates to Anglo-Saxon times, and the earliest surviving record of it is from 1086, when it was held elsewhere. It is recorded as having its current location from at least 1170. Originally paid to the Crown, on 20th July, 1629, the rights to the ceremony and its proceeds were sold for £40, and thereafter granted by letters patent to Sir Frances Leigh and his heirs by Charles I.

Other Wroth money (also called Warth or Ward money, and Swaff penny) ceremonies previously existed in other parts of Warwickshire, but

Knightlow's is the only one that survives. The New Forest in Hampshire had a traditional payment of 'Wrather Money', recorded in the 1670 *Abstract of Forest Claims*, also as *rother* or *hryðer*, which would mean 'cattle money', an actual payment received in cattle (other similar payments existed there, such as 'oves', which was paid in eggs). It was subsumed into broader Forest rent payments from about the mid eighteenth century.

The final stage in the development of the modern Martlemas occurred in 1918 at 11am, with the cessation of hostilities of the First World War on the Western Front, and the establishment of Armistice Day to commemorate it. Ever since, on the eleventh hour of the eleventh day of the eleventh month, a two-minute silence is held. Often this is combined with the laying of a wreath or wreaths on local war memorials.

Since the Second World War, a partner ceremony has been held on the nearest Sunday, being the second in November, known as Remembrance Sunday, in which a more formal ceremony is held at war memorials, and usually with another two-minute silence. The General Synod of the Church of England to this day recognises Hallowtide as concluding with Remembrance Sunday, whenever this occurs later than Martlemas.

The addition of this period of national remembrance for the dead, and of official Anglican incorporation into Hallowstide, has cemented the Martlemas period (and, by extension, Old Halloween) into the English Hallowmas season. Many, in consequence, continue to drink heartily or hold large dinners on Martlemas, after a remembrance service in the morning, though fewer than before keep to the traditional roast goose, or to good black pudding.

We begin, now, the conclusion of All Hallows, and so move on, after a brief tale, to St Brice's Day.

29

THE MARTLEMAS MURDERS

The Richmond Arms Pub at Godalming in Surrey, which, at time of writing, serves an excellent Sunday roast, has for many years accrued sightings of a peculiar pair of ghosts at the bar. The sightings always begin around All Hallows Eve, and always come to an end (where this pub is concerned) by midnight on Martlemas Eve, when 10th November becomes the 11th.

These ghosts seem, initially, to be a merry pair of fellows, jolly and hearty and spendthrift. Accounts vary wildly; sometimes, people at the bar are vaguely aware of them in the corner of their eye, though they disappear when looked at properly; other times, they are heard or 'felt', but not seen. Some say they drink people's pints when the owners aren't looking, or knock over glasses and leave beer taps running; others have heard them inside, long after closing, when the doors are locked up tight. Occasionally, they have full-fledged conversations with unsuspecting punters, even buying them a drink before vanishing. Generally, they are dressed in non-specific but old-fashioned clothes – one smart and one scruffy. Sometimes, the smart one is described as wearing a top hat or frock coat, while the scruffy one wears a smock (both of which are dismissed as Halloween costumes by the unsuspecting witness).

The strangest accounts are quite hideous. They describe the pair as looking perfectly merry, fleshy and normal on one side, but when they turn their heads to talk, or the witness walks around them, the other half of their face has been cut to pieces, dissected, with parts of them exposed like anatomical models. One first-hand account likened them to Gunther von Hagens's 'Body Worlds' exhibitions of plastinated corpses.

Another tale told of a bartender in the 1970s who took their order and received payment in the usual way. The bank note he was given, however, was old and out of date, with smudges of blood on it. When the bartender looked up from the till to object, the ghosts were nowhere to be seen and his hand was empty of payment.

One old man I spoke to had a half-memory of the story behind it all. 'They were a pair of murderers who were executed, and after they were dead and buried they came back the next week and terrorised the town.' Apparently, they were seen stalking up and down the streets, banging at the doors and windows of pubs, trying to get into homes, climbing onto rooves. 'They broke into the church and smashed the place up, did a sh*t on the altar I heard. In the end they had to be dugged up and their heads had off with a spade. But then their ghosts came still when their bodies couldn't.'

This fits with the revenant tradition of the undead – reanimated corpses, usually of violent or wicked people, who return after burial to terrorise the community they've left behind. In English folklore, they are also known as shag-boys, hogboys and after-gangers, and there are multiple accounts from as early as the eleventh century.

Sightings of the Godalming ghosts wax and wane in popularity. The earliest I've found date to the start of the twentieth century. They peaked in the 1930s, with a resurgence post-war, and a small rise again in the early 1970s. The most recent account I've heard is from 2022.

As with so many other instances, these ghost stories stem from a brutal historical event, the original of which has been long since forgotten in the public consciousness. This is the first time, I believe, that what I am about to tell you has been recognised for what it is and written about for a mainstream, modern audience.

William Chalcraft and George Chennel the Younger were archetypal serial killers, long before such things were known or understood, and more than seventy years before Jack did his ripping. A serial killer can be defined as someone who has murdered more than three people, with a window of time between the murders, and with the entire period from first to last taking place over at least a month, usually longer. Laurence Miller, in his 2012 textbook *Criminal Psychology*, specifies 'Dominant-submissive pairs' as one of the 'four types of partner or group serial killers'. In this case, there will be a dominant and driven person, partnered with a submissive and compliant person, the former being more intelligent and organised than the latter, and the latter looking up to the former and eager to please them – a co-dependent relationship with a common goal.

So it was with Chalcraft and Chennel.

The newspapers of the time indicate various other murders that the pair were believed to have been involved in, but as no evidence existed to confirm the link, they did not go into specifics. No doubt there were others that were never recognised at all. I shall briefly outline four cases, each of which we can be comfortable assigning to them, though in the end, they were tried only for the last – their grand finale – that which burned itself so deeply into the mind of Godalming that its shadow would survive long after the literal events were forgotten.

On Sunday, 18th August 1816, 8am, the body of an elderly farmer named Stillwell was found with his throat slit in his own home. The house, Dockenfield, sat on the isolated edge of Holt Forest at a small village called Farnham Hole, near Farnham town. The deceased was known to have possessed some money, and having lived in an almost retired state, it was supposed by the authorities that he was 'attacked by some villains, whose object no doubt was plunder', as *Drakard's Stamford News* reported on the 23rd of the month. Two strangers were witnessed in the vicinity, and the presumption was that they, whoever they were, must have been the culprits.

Six months later, on the morning of Friday, 7th February 1817, another body was found. As per the *Windsor and Eton Express* of 9th February:

> Mr. Longuet, Minister of the Catholic Chapel at Reading, was found murdered on Friday morning, on the Oxford road, halfway between Pangbourn and Reading [...] he left about 8 o'clock in the evening, on his horse, with his umbrella fastened at his back. It appears that he was murdered in the middle of the high-road, from the quantity of blood scattered about. His head is nearly severed from the shoulders; there are several wounds in the face, one of his ears nearly off, and stabs in various parts of the body. His pockets were turned inside out, but a gold watch he had was found upon him, and also the silver buckles in his shoes.

The *Oxford University and City Herald* of the 22nd gave more details:

> Mr. Longuet was a Roman Catholic Priest, and a teacher of the French language, residing at Reading. On Thursday se'nnight he paid a visit to the family of Thomas Morton, Esq. who resides about six miles from

> Reading. Mr. Longuet quitted Mr. Morton's house between eight and nine o'clock; previous, however, to his quitting it, Mr. Morton came to the door with him, and observing that it was a very dark night, endeavoured to persuade him to continue there all night. This hospitable offer, however, was unfortunately for the poor gentleman rejected, accompanied by these words: 'I know the road very well; and although it appears very dark now, it will be much lighter to me when I get from the light of a candle.'
>
> He then bade Mrs. Morton a good night, and pursued his journey. He had not proceeded more than three miles before he was attacked by some villains, who barbarously murdered him, apparently with some sharp instrument; for when he was found on Friday morning, his head was nearly severed from his body, and he was dreadfully mangled, cut, and stabbed in various parts of the body. His body was cut open, and in his heart were no less than five stabs.

All reports emphasised how liked and respected Longuet had been, and how good a man he was. An amount of £13 had been stolen from his pockets, and though there were multiple reports of the murderers being apprehended – first, two or three soldiers from the nearby Oxford Blues, then a man named John Woodisson, and finally a bargeman named Franklin – none of them held up to scrutiny and nobody was charged with the crime, despite an astonishing reward of £250 being offered.

Another six months passed, and again, during the hay harvest on Thursday, 14th August 1817, another 'atrocious murder was discovered'. As *The Observer* put it a couple of months later:

> As Mr Munday, a respectable farmer, residing within a short distance of Petersfield, was walking about 10 o'clock in the morning over one of his hay fields [adjoining the turnpike road, within a quarter of a mile of the town], he found one of the hay cocks very much tumbled; and was putting it in its original form as he left it on the preceding night, when the prongs of the fork came in contact with a hard substance. Mr. Munday removed the hay, and, to his great surprise and terror, found the mangled corpse of a man, partly naked. The body presented a most shocking spectacle, being nearly covered with deep cuts, one of them very large on the right side; another, which appeared to have been done with a long knife, pierced below the right eye to the back of the head: and the right hand was nearly cut off. The hat and the breeches were missing [...] The surgeon who examined the corpse discovered 21 wounds about the body. It was apparent that the deceased

> had made a great resistance, and being a very strong powerful man, it was conjectured that there were more than one person concerned in the foul transaction.

The cadaver's name was Searson. From Lincoln originally, he had recently been in London, having sailed down for work. Whilst there, he'd apparently fallen in with an unidentified man or men. They'd then travelled together to Ditton Marsh, where they supposedly attacked a farrier, robbed him, stripped him and left him for dead. The farrier survived, however, and was able to identify a knife and key on Searson's body as belonging to him. At some point, it seems, the mysterious strangers turned on Searson and killed him, or perhaps he had never been an accomplice at all, with the murderers adding the clues to Searson's corpse as a red herring.

The *Hampshire Chronicle* of 1st September 1817 describes:

> ... dreadful cuts perceived about Searson; dreadful gashes appear from both ears to the mouth, as also on his shoulders, as if they were inflicted whilst attempting his throat, and which he, it would appear, resisted by holding his head down. Between his eyes a dreadful cut is perceived, supposed to have been done to make him hold up his head. But the blow that finally deprived him of life is a most dreadful wound in his side, directed upwards towards the opposite breast; to stop the blood that was running from this wound when the body was found, a wisp of straw was introduced.

These murders, despite causing extreme consternation throughout the vicinity, remained unsolved and unconnected, with little forward movement in the investigations.

Then came Halloween.

George Chennel the Elder was a successful and well-respected shoemaker in Godalming. George Chennel the Younger was his son and was neither. George Junior was a handsome and charismatic man, but he also was a drinker, and had a wildness to him. The papers of the time described him as 'a stout made man', of about 40, 'rather inclined to be corpulent, with the outline of a good face, apparently rendered heavy and dull by the effects of indolence and regular habits'.

Young Chennel had been considered of good character in early life. An exceptionally quiet and gentle schoolboy, his reputation as a parsimonious sort who was likely to succeed grew as he did. His mother died when he was 10, and it was then that his father employed one Elizabeth Warren as a live-in housekeeper, to assist with caring for young George. Elizabeth doted on him and was, by all accounts, as loving and attentive to him as any mother could have been, both in his childhood and adulthood.

At 30, he became acquainted with the daughter of a respectable farmer, residing at Chillingford. They soon married, whereupon they received the then-astonishing sum of £2,000 between them from her father, and with this Chennel set himself up as a farmer in his own right. It was said locally that this was the start of a change in him. That, by degrees, Chennel the Younger grew into 'habits of extravagance'. He became overfond of hosting high society, and as his funds began to fail him, he 'began to frequent public-houses, to neglect his family, and to addict himself to the society of the lowest class of females'. The good nature and reputation he once had held soon soured to one of dissipation, though he was never considered violent or quarrelsome, and was always averse to fighting or open hostility.

The downturn in Chennel's fortune and character, not to mention the boozing and apparent frequenting of prostitutes, had resulted in a separation from his wife towards the middle of 1816. He had become a sullen, bitter man in consequence, and reports of the time describe him after this as 'in the constant habit of using invectives against his father and the old woman', meaning Elizabeth, who by then had been his father's close domestic companion, and a surrogate mother to himself, for thirty years.

William Chalcraft had a keen eye and intelligent face. He had a bad reputation in his neighbourhood – fond of drinking establishments, but a disinterested husband and father. For some time, he had forced his family to rely on parish charity, giving them only a very small portion of his wages and keeping the rest for himself and the alehouse.

Ever since Chalcraft had taken up an apprenticeship with George Chennel the Elder, he had been in thrall to his master's son. They became firm friends, despite the social gulf between them, and Chalcraft could always be found by young Chennel's side, laughing at his jokes, agreeing with his every word.

It was on Halloween of 1817 that they decided to kill the old pair.

Over the days that followed, when deep in drink, Chalcraft could often be heard mumbling that 'there would be a bigger blow up before long than Godalming had ever seen'. The Friday before the murders, young Chennel had been raging in the Richmond Arms that he wished his father's housekeeper dead, and if he saw anyone murder her, he would not tell of it. Nobody took him seriously. He said it often.

At about 7pm on Martlemas Eve, Chennel the Younger entered the Richmond Arms and called for beer and tobacco. He drank and he smoked and he left about ten past nine to go to his house 'to look after a girl'. He was seen thereafter with Chalcraft.

At 9.30, a passer-by heard a woman scream, and a crash from Chennel Senior's house. Chennel the Younger had been seen loitering in the passage. A female associate of theirs named Sarah Hurst was witnessed pacing up and down outside. Chalcraft was seen nearby afterwards.

Young Chennel had returned to the Richmond by 10, and called for more of the same. When the beer was finished, he called for a glass of brandy and water, then a second, then a third, which he drank with the landlord (one James Tiddy). Still his hands shook. 'We shall want some beer for a cooler,' announced Chennel, and this they had. And another.

The corpses were found next morning – Chennel the Elder in his bed, poor Elizabeth Wilson in the kitchen. As Mr Parsons, the surgeon, would later testify in court:

> The throat of Mr. Chennel was cut from the right ear to his left. There were several indentations, which were done, in my opinion, by a hammer, or some blunt instrument; the skull was fractured in several places. The throat of Elizabeth Wilson was cut, but not so deep as Chennel's; her head has bruises on it similar to those on Chennel's head.

The first to arrive on the scene, ostensibly to start his day of work, was Chalcraft himself – who immediately drew suspicion with a pantomime performance of calling for his master, then asking the neighbours for help because he'd found blood in the kitchen. He failed to inform anyone of the body of Elizabeth Wilson, however, and he could not have seen one without seeing the other. When asked about this, he replied, 'You would have done as I did, if you knew the pedigree of the affair as I do.'

Before long, people started to notice that the blood had somehow also gotten onto his clothes. When asked why he didn't go up to check on his master, he replied, 'I could not for all the town, as I've ne'er seen any man murdered but the one at Petersfield.'

'Do you mean you saw that man get murdered?'

'No, no. I meant after he'd been murdered. I only saw him after.'

Though the till had been forced open and emptied, a full £6 in notes were found untouched in the late Mr Chennel's breeches. A hammer with blood on the handle was soon found. Upon comparing it with the fracture, it appeared to be the blunt weapon concerned. A case knife, likewise covered in blood, was with it.

Chennel the Younger was called for, and when woken and informed of the discovery, cried out, 'Lord, have mercy upon us, is he quite dead?' On first entering his father's bedroom, he gave a brief sideways glance at the corpse, before sitting down and burying his face in his hands. When James Wrale, the town constable, searched young Chennel's lodgings, they found, at the bottom of a large trunk in his bedroom, a pair of bloodied stockings and a pair of shoes, wet and dirty.

Benjamin Keen, officer, aided Wrale in the search, and found two £1 notes along with some silver. One of the notes, likewise, had two spots of blood on it. T.S. Allathorp, a warehouseman, would later testify that he had paid those very notes to Chennel the Elder the day before Bonfire Night, and they had been free from any bloodstains then.

Needless to say, the pair were arrested and held in the jail to await a trial.

On Wednesday, 26th November, the parents of the murdered Z. Searson arrived in Godalming. A bundle, recently found in a pool of shallow water near Esham Mill, about 2 miles from the town, was produced and shown to them. It consisted of a shirt, wrapped in an apron – immediately Mrs Searson exclaimed, 'That is my poor lad's shirt', and wept.

She had made the shirt for her son herself, along with a number of others in advance of his setting out to sea. The apron in which it was enclosed had already been identified as belonging to either Chennel or Chalcraft. Further items found in their rooms were also identified as belonging to Searson, his hat was found on the road from Petersfield to Godalming, and ever more witnesses came forward claiming to have seen them in the area that day – likewise in Farnham Hole, a year previously.

Soon after the murder of Searson, Chennel the Younger had been drinking at the Angel Inn, where he'd fallen into conversation with the waiter there, a Mr W. Coombes. Chennel referred to a certain 'business' he was attending to, how the business was necessitated by his diminished funds, and he could no longer pay his rent. Coombes commented that his costs shouldn't be too high, 'When your business is arranged, you will go and live with your father'. Chennel answered, 'I will go home to eat and drink, but not to sleep; otherwise, Old Bet would know what hour I got home. I hope some morning that I should get up to find her with her throat cut, and if I were to meet the man coming out of the door who had done the murder I would tell nothing of it, though I were hanged for it myself. Aye, were I to find both her and my father cut so I would not be the least sorry, nor should I think it any sin, even if I had committed the murder myself.'

The case against them was strong, and they'd overplayed their hand.

When she was arrested, Sarah Hurst, the female associate who'd been seen keeping watch, had initially accused her husband Thomas (though, it transpires, their marriage was bigamous on his part and so not legally valid) and a man named Scooly, a former servant of the late Chennel Senior. Both had alibis, and under questioning her story collapsed. She confessed all.

The trial was scheduled for April but had to be postponed. According to the *Bury and Norwich Post* of 8th April 1818, 'The female, Hurst, (who confessed that she was an accomplice) is in a deranged and convulsed state, and therefore unable to give her evidence'. It was around then that the man she was living with as husband, who she'd falsely accused, chose (not before time) to leave her. She saw no more of him.

When the court case finally came, Hurst had to be revived by smelling salts halfway through her testimony. The witness evidence against the pair was vast, consisting of over thirty people called to take the stand, all in agreement.

Chennel was cool-headed and resolute in his claim that he was Not Guilty. He would remain as such throughout, dressed in a black jockey coat, striped waistcoat and black neckerchief. It is my opinion that he'd been casually planning it for some time, and had intentionally sought to seed the ridiculous idea that, should he find strangers murdering his father and surrogate mother, he would take the blame for it himself rather than say as much. According to reports of the time, such as that in the *Perthshire Courier* (20th August 1818), 'he displayed, on his entrance into Court, the utmost indifference to his situation, and did not appear to be much touched by anything that occurred'.

His defence was rambling and often irrelevant:

> He delivered [his] story, introducing the most minute circumstances, and the most trifling dialogues, without the least stop or embarrassment, in a firm voice, and with great composure of manner. The only symptom of anxiety or agitation that appeared was a quivering of his lips, which he found it necessary to wet frequently with his tongue.

Chalcraft, predictably in such a dynamic, was the opposite, and had little to say for himself. He appeared in a smock, with a coloured handkerchief about his neck, and 'all the rustic appearance of his situation'.

In summing up, the judge allowed Chalcraft and Chennel to sit on the sides of the dock, as both were showing signs of collapse due to fatigue.

He pointed out to the jury the difficulties in taking Hurst's testimony at face value, and in being careful over taking Chennel the Younger's talk of murdering his father (which began about the time of the murder of the old man in Farnham Hole) as entirely sincere. Beyond that, he merely repeated the various testimonies, and after two and three-quarter hours, he let the jury leave to consider their verdict.

They returned almost immediately. Guilty.

Chennel and Chalcraft remained impassive. The judge declared that they were to be taken to the prison from whence they came, and Friday next carried to the place of execution, there to be hanged by the neck until dead, and their bodies afterwards to be anatomised and dissected. The prisoners were then led away, Chalcraft protesting that he was 'as innocent as the child unborn', and Chennel saying nothing.

Chennel and Chalcraft were executed on Friday, 14th August, 1818, in a meadow adjoining the town. The *New Times*, published the next day, described events in detail, and I shall quote it extensively:

> Never perhaps were two men put to the Bar under a charge of so dreadful a nature as that against Chennel and Chalcraft, who displayed so much indifference to the awful circumstances under which they were placed. Chalcraft, at certain times during the trial, appeared much agitated, but it was the agitation rather of a guilty man endeavouring to appear intrepid, than of an innocent one writhing under unfounded accusation. His features were unaltered by confinement, his look was erect to the last, and he parted from the dock with a bold avowel of innocence. Chennel, who, if a person might judge from physiognomy, seemed to have feelings sufficient to bear him unmoved through every species of crime, never for a single moment relaxed into anything like remorse.
>
> When Mr. Serjeant LENS, in the most pathetic manner, commented upon the enormity of his guilt, in lifting a murderous hand against an aged parent, whom every tie of nature and of law should have induced him to protect, the prisoner heard him with the most listless indifference. Never, perhaps, did any man display such hardness of heart. His eye was as completely free of anything like remorse as if he was about to receive the crown of martyrdom in a cause which promised salvation to those who suffered it. He left the Court with a firm step, as did his companion Chalcraft. From their conduct, it was the general belief, that exhortation, or the approach of death, would have little effect in altering the manner

of the prisoners, or producing a confession of their guilt. Chalcraft, in passing through the Court, after leaving the dock, said to Chennel, 'Now George, you can clear me, if you please.'

During a great part of Wednesday night, and on Thursday morning, Chalcraft continued to declare his innocence in the most solemn manner. Chennel remained sullen, without saying any thing in allusion to the crime for which he was about to suffer. He expressed no desire to see any of his friends or relations until Thursday morning, when he requested that his wife and child might be sent for. Chalcraft appeared to have strong hopes of acquittal. The long confinement he had endured made no alteration in his countenance, but in a few hours after sentence was passed on him, the approach of death had so powerful an effect that he could hardly be recognised as the same person who appeared at the Bar a short time before in so much confidence and health.

[…]

They were visited by their wives and children, and by those who witnessed the circumstances of this agonising interview, it was said that nothing could be more affecting. Chalcraft's wife entered his cell with six children, the youngest of whom was but 12 months old. The poor creature appeared to sink under the accumulated miseries of her situation. She was drowned in tears as she passed through the gaol, and the children too wept most bitterly. The moment she was introduced to his cell, she dropped upon her knees, and begged of her husband, in the name of Heaven to confess his guilt if he had any concern in the murders. Chalcraft's answer to this solemn appeal was a firm avowel of innocence. The unfortunate woman was heard after to say, that if her husband had confessed when first apprehended she should die quietly, but now her mind could never more be at rest. The wife bears an excellent character in Godalming. […] She was the second wife of the wretched culprit, and had been for some time a burthen to the parish, as the earnings of Chalcraft were not sufficient for the support of the family.

Chennel had not lived with his wife, the daughter of a very respectable farmer, for the last eighteen months or two years. On Thursday evening, about half-past five, she, together with her child, eight or nine years old, was admitted to the cell. Chennel stood at one corner of it in sullen silence, but the moment he perceived their arrival, that almost brutal insensibility which marked his behaviour from the time of his apprehension to his execution, forsook him. He became for a moment humanised, and tears ran down his

> cheeks. His wife and child burst into lamentations also, and it became almost too much for humanity to bear. Though Chennel's conduct for a long time was such as must naturally have withdrawn from him the affections of a wife, all the tenderness of that connexion seemed to revive at the awful and melancholy spectacle of a husband on the eve of eternity, about to suffer the most ignominious of all punishments for the most horrid and unnatural of all crimes. After some time passed in expressions of mutual forgiveness and affection, the wife retired in a wretched and afflicted state of mind.

As the days passed, they were attended on earnestly by the clergy. Chennel remained impassive, and refused to pray throughout. Chalcraft, however, joined in prayer with great warmth and devotion, but never gave the smallest intimation of guilt. Finally, the bell tolled:

> At a quarter before nine o'clock, the prisoners were brought forth, and conducted to the cart, in which they were to be conveyed. Chennel, in ascending, discovered some symptoms of weakness, but they arose more from the manner he was pinioned than from any apprehension of approaching death. He stumbled a little, but soon recovered his wonted firmness, and took his seat with as much composure as if he was going upon some usual business. Chalcraft followed immediately after, and both seemed desirous to avoid, as much as possible, the view of the vast multitude who surrounded them.

They then marched, all of them, in a sort of pageant procession on horseback, parading the guilty men for the amassed crowds of 20–30,000 along the 4 miles of road from Godalming. At the head was the High Constable. Behind him came a carriage containing the Under Sheriff and a chaplain, with two officers alongside. Then came six javelinmen in twos, then the caravan with the prisoners and three officers on either side. Behind the caravan went the gaoler, with one officer on either side. Behind them came another six javelinmen, likewise in twos, followed by a number of constables in twos – the whole procession was further flanked by constables on foot, in single file on either side.

> The order of the procession being arranged, and in the best possible manner, as well as to guard the prisoners as to prevent tumult or inconvenience, the whole began to move with melancholy and affecting solemnity. Throughout the vast mass of people in attendance, no

sound could be heard except the step of feet, and, from time to time, a deep sigh, proceeding perhaps from some person who had known the unhappy Chennel in the days of youth and innocence. This awful stillness was sometimes interrupted by the solemn voices of the Clergymen, endeavouring to excite the criminals to repentance [...]

Chalcraft, upon hearing the first verse – 'Cry aloud, spare not, lift up thy voice like a trumpet, and shew my people their transgression, and the house of Jacob their sins,' seemed to be seized for a moment with the spirit of the passage. He raised his eyes to Heaven, and in the attitude of humble and contrite feeling, implored pardon for his sins. While the cavalcade was on its progress to the fatal spot, he prayed with the Clergyman, and appeared deeply impressed with the exhortations that were addressed to him.

Chennel, the most cold and immovable of all men that were perhaps ever conducted to execution, seemed to pay little or no attention to what he heard. He never uttered a single word of prayer from the time he left the gaol until his arrival at the entrance into the field where the gallows was erected, when he said, in rather a subdued tone of voice, 'the Lord have mercy on me'. The Rev. Mr. Mann, after praying for a considerable time, and using all means which prudence or piety could suggest, asked Chennel whether he knew by whom the horrible crime was committed? He answered with obdurate coldness that he did not; and Chalcraft immediately replied, with much apparent emotion, 'You do, George; you do.'

The gallows was erected in a place called Godalming marsh, immediately adjoining to a farm, formerly in the possession of Chennel. It is surrounded on all sides by hills, the whole of which, to the very top, were partly occupied by spectators from the adjacent country. The criminals being brought under the gallows, Chennel, who did not lose in the smallest degree that cold indifference of manner which he displayed in the dock, looked up at the preparations that were making, and heaved a deep sigh.

This was the only symptom of emotion he discovered from the moment he quitted the prison until he expired.

He was again asked whether he had anything to disclose, and he answered, as usual, that he knew nothing about it, and could tell no more than he had told before. In a moment after he ascended the steps with a firm pace, and was placed upon the temporary platform, on the right hand, the rope being adjusted round his neck, and the cap drawn over his face.

In this position he remained, quite erect and firm, for a few moments, while the Rev. Mr. West was addressing himself to Chalcraft, who sat at the other end of the caravan. He exhorted him, now that he was going to appear before that God from whom nothing could be concealed, to make a full and open confession of his crimes; that it was the most acceptable sacrifice he could make to Heaven, and the best atonement he could make to society. Chalcraft still declared his innocence. One of the officers present reminded him, that he had promised before to tell everything he knew concerning the murder. Chalcraft's answer was, that he had told all he knew.

Before Chennel mounted the scaffold, whenever any words were addressed to Chalcraft, calling upon him to make a disclosure, the other turned an anxious eye towards him, as if fearful that he might come to a declaration of what he knew. To every person who witnessed their conduct, it appeared as if they had entered into a solemn league to carry with them to the grave the secret of their guilt.

Chennel appeared to have been a man never accustomed to the exercise of religious duties. The awful situation in which he was placed produced no emotion, no apparent feeling of remorse, or repentance. He was as unmoved as if a total forgetfulness had taken place of all he had committed, and of all he was about to suffer. Not a word escaped from him that could afford the momentary consolation of suspecting that he wished that horrid deed undone, for which he was going to suffer death.

Chalcraft gave less of that species of pain which must touch every man of feeling, who witness the departure of a criminal still reeking from his sins, and too obdurate even to speak the language of repentance. Mr. West, as they were going to mount the car, said to Chalcraft, 'This is an awful moment.' 'Yes,' he answered, 'but I hope we shall soon be in a better place.'

Both criminals being now placed next to each other, and every necessary preparation made, the Clergyman spent a short time in prayer. The fatal signal being then given, the unhappy culprits were launched into eternity. They died without the least struggle, and after hanging for about an hour, were cut down and delivered for the purpose of dissection, one to Mr. Haines, and the other to Mr. Parsons, surgeons of Godalming. It was said that their bodies were to be exposed for the purpose of public example at some place in town where the murder was committed. Not having remained long enough, we cannot say whether this has been done.

Fortunately, if morbidly, a writer for the *Hampshire Chronicle* of 24th August was also present, and described it thus:

When the procession was on the road from Guildford to the place of execution at Godalming, Mr. Mann earnestly entreated Chennel to make a confession, and told him he had no right to expect mercy unless he acknowledged his crimes, if it were only for the purposed of preventing innocent persons from suffering for the crimes which they had committed.

He then put the question to Chennel in the most solemn manner, 'Did you or did you not commit the murder, or assist at all in it?' Chennel lifted his eyes, and said, in repy, 'I never had any concern in the murder.' Chalcraft turned his head round, and looking at him very expressively, answered, 'You do, George, you know you do.'

[...]

After their bodies had been cut down, they were received into the waggon which [had] conveyed them to the place of execution, and extended on the elevated stage which had been constructed in the vehicle. The procession of officers and constables was then reformed, and the remains of the murderers were conveyed in slow and awful silence through the town of Godalming, until they arrived at the house of the late Mr. Chennel.

Here the procession halted, and the bodies were removed from the waggon into the kitchen of the house, one of them being placed on the very spot where the housekeeper, Elizabeth Wilson, was found murdered. After this the surgeons proceeded to perform the first offices of dissection, and the bodies in this state were left exposed to the gaze of thousands, who, throughout the day, eagerly rushed in to view them. The effect of this awful scene may be imagined, but not described.

Forgive the huge excerpts, but I hope you agree that the first-hand accounts are far more appropriate than any embroidering I could provide.

Jack the Ripper is often referred to as the first modern serial killer – so called not merely because he killed multiple people over a drawn-out period (no shortage of such cases in the historical record), but because the cases were well documented enough that he can be demonstrated as clearly fitting a textbook psychological and behavioural profile that has since been recognised as fulfilling a recurring homicidal pattern. Chennel and Chalcraft have never before been recognised as such, or even explored in print, but it seems arguable that they fit the bill far earlier than Jack.

In criminal psychology, a 'stressor' is the name often given to the traumatic event or change in circumstances that precedes a serial killer's first kill and concomitant serial kills. Some consider this to be the event which unlocks the latent potential for such behaviour, and sets the killer on their course. In the case of Chennel, the dominant, the stressor was plausibly the separation from his wife, which was not only highlighted by contemporary reports as having provoked a change in him, but seems to have happened shortly before the murder of Languet in Reading.

This first murder was much messier than the later ones, and though he succeeded in getting a considerable sum in cash, he was perhaps too panicked or excited to think clearly enough to take the gold watch and silver shoe buckles. The wounds indicate a rushed, frantic, undisciplined attempt to slash the throat and stab the victim, and this is the same type of attack we see on Searson, though Searson was more thoroughly robbed and more quickly despatched (despite putting up a struggle), indicating the killer was learning. We see a similar MO in the intervening murder (which went far more easily), and the approach seems to have been perfected by the time of the Martlemas Murders. This pattern fits that of a developing serial killer.

Throughout the trial, the dominant–submissive relationship between Chennel and Chalcraft is clear, with Chennel having an extreme psychological hold over Chalcraft, who never confessed in full, despite his clear desire to – even to the extent that he is on record as begging Chennel to allow it. Likewise, the impassive, emotionless state that Chennel held to throughout the arrest, trial and execution – which so shocked the commentators of the time – is now immediately recognisable as criminal psychopathy.

Chalcraft's constant claims to innocence, and statements that Chennel could get him off if he wished, are interesting. Perhaps Chennel was the killer in each case, and Chalcraft merely watched and aided, completely under his sway. Whilst it could have been Searson who attacked the lone survivor with Chennel, before getting killed himself, I think it more likely that it was Chalcraft and Chennel who did so, and who then successfully murdered the innocent Searson when coming to him later, perhaps leaving some of the worthless possessions from the earlier theft on his body to confuse things.

Six victims, one of whom survived. All were single males, bar the penultimate, and all were attacked in the same way before being robbed. Chalcraft and Chennel were definitely present at each and overtly tied to at least three. It seems that all was building up to Chennel's murder of his parents, and he had clearly been thinking about it for some time, likely emboldened by the murders he kept getting away with. But he overplayed his hand, and there was never any question of his innocence.

This is a fascinating case, not only in that it so vividly fulfils the remits and patterns of the now ubiquitous serial killer model, but also because it has been so thoroughly forgotten. Though the execution itself has been cited in a couple of obscure books about dissection, almost nothing has been written about it since 1818, with the connections to earlier murders never mentioned at all.

It is this that makes the ghost traditions surrounding it so striking. Long after the reality of the murders, long after the facts of the case have been forgotten, the lurid ghost stories surrounding them have survived. It is a perfect example of the importance of telling, recording and remembering such tales, because we simply cannot know what obscured truths they hold, or what hidden events they memorialise.

In the surviving oral tradition we can see many details, not just the vague characters, dynamic and clothing of the murderers themselves, but specifics such as the stolen money with bloodstains on it, the fact of them having been anatomically dissected, or their sin being murder. Perhaps the most extreme of the stories is that of their bodily revival as revenants a week later, whereby they stalked through the town having dug themselves up from the grave, desecrated a church and tried to gain entry to buildings, whereupon come daylight they were dug up and beheaded to stop them returning.

On that note, I will finish with the following excerpt from the *London Moderator* of 2nd September 1818:

> It will be recollected that on Friday, the 14th of August, CHENNEL and CHALCRAFT were executed pursuant to their sentence, for the murder of Chennell's father and housekeeper, at Godalming, Surrey, in a meadow adjoining that town; and after their bodies had hung the usual time they were conveyed to the house of old Mr. Chennel, where the deed was perpetrated, in order to be dissected. On the night of the very Friday week following, the Church of the town of GODALMING was broken open and robbed of everything of value, that could be taken, even the cloth which covered the sacred altar, as well as the tassels belonging to the pulpit; and not satisfied with this, the bestial villains aggravated their offence by committing their nuisance in the pulpit. It is to be hoped that ere long the law will overtake them, when they will receive that punishment which they so justly merit.

No further mention of Chennel or Chalcraft is made in the archive.

30

ST BRICE'S DAY

St Brice was the successor to St Martin in the bishopric of Tours in AD 397. They were not close friends in life, but in canonisation they are forever twined, and Martin plays a key role in Brice's hagiography. St Brice's Day concludes the Martlemas season, and as with the rest, it is defined by feasting and meat, though the exclusive association Brice has is with beef.

It is easy enough to find an outline of the career of St Brice, so I will not go into too much detail here. In short, he was a wild and rammucky youth, dissolute and wanton, drinking and eating and fleshing to excess, a lover of both quality and quantity in all aspects of life. After varying amounts of debauchery in his hearty prime, he rose in the clergy at Tours under the reign of Martin, where he remained more or less as he always had been.

Through miraculous means, as the story goes, Martin overheard Brice (with whom he had a fractious relationship) being less than kind about him (essentially calling him a mad old fart who talks to the sky), and so as a double-edged punishment, Martin named Brice his successor as bishop. Brice came to power soon after.

Brice continued in his pomp and his circumstance, but earned the enmity of the mob. Those who rise highest fall farthest, tall poppies are cut to size, and crabs ever pull each other back to the depths of the bucket. And so it was that the rabble of Tours rose up against Brice, accusing him of continuing his sordid ways, and in particular, of being father to a certain unacknowledged new-born baby that had recently popped out of a particularly attractive nun. Brice undertook all manner of miraculous tests to 'prove' his innocence at Martin's tomb, including carrying hot coals while remaining unburned (redolent, perhaps, of certain seasonal fire ceremonies already discussed), and even the baby itself, so the story goes, found supernatural voice to announce out loud that Brice was not his father.

Public opinion, alas, has little to do with reasoning or apparent evidence, and the egregore's mind was made up. Brice was forcefully expelled from office by his underlings, and went into a wreccan exile for seven years; first to Rome, where he petitioned the Pope for his return, before moving on to wander the world in an extended walkabout, either in penance, or as a last hurrah to get the wildness fully out of his system (depending on who you listen to). The folk version of his story has him coming to Britain in the third year of his journeying, seducing a strikingly beautiful native girl, and leaving her full with child when he continued on his travels.

After seven years and two usurpers, he returned to Tours to retake the bishopric, and apparently did so without opposition and in full contrition. He remained there until his death at the age of 74 in the year AD 444, well thought of and pious, gaining sainthood soon after and becoming forever tied up with the afterlife of his predecessor.

A popular saint amongst the Anglo-Saxons, his cult waned after the Conquest, with the notable exception of the area around Dinnington, in Somerset. The village is home to a family named Brice (from whom I happen to descend), who have been present in the vicinity since at least the 1200s, when one of their number is recorded as a reeve at Glastonbury Abbey, with a later branch spreading into the New Forest in Hampshire from the 1500s. The small church of St Nicholas in Dinnington is home to an impressive number of Brice graves (the soil is, quite literally, rich with my ancestors), and the church itself is centred around the armorial ledgerstone tomb of one Worthington Brice (my 10x great grandfather; d. 1649), a companion of the king during the Civil War, whose son fought as a Cavalier.

I last visited some years ago, and in the church was a large visitors' book, a ring binder with some printed pages on the history of the building, and a scrapbook of relevant local remembrances of the area. It is a fascinating miscellany, and there are many details from and regarding Brices. It gives a fragment of folklore that I will repeat here in full:

> The spectral shade of Worthington Brice is still to be seen at St Nicholas on Brices day, and lights and incense are often said then to emanate from within on that eve and day. It is for this reason that many in the parish leave lighted candles in the porch or on the Brice graves outside, though they rarely stay lit for long in the wintry weather. The family tradition is that they are anciently descended from the former Bishop of Tours who

> supposedly visited the area to lie with a local girl when in Britain during his exile. Needless to say this fanciful story has no great authority, though the family ne'ertheless have kept up the customary observances of his day since time immemorial despite not being Anglo-Catholic themselves, and claim as heirloom a supposed relic of the saint rescued from some pre-Reformation shrine.

Another St Brice's Day ghost tradition can be found in Welwyn in Hertfordshire, which was one of many places involved in the infamous 1002 St Brice's Day Massacre, in which King Ethelred the Unready ordered the slaughter of all Danish mercenaries in Britain outside the Danelaw. According to Nicholas Blatchley, writing on the Herts Memories website (hertsmemories.org.uk), 'As a result, White Horse Lane, on the border between Welwyn and Datchworth, is regularly haunted by a headless white horse carrying the ghosts of the [St Brice's Day] victims, and horses and dogs are said to be reluctant to go into the lane'. Most of the year, any mounted spectre one encounters on that road is probably 'the ghost of a royalist farmer, Edward Pennyfather, who was killed along with his white horse by Roundhead soldiers during the Civil War'. On St Brice's Eve and Day, however, it is the slain Danish warriors themselves who can be seen.

Aside from Brice family ghost stories, the book in Dinnington also contains a recipe for 'Brice's Day Beef' – an effective way to make cheaper or smaller cuts and scraps go further, or to use up beef remaining from Martlemas feasting or Sunday roasts. As with Martlemas Beef, it is almost completely unknown today, and of the four recipes I have obtained, the other three were all orally transmitted. This fourth was apparently found in a commonplace book of 1921, which in turn stated that it was copied from a diary entry for 13th November, 1817, in which it had been described as 'Brice's day beef [...] a very old dish'.

(There is also a report from a Miss J.B. Partridge in May of 1911, given in *British Calendar Customs: England Vol. III*, that 'at Bisley, Gloucestershire, pig's cheek and parsnips was the customary dish' for St Brice's Eve, on 12th November. She adds, 'I gather that the custom is dying out', which means that it survived into the twentieth century at least. I have found no further reference to it anywhere.)

The key to Brice's Day Beef is that it should be served as beef in its own right, alongside accompaniments, rather than as a comprehensive one-pot meal or casserole – any ingredients added other than beef and beer (such as garlic, onions or carrots) should be diced very finely, and stewed long enough that they disappear into the sauce. I find it's best with very large hunks of beef that have been seared on a high heat, but it also works with leftovers. It should ideally be served with roast potatoes and a vegetable of your choosing. I usually add a Worcestershire sauce, and/or extra beef stock. The recipe, perfect for a slow cooker, is given as follows:

> Cut up the remaining roast beef to slices and place in a pan with dripping or butter. Add an onion sliced very small and carrot if desired. Let all brown. Add bay and thyme and add wild garlic if desired. Add beer and any stock by degrees. Salt to taste and pepper thoroughly. Seal in a good strong pot and let bubble for some hours at as low a flame as can be maintained. Some add mustard if the beef is poor.

The specific timing makes a relationship with Martlemas Beef likely, and I would suggest that the scraps of meat which proved unsuitable for smoking on Martinmas itself would instead have been used for this dish, potentially stewed in beer (etc.) left over from the Martinalia festivities. Red meat and alcohol have also long been associated with gluttony, vice and excess; it is possible that this symbolism is also relevant, recalling St Brice's hedonistic lifestyle. Whatever the origin, it is a genuinely lovely foodstuff – I heartily encourage you to try it (though some beers work better than others).

The three tear-stomach feast days of Martlemas, then, alongside the ghosts and the flames that we see across all of Hallowmas, each have a specific food association of their own: black pudding and goose for the 11th, pigs cheek and parsnip for the 12th, and beef and beer for the 13th.

But Brice's Day once held another type of beef.

31

AS MAD AS A STAMFORD BULL

On this Day there is no King in Stamford; we are every one of us High and Mighty. Lords of the united Parishes in a General Bull-running [...] we are every one of us a Lord Paramount, a Lord of Rule and Misrule, a King in Stamford [...] We are punishable for no Crime but Murder, and that only of our own, and no other Species.

Francis Peck, 'The Speech of a Notable Bullard about Forty Moons Ago', from his pamphlet *c.*1743.

The bull-running custom was at one period the idol of the people of Stamford; it was to them what the Olympic games were to the ancients of Rome.

George Burton, *Chronology of Stamford*, 1846.

The most famous St Brice's Day tradition in all of England was the infamous Stamford Bull Run. While not quite unique in Britain, it was nevertheless extremely rare. Whilst bull baiting was popular across the land, the only other known example of a British bull run was the August one held in Tutbury in Staffordshire, which some say was even more raucous than that in Stamford, though Stamford's was older, and far more twined with the local identity – we shall not detail the Summer Tutbury Run any further.

It's impossible to say whether the St Brice's Day association with beef is a result or a cause of the Stamford Bull Run, just as it's impossible to say when, how or why the run originated. The local legend is the only explanation offered, and it may or may not bear relation to truth.

As it goes, in the time of King John, about 1209, one William de Warrenne, Lord of Stamford, was innocently gazing from his castle walls on St Brice's Day, when he spied a pair of bulls in the castle meadows fighting over a cow. When a butcher and his mastiff tried to break it up, one of the two bulls managed to escape into the town, where it charged and tossed and gored men, women and children alike. De Warrenne immediately mounted and joined the chase to subdue the beast, having so much fun in the process that he gave the town's butchers grazing rights over the meadow (known as Bull Meadow thereafter, until it was changed, quite recently, to a rather insipid 'The Meadows') in exchange for a commitment from them to provide a mad bull every year on 13th November to repeat the festivities.

The earliest hard evidence for the bull run, however, dates to 1389. The document, from Stamford's Guild of St Martin, states, 'On the feast of St. Martin, this gild, by custom beyond reach of memory, has a bull; which bull is hunted by dogs, and then sold; whereupon the bretheren and sisteren sit down to feast.' The guild itself had been established within living memory, just sixty years earlier in 1329, and so the phrase 'custom beyond reach of memory' likely places the bull run as pre-dating the guild, and back somewhere into the 1200s, if not older.

The date cited is interesting. As we have discussed already, St Brice and St Martin are closely associated, and many reckonings include St Brice's Day as a conclusory part of the wider Martinmas period, though of course, St Martin's Day also has an association with beef.

The first full description we have of the event is also the first expression of disapproval (apparently, it provides 'no pleasure except to such as take a pleasure in beastlinesse and mischief'). The piece dates to 1646, in the Puritan Richard Butcher's *The Survey and Antiquitie of the Towne of STAMFORD, In the County of LINCOLNE*. He places it firmly on 13th November, 'six weekes before Christmas' and outlines the ceremony thus:

> The Butchers of the Town at their own charge [...] provide the wildest Bull they can get, this Bull over night is had in to some Stable or Barne belonging to the Alderman, the next morning proclamation is made by the common Bell-man of the Town [...] that each one shut up their shops-doores and gates [...] That none have any Iron upon their Bull-clubs or other staffe which they pursue the Bull with. Which proclamation made and the Gates all shut up, the Bull is turned out of the Aldermans house, and then hivie, skivie, tag and rag, Men, Women and children of all sorts and sizes, with all the Dogs in the Town promiscuously running after him

> with their Bull-clubs spattering dirt in each others faces that one would think them to be so many Furies started out of Hell.

Opposition to the bull run, then, is one of the oldest elements of it that we have evidence for. Initially, the opposition was from seventeenth-century Puritanism, but it later came under fire from Enlightenment thinking in the eighteenth century, from the temperance movement in the nineteenth century, and finally (and, alas, rightly) from the growing animal welfare movement of Victorian England. Those interested in further reading on the history of the event could do worse than seek 'November Bull-Running in Stamford, Lincolnshire' by Martin W. Walsh, originally published in the *Journal of Popular Culture*. The beautifully produced *Stamford Myths and Legends* by Martin Smith (1991) also provides an entertaining but thorough overview.

The event more or less continued to hold to the pattern outlined by Richard Butcher until its eventual suppression, with various extra details and habits accrued along the way. An interesting element was the practice of smearing, according to Peck, bull faeces (called Bull-Dirt) on all and sundry, 'The Streets are filled with Heroes who bandy the Dirt about their own Dublets, and take care that every Body who appears with a clean Face shall not want a dirty one; for He that gets no Bull-Dirt, gets no Christmas Pye'. Here, the daubed-on muck becomes a vital ritual for a good Christmas, reflecting the role St Brice's Day played as the end of the transitional period of Hallowmas, bridging the gap from autumn to winter.

The core of cruelty at the heart of the bull run was in the efforts to provoke ever-increasing madness in the beast. There are reports of firecrackers, water hurled at his face, pepper in his nose, and gunpowder lit or vitriol (sulphuric acid) poured on the animal's back, his tail and horns cut off, prodded at with needles, beaten with sticks. The exhausted bull would then be baited (at the bull ring near Lammas Bridge on Bath Row) or slaughtered, whereupon, as Francis Peck puts it in his 1727 *Antiquarian Annals*, the 'body is shared by the Heroes, and in old time, he who first rode upon the Bull's Back, had the head [... and] The Great Gut, or pudding, commonly known by the name of Tom Hodge, be given to the most Worthy Adventurer'.

As the custom aged, so it developed. In time, the main object became to push the bull from the town bridge before killing and roasting it into a great feast of bull-beef. If the bull showed itself a 'beast of spirit', however, and could not be 'brigged', then it was allowed to live. On the other hand, a 'bad bull' that was brigged too soon (by midday, generally) was an extreme underwhelm, and often resulted in a second bull for Christmas for the 'bullards', or bull-chasers.

The bullards themselves started to develop flamboyant and grotesque costumes, unveiled on the day and hyped up a week beforehand by their 'imps', who ran through the town bellowing, 'Hoy bull, hoy!' Peck described them as 'habited Ten Thousand Times more hastily than so many Witches on a Plow Monday', and there are obvious parallels with Bonfire Night and Mischief Night. Private or 'stop' bull runs began to be held throughout the winter months, usually in small alleyways for small groups, sponsored by taverns or trades, sometimes using a stuffed Guy-style effigy to attract the bull.

A fascinating addition was the growth of the Bull Queen, or Bull Woman, who would preside over the entirety of the festival dressed in blue and carrying a 'blue ball stick', taking on the responsibility of raising the money to provide the bull. Though it is unknown when exactly this tradition began, some date it to 1789 when, during an attempted suppression of the custom with the 2nd Dragoon Guards, the bull was unexpectedly brought into the town through St George's Gate by one Ann Blades, who the soldiers were loathe to challenge. As the bullards seemed placid, the officer in charge dismissed his men, at which point, Ann let the bull loose and the dismissed troops joined in the chase!

By this time, the bull run had become an increasingly working-class affair, and polite society began to shun and disapprove of it in their droves. This trend would continue over the next half-century, characterising the event as one defined by class warfare and leading directly to its undoing. Ann Blades, meanwhile, remained Empress of the Bullards (or 'Nan Roberts') until her death in 1808, when she was succeeded in this office by Mrs Jorden until 1828, when she apparently burned her blue clothes of office and joined the Methodist Church.

Throughout the 1830s, increased attention and campaigns from the Society for the Prevention of Cruelty to Animals hastened its demise, and by the end of the decade more and more dragoons were being drafted in to suppress the run, with the fighting and violence growing concomitantly. When ever-increasing military force failed to snuff it out, the authorities realised they could simply put the cost of the soldiers and constables onto the townspeople. The 1839 run went ahead but cost the citizens £300. Words were had thereafter, and the runs ceased.

But the memory did not. Bull Suppers remained a common St Brice's Day event into the twentieth century, as did hearty public performance of the famed 'Bullards Song'. According to the *Stamford Mercury* of 4th November, 1930, the song is said to date to 1817, when four Stamfordians (Anthony Peasgood, James 'Doctor' Woodhall, Ireland and Barton) wrote and performed it on the old bowling green. It became an instant hit and was immediately embraced by the town:

To conclude, 'Here follow the words of the once-famous ditty. It should be noted that the word "Stamford" was always given in its ancient pronunciation, viz., "Stahmford"':

Come, all you bonny boys
   Who love to bait the bonny bull,
Who take delight in noise,
   And you shall have your belly-full.
On Stamford's Town Bull running day,
We'll show you such right gallant play,
You never saw the like, you'll say,
   As you have seen at Stamford.

Earl Warren was the man
   That first began this gallant sport;
In the castle he did stand,
   And saw the bonny bulls that fought;
The butchers with their bull-dogs came,
These sturdy stubborn bulls to tame,
But more with madness did inflame,
   Enraged they ran through Stamford.

Delighted with the sport,
   The meadows there he freely gave,
Where these bonny bulls had fought,
   The butchers now to hold and have;
By Charter they are strictly bound,
That every year a bull be found:
Come daub your face you dirty clown,
   And stump away to Stamford.

Come, take him by the tail boys, –
   Bridge, bridge him if you can;
Prog him with a nail boys;
   Ne'er let him quiet stand:
Through every street and lane in town
We'll chevy chase him up and down;
You sturdy bung-straws ten miles round,
   Come stump away to Stamford.

Bring with you a prog stick, –
  Boldly mount then on his back:
Bring with you a dog, Dick,
  Who will also help to bark.
This is the rebel's riot feast,
Humanity must be debased
And every man must do his best
  To bait the bull in Stamford.

Early versions preclude the final verse and replace 'daub' in verse 3 with 'dight'. Some later versions replace the 'bung-straws' of verse 4 with 'strawyards', and the word 'prog' with 'prod'.

And so, in 1839, after centuries of mounting opposition from various authorities (religious, social, ethical and legal), it was the financial that finally succeeded. I am less interested in the pre-1839 history of the custom, however, which has been thoroughly researched already, and far more interested in the post-1839 afterlife, which has barely been scratched and which has yielded some surprising results.

Though the raucousness of the bull run was concluded, informal feasting and revelry on St Brice's Day continued for many years. Not only that, but the hitherto mundane practice of 'bullock whopping' (driving bullocks through the streets to get them to the slaughterhouse) immediately took on an entirely different character in Stamford. What had hitherto been a fairly perfunctory rite suddenly became communal and celebrated, filling the void that the bull run left behind.

An account of the bullock whopping was given by Jessie K. McHugh (née Graham), of 10 Edinburgh Road, in the *Stamford Mercury* of 26th January 1979:

> Anyone of my age and generation will have a vivid picture of bullock whopping days.
>
> I was born at 38 North Street – near where Tilley's Garage now stands.
>
> On what we called 'Bullock Whopping Day' [near to 28th October] Broad Street was roped off but not at the bottom end of Lowe, Son and Cobbold's passage (as we called it in those days). All the farmers came to sell and buy.
>
> Where we lived we had a large yard and as the bullocks were being taken to the slaughterhouse they used to run straight into our yard and if my mum's door was open, in to the house. Then we would run upstairs to get out of the way. Men used to drive them out of the house. My mother always said that the animals knew where they were being taken to.

> Often when walking down Lowe, Son and Cobbold's passage we would have to run back as the bullocks had got away and were coming up towards us. My brothers and sister enjoyed every minute of it!

An editor's note goes on to explain:

> Bullock whopping was a pastime for anyone who had a stick to whop the bullocks which stood in the streets at some of the famous Stamford fairs, notably [on the feast day of Saints] Simon and Jude [28th October]. It is believed that bullock whopping ended when the selling of beasts in Broad Street finally terminated in 1929. The Mercury carried a picture of the last selling of animals in Broad Street although it had been prohibited by the Town council in 1928, when they decreed that the fair must be transferred to the cattle market.

Based on this account, it seems that the communal chasing and beating of a bull down Broad Street before its slaughter on 13th November, fairly elegantly moved two weeks earlier to the end of October, and became the communal beating and driving of bullocks down Broad Street to lead them to slaughter. The atmosphere of revelry, bull sticks, and a special and celebratory saint's day are all there, but it was clearly economically justified (and socially restrained) enough to pass without issue for ninety years after the St Brice's Day Bull Run was ended.

But that's not all. While Bullock Whopping Day was still in full swing, a revival occurred.

The ceremonial revival of the Stamford Bull Run began on 9th June, 1924, as part of the Stamford Whit-Monday Carnival, held annually at Burghley Park in aid of the Stamford & Rutland Infirmary. The *Stamford Mercury* of 30th May affirms the intention behind the bull-running revival, and it was such a success that it became (for a time) synonymous with the carnival, which is still held annually today (though it has lost its Whit Monday association, its date has been moveable throughout the decades, and at some point the revived bull run appears to have been dropped from the parade).

Perhaps the most important element of this 1924 revival is that it included, as both ceremony advisor and actually as part of the costumed bull-running procession (he 'took part [...] in fancy costume'), someone who had been at, and could remember, the last full-scale bull run back in 1839.

Mr James Fuller Scholes of Pretoria House, Foundry Road, was born in 1834. The year before taking part in carnival, according to the *Stamford Mercury* of 19th October, he was taken up in an aeroplane for his 90th birthday (which he 'thoroughly enjoyed') and rendered a performance of the 'Bullards Song'. He died in 1929, and in his obituary the *Leicester Evening Mail* of 7th February described him as a 'Jack of All Trades and Master of How to Live', who 'never took medicine' and was the 'Last Link With Days of Bull Running'. They quote him from a recent interview, where he clearly states, 'I can remember my mother showing me the bull and the horses and the bullards who chased the bull. She kept the Chequers Inn, in St. Peter's Street, and showed me the bull-running sport from a bedroom window. I was four years old then.'

The carnival continued, though Bull Whopping Day did not, and the *Leicester Evening Mail* of 26th September 1931 affirms that the highlight of the festivities was still when 'the ancient pastime of bull running was revived, preceded by a carnival procession through the streets. This part of the proceedings, which caused endless amusement, was undertaken by the Crown Vat of Frothblowers' (the Ancient Order of Froth Blowers were a whimsical social and charitable organisation whose motto was 'lubrication in moderation'). The *Market Harborough Advertiser* of 2nd October confirmed the 'most exciting feature of the day was the "Bull running," a mimic representation of the sport'.

According to the published photographs, alongside the bull run, the event consisted of a comically dressed Town Cavalry on hobby horses, who charged the crowd and captured the town mayor – ostensibly on the charge of allowing the infirmary finances to falter, but one wonders the degree to which this could also have been a self-conscious play on the Dragoon Guards shutting down the original bull run. The *Nottingham Evening Post* of 28th September reports that he was captured on the first day and released on the last, when prominent attendees of the carnival were burned in effigy on a bonfire.

The Froth Blowers liquidated in 1931, and the bull run seems then to have continued as a part of the carnival, but taken over by the local branch of a Christian youth group called Toc H. A historic photo of one of these bull-run parades was published in the *Stamford Mercury* on 2nd February 1979, depicting the top-hatted bullards (all young members of the Stamford Toc H) with their bull, holding up a banner proclaiming, 'YE OLDE STAMFORD BULL RUNNING – humanely revived'. The bull that year consisted of Mr George Anderson as the head, and Mr Ron Oak as the rear. Quoting the article:

> Mr Anderson said that Toc H contributed a bull made of old blankets and horns from the town's slaughterhouse to an August Bank Holiday before the Second World War. The carnival procession, he said, started in Broad Street and wound along St Martin's until it turned into the Burghley Park cricket grounds. The 'bull' got more running than he anticipated. In an attempt

> to be realistic, Mr Anderson said, he paused during the parade to look in a shop window. At that time, he said, cattle weren't an unusual sight in the town. 'In the old days if you saw a cow look in a window you got it away from there as quickly as possible in case it charged its own reflection.'
>
> The blanket bull looked all too real to a passing farm labourer who had has a few drinks. 'He clubbed me over the head and I went down on my knees,' Mr Anderson said. 'I thought if I stayed there I might get hit again so we ran all the way to Burghley Park.' Despite their performance, the group failed to get a prize, said Mr Anderson.

One Leonard C. Dolby also took part in the parade, as did other boys from St Michael's (Stamford Boys' Senior School). In the *Stamford Mercury* of 2nd February 1979, he describes it as:

> … a well-organised carnival parade, by our headmaster, Mr H.J.B. Niblett, and Mr 'Dud' Henson of Gibson's foundry. We were dressed as bull-runners in red bandanas and white flannels, as far as possible, and had our faces blackened by burnt corks […] I know we all enjoyed ourselves tremendously […] Unfortunately I cannot remember the exact date […] We were given lectures on the Stamford bull-running and learned to sing a bull-running song at school.

Though Scholes had passed on, the original bull runs were still remembered vividly in the oral tradition of the town at this point. In the 24th July edition of the *London Daily News* in 1931, Mrs Florence M. Barker from Middleton Cheney, Banbury, writes:

> My father has in his possession, a drinking horn which bears the following inscription in old English lettering: 'This horn tossed John Berridge when bull-running at Stamford, December 26th, 1815.' The said John Berridge was the son of 'Marm' Berridge, the mistress of Lady Exeter's girls school at Stamford, and the father of my grandmother, whom I have heard tell the story of how, 'it was not satisfied with tossing him once, but caught him again as he came down.' She also talked of the barrels of sand which were placed at intervals along the streets used in the 'bull-running,' and were used as refuges by the intrepid 'matadors'.

The bull-running revival seems to have stopped along with the rest of the carnival, when it was put on hiatus during the Second World War, and there's no mention of bull running as a part of the carnival when it revives thereafter, so it seems as though it may have ceased. A little over twenty years passed before another small-scale informal bull running was held, on 27th April 1961, to advertise the Stamford Rugby Football Club's fundraising flannel dance at the Stamford Hotel. The head of the bull costume was A. Haynes, the rear was P. Trath, and the accompanying matador was J.M.G. Chappell.

It is possible this revival inspired (or was inspired by) the donation, reported in the *Stamford Mercury* of July 28th that year, to the local museum of 'a brass medallion connected with bull running (found in an old long-case clock)'. Such artefacts were found frequently throughout the twentieth century, and demonstrate a deep and living connection with the practice that never died out. Not long after, as reported in the *Stamford Mercury* of 4th July 1969, 'The Mayor, Councillor R.J.R. Seamer, was last week presented with a memento of the days when bull running was practised in Stamford by Mrs J. Short, of Hudds Mill Cottage, Uffington Road, Stamford'. It seems that a few weeks previously, Mrs Short's son-in-law, Mr Novak:

> ... was digging in her garden and unearthed a small metal object bearing the coat of arms of Stamford. This was passed to Mr L. Tebbutt, Stamford's Librarian and Museum Curator, and afterwards to Mr H. Bedford, the Town Clerk. After some research they came to the conclusion that it was the top of the Rod of Office, carried by Ann Blades, Queen of the Bullards.

No explanation of how the head might have ended up in the garden is offered, except for a vague suggestion she may have lived there in 1839, but the site is close to St George's Gate, 'where she is recorded to have made her appearance'. The article goes on to confirm:

> The top has now been fixed to a staff and will be placed with the borough regalia. [...] In addition the Town Clerk presented to the Mayor a pair of bull's horns taken from a bull which had run through the streets of Stamford in 1836. These horns had been bequeathed to the Corporation by the late Mrs K.B. Atter, whose husband, Mr Walter Atter, was the brother of the former Town Clerk [...] Mr Charles Atter. [...] The horns, mounted in silver, bear an inscription to say that they were presented on November 13, 1836, which is only three years before the last bull running took place.

None of this is yet ancient history.

Again, the *Stamford Mercury* of 16th May 1975 reports:

> Mr and Mrs Maxwell Leigh, of Cape Town, returned a hoof, reputed to be from the last animal to take part in Stamford's famous bull running. The silver-mounted hoof will now take its place alongside the pair of horns at the Town Hall, which are also from an animal in [one of] the last bull run[s], in the 1830s. Mrs Leigh who is related to Mr Laurence Tebbutt, of 28 St Paul's Street, Stamford, inherited the hoof, which was taken to South Africa by her grandfather, Henry Tebbutt, in 1889.

The run was revived again in a more complete form on 4th July 1987, as the opening event of the Stamford Festival. For months, the Bull Run Committee had promised a complete revival of the original run with a genuine trio of bulls, prompting letters of outrage and provoking the ire of the League Against Cruel Sports, who threatened legal action and sent witnesses to the event to prepare for court proceedings, despite repeated assurances from publican organiser David Ladd that all would be safe and legal. The office of the Lady in Blue was revived, and held by Jayne Addison, who won it in a competition at the Green Man Pub.

On the day itself, the Lady in Blue processed to the closed Broad Street in the back of a vintage sports car, officially opening the event in fine, traditional bull gown to much adulation. Up to 100 red-shirted runners were assembled before three trucks, each containing a stamping, grunting beast.

The church bells rang, the truck doors swung open, and out ran… costumed pantomime cattle; namely two bulls – Billy (manned by Butch Baker and Aubrey Johnson) and Horny (Chris McLaren and Neil Patten) – and a comedy cow named Gertrude (played 'strictly for laughs' by Steve Fowkes and Dusky Doyle). This trio is, of course, a nod to the original founding legend. The run was performed to the delight of all, followed by a full parade with ornate floats. Some good pictures, alongside accounts of the event, were published in the *Peterborough Standard* on 9th July and the *Leicester Daily Mercury* on 6th July.

The most recent revival (which erroneously presented itself as the first since 1839) was a colourful parade with papier mâché bulls and other fantastical animals, held during the Stamford Georgian Festival in September 2013. The four-day event then took place every other year until 2019, with a bull-run procession at each. At the time of writing, there are no plans for another, and covid seems to have taken the wind out of it, the website being long since defunct.

I attended the 2017 Stamford Georgian Festival, which had as its grand finale a light and projection show with intermittent interpretive dance set to music, alongside a booming narration about the history of the town. Much of it centred on the bull run, with a misrepresentative and revisionist account given alongside an intense soundtrack. It was approached from a purely moralistic position and presented as a source of shame, with the vague implication that it was all the result of archaic toxic masculinity 'handed down from father to son'.

Suddenly, the scary music became inspirational and positive, and the narration changed from a gruff male to a clear female voice, explaining that the town's opinion then altered, the bull run ended, and everything became nice and modern. The military authorities were presented as heroic for 'enforcing change' as 'the time had come for the town to move on'. The reality, of course, is that they subdued the working-class townsfolk at the barrel of a gun, and then fined them into submission because the middle-classes no longer enjoyed the event. The light show finished with a self-congratulatory screed at how advanced and superior we all are now, and how barbaric they all were then.

This whitewashed history ignored the essential class-warfare element of the gradual killing off of the bull run (history is written by the victor, after all, and the middle-classes have very much won the modern age), and completely removed the notable and socially empowered role that women played in the custom. These are vital and relevant factors, complex and nuanced, which have the capacity to expand our human knowledge of the past. This performance, however, sought not to understand the town ancestors, but to castigate them. Not to explore local heritage, but to obscure it. Not to seek out symbolic continuity, but to demonise the dead.

In recent decades, Stamford seems to have become insecure and uncomfortable with its heritage, and unable to talk of it without performatively finger-wagging a judgement. I sincerely hope that the town eventually revives a raucous, symbolic bull-running on 13th November and does so not to denounce the barbarism of the past, or to celebrate the progressivism of the present, or to retrofit their history into something more socially acceptable. Rather, I hope a revival would simply acknowledge that for over 600 years this distinctive tradition defined the character of Stamford and Stamfordians, and that this alone is worth, once a year at least, engaging with unapologetically – with folk cheer and carnival heartiness and pride, rather than middle-class moralism. At the very least 'The Meadows' should have its proper name restored, and be known by all as Bull Meadow once more.

A photo of the pre-war Toc H bull-running carnival published in the *Stamford Mercury* of 19th January 1979 shows that on the boys' school float, pulled by a horse, there was a large and peculiar contraption for making 'Bull-Pills' (which Leonard Dolby recalled so fondly that 'at the time' he 'almost believed in its properties' – some sort of sweet, perhaps?). The notice atop it read:

THE PRIORY BULL PILL
This remarkable tonic, the 'Priory Bull Pill,'
Is a mixture compounded of mirth and good will,
  And its principal mission
  Is to nourish tradition,
And keep the bull running in Stamford Town still.

There are many who would benefit from a dose today.

32

AND THE REST

And so we find Hallowtide concluded, and the two weeks (ish) that remain of November become a matter of eagerly waiting for Advent and December, and with it, the great slide down into Christmas.

One major event – in the London calendar anyway – that usually occurs within the Hallantide season (but which I have excluded from this book as essentially unrelated) is London's Lord Mayor's Show. Historically belonging to 29th October, it moved to 9th November after the shift from the Julian to the Gregorian calendar, and since 1959 it has been held on the second Saturday in November. Despite this, it has never naturalised into Hallowmas.

The office of Lord Mayor of London dates from 1189 (it is an entirely separate office from that of the Mayor of London, which has only existed since 2000), and the original charter establishing it required that upon beginning his term, the Lord Mayor had to travel to the royal enclave at Westminster to present himself to the monarch's representatives and swear an oath. This had developed into a full pageant by 1215, with the title of Lord Mayor appearing in the 1300s, and the show becoming a major public event by the sixteenth century – in some respects, a highlight of the London year.

It was held in abeyance during the Commonwealth, and cancelled for the funeral of Wellington in 1852. Though it continued throughout the Black Death and the Blitz, it was again cancelled for the coronavirus pandemic in 2020. Aside from these blips, it has been held annually for over 800 years.

An entire book could be written (and many have) on the intricacies of the Lord Mayor's Show, the City of London itself (as distinct from Greater London) and the London Livery Companies who are the ancient trade institutions at its heart. The Great Twelve City Livery Companies are the oldest of many (the very oldest date to the 1100s, but there are over 100 in total) and attend by right, with all the rest (including my own, the Worshipful Company of Arts Scholars) by invitation, alongside certain privileged regiments, such as the Honourable Artillery Company and the Royal Fusiliers, and any other organisations or charities the new Lord Mayor wishes to invite. I recommend the *City of London Freeman's Guide*, by Paul D. Jagger, for those interested in learning more about this.

The show as it exists today is part pomp and ceremony, part carnival, with floats, regalia and pageantry aplenty. It has been broadcast live by the BBC since 1937 (making it the longest-running television broadcast in the world). It usually starts around 11am and is finished by 3.30pm. Though the procession is more than 3 miles long, the route is much shorter, and those at the front are always finished long before those at the back have even started. Come the evening, there is usually a fireworks display.

A notable element is the inclusion of Gog and Magog. In the mytho-legendary history of Albion, Britain was established by Brutus of Troy (hence the name), who battled several giants and monsters to win the land. The largest of these was Gogmagog, who was defeated by Brutus's companion, Corineus (after whom Cornwall is named), in some traditions also a giant. Effigies of Gogmagog and Corineus were included at the coronation of Elizabeth I, and these (or similar versions made of lighter material) were carried as part of the Lord Mayor's Show thereafter, gradually becoming known as Gog and Magog rather than Gogmagog and Corineus (one version of the story accounts for this with the tradition that, when Corineus defeated Gogmagog by throwing him from a cliff, the giant split in two on the rocks below, each half growing into a separate being. Brutus named them Gog and Magog and bound them to the City as its guardians).

A new pair of effigies were carved from pine by Captain Richard Saunders in 1709 and kept in the Guildhall, but were destroyed by bombs during the Second World War, and replaced in 1953 with versions by David Evans. In 2006, Olivia Elton Barratt, Prime Warden of the Basketmakers Company, decided to remake the Guildhall carvings in woven willow, so that they could be included in parade again. Forty members of the Basketmakers' Association gave time and expertise in constructing the 14ft-tall giants in a workshop in Essex, with willow donated by Musgroves of Somerset. They are now included in the show annually, accompanied by members of the Worshipful Company of Basketmakers and the Guild of Young Freemen.

Historically, a number of 'Mock Mayors' were also elected on 9th November in various parts of the country – not dissimilar to Lords of Misrule, these carnival figures still exist in some locales today, elected annually on numerous dates throughout the year, as figureheads for village fetes, parades and other jolly events. The town of Ashburton in Devon still has something much older than a mayor (be they Lord or Mock), and every 28th November, its ancient Court Leet appoints the new Portreeve, an office it has had since AD 820. Though the title is used ceremonially by various towns in Britain, Ashburton's is the only official one, and is a truly Anglo-Saxon survival legitimised today by an Act of Parliament.

The remainder of November has had other festivals, but none survive today in any meaningful sense. One such was Queene's Day, 17th November, which commemorated Elizabeth I's accession to the throne and was a hugely popular national holiday for over 300 years. It involved much ringing of church bells, alongside feasting and parades, and after her death it became a tool for criticising both Catholicism and the Establishment. It was apparently revived by the Devon village of Berry Pomeroy in 2005, with celebrations starting at Evensong in the parish church and finishing with the burning of the Devil in effigy, on a bonfire in a neighbouring field. The revival does not appear to still be current.

The largest to have been forgotten are the days of St Clement and St Catherine on 23rd and 25th November, respectively, whose traditions of Clementing and Catterning have already been discussed. They were rarely observed in areas that engaged in soul-caking – it tended to be an either/or situation. These two days have large and fascinating histories behind them, more especially as each was taken up by certain tradesfolk – St Clement by blacksmiths and metalworkers, and St Catherine by lacemakers, ropemakers and wheelwrights (being their respective patron saints). St Clement's Day had extensive parades, rituals and festivities enacted by blacksmiths, reminiscent of many of those already covered, where gunpowder was beaten on anvils and metallurgic revelry abounded. As these trades and tradesmen have faded from daily life, however, so too have their festivities.

We still see a few fragmentary survivals, though. In Burwash, East Sussex, an effigy of 'Old Clem' is still mounted above the door of the inn for an annual Clem Feast. Finch Foundry, near Okehampton in Devon, holds a grand St Clement's Day celebration, attracting ironworkers from across the country with competitions and displays, stalls, morris dancing, mince pies and mulled wine. In Hastings, the Bonfire Society has revived an annual procession with Clem and Catherine, including traditional songs and Cattern cakes – Catherine, of course, is still annually commemorated in firework-wheel form every Bonfire Night. No doubt there are other examples, but the light is dying, and time grows short.

Finally, this liminal period of pre-Advent concludes properly with Stir Up Sunday, the last Sunday of November and the traditional time to begin your Christmas puddings. The day's name comes from the opening words of the collect for the day in the Book of Common Prayer ('Stir up, we beseech thee, O Lord, the wills of thy faithful people'), but it is popularly associated with stirring up bowls of mincemeat and dough for Christmas puddings, and is an opportunity to have drinks, food and general festivity.

So Christmas begins, and we finish for another year.

But this book is one of Halloween, and as the spirits of the season may have dissipated a little during the last few chapters, we'll conclude with a clutch of resolutely Hallowmas tales, none of which I've been able to fit in elsewhere, but all of which have relevance.

Are you sitting comfortably?

Then it is time to begin the end.

33

SOME FINAL HALLOWMAS TALES

This old story was put to verse for Halloween of 1946 by a 'well-known Sutterton man, who wishes to remain anonymous', being later published in the *Spalding Guardian* of 27th December as 'The Laying of the Sutterton Ghosts'. The tale tells of medieval Lincolnshire Halloween festivities, with the church bells ringing and a great communal bonfire on the land of Sutterton Grange, residence of the local squire, around which the villagers enjoy their revelry. It tells of a weary traveller arriving to stay for the night, his dog merrily yapping at his feet, his pack filled with exotic wares from across the world. He lays out his riches and locals come to fawn and admire. Gifts are bought by courting lovers, doting husbands and proud parents alike – some in seasonal spirit of romance, others in preparation for Christmas.

But one among them looks on, not with wonder, but spite – for desire can quickly turn to envy, to bitterness and worse. This one is named by our poet as Hodge, the squire's ploughman, who gazes nastily on the loving young couples.

The laughter continues, the hot drinks are drunk, the hot foods are eaten. The traveller packs away his goods and retires to his room at the top of the house, and Hodge does likewise; his room in the attic, a few doors down.

As the bell tolls midnight 'twixt Eve and Day, Hodge takes a step towards the traveller's room, his mind full of thoughts of the treasure that lies within. Hodge turns the handle of the traveller's door. Hodge pushes silent into the darkness within.

When the household stirred next morning, they found nothing in the traveller's room but a bloodstained floor, and not even that in Hodge's. The traveller's dog was found yapping at the depths of a nearby pond.

They say to this day that on Halloween night, the traveller's dog can still be heard yapping by the pool, and the figure of that traveller can sometimes be seen, tied to his remains, lost in the mere. Others report seeing him, skeletal, bent over the gate in a nearby field, his dog at his feet. They say also that Hodge can be seen far off in the distance, riding a spectral horse, doomed now to do so for eternity, ever rushing to escape his restless fate, never finding satisfaction.

Lincolnshire is long and rich in Halloween stories, and it's no surprise to find All Hallows ghosts in nearby Skirbeck, as we see from the following report in the *Lincolnshire Chronicle* of Friday, 25th November 1864:

> Some person, fond of a joke, has been hoaxing some of the inhabitants of Skirbeck by playing the 'ghost.' It is said that this 'spectre in white' made its first appearance about a fortnight ago, between Main-ridge Bridge and the foundry of Messrs. Tuxford. Since then it has been seen almost nightly – at least so it is said, and crowds of people have gathered together for the purpose of catching a glimpse of it. On Sunday evening last as many as 200 people, it is said, were strolling along the drain side with this object in view.
>
> While many of the credulous, however, really believe it to be a veritable ghost, the more rational regard it simply as a hoax that is being played by some person draped in a white sheet. A stout ash plant or a good horse-whip, skilfully applied, would no doubt soon solve the problem, and cure these nocturnal wanderings and allay the terrors they have created in the minds of the superstitious.

Here we see the same newspaper response as we did with the Pig-Headed Bride and the Richmond Ghost over fifty years earlier – a mirthful scorn, and the presumption of an obvious hoax (despite '200 people' following the thing and not finding any evidence of foul play). The ghost would've begun its haunting around Brice's Day or Martlemas and carried on throughout the Christmas season, as the follow-up report from 3rd January states:

> It is rumoured that this nocturnal biped, not content with alarming the inhabitants on Maudfoster's Bank, has latterly been performing his mad pranks in the environs of Boston, and numerous stories are afloat as to the assaults, &c., committed by him, most of which, however, we believe to exist only in the imagination of the alarmed persons. Suspicion has fallen upon a highly respectable young man in the neighbourhood of Maudfoster, whose proceedings are narrowly watched.

Again, a 'respectable young man' is to blame, with no explanation actually given. As there are clearly many, many people encountering the thing, and apparently nobody who has been able to debunk it or reveal the person responsible, it seems somewhat hubristic to maintain the disdain six weeks later. The Skirbeck Ghost appears only to have hit the headlines during that one Halloween/Christmas season, and I can find no further reports.

Another potential Halloween ghost tradition can be found in the following account from Somerset, referring (apparently satirically) to a recently built concrete tax office in Keyford, next to Frome, in a letter from J.W. Thompson published in the *Somerset Standard* on 15th August 1930:

> Upon [the building's] foundation, according to tradition, flourished, in the days of Elizabeth, one of the most magnificent oak trees in England, and was the trysting place of youths and maidens as far away as Blatchbridge. And under this tree one Autumn evening was enacted a terrible drama. A gaily-adorned highwayman, mounted on a coal-black steed, and well primed with cider, which he had imbibed at Maiden Bradley, dismounted and demanded a kiss from one of the comely maidens present. Her sweetheart rushed at the drunken bully and struck him a violent blow in the face, whereupon, in his rage, the highwayman drew his pistols from their holster and shot the lovers dead. And under H.M. Tax Offices their bones still moulder, for they were buried there three days after the murder. So, you see, a first-class ghost can now be imagined each Hallowe-en to be seen prowling around its embattled entrance.

Leaping forward to Halloween of 1987, the graveyard of Chaldon Parish Church, in Surrey, was vandalised with a repair bill of £450. Stories among local children had it that this was either Devil-worshippers conducting black magic or undead creatures loosening themselves from the depths – both stories remain current in the area, and still at Halloween they're said to be abroad and visible if one attends the churchyard at midnight.

A similar tradition appears in the Leicestershire village of Mountsorrel, just south of Loughborough, where Devil-worshippers are said to be seen in the churchyard at midnight on Halloween, raising the dead and reanimating corpses. This seems to stem, again, from the graveyard getting vandalised on the weekend before Halloween in 1978, this time causing £900 of damage. Fifteen stone crosses were pushed over, five smashed beyond repair, and a large pentagram marked out with bandages stolen from the sexton's office.

A story from the aptly named village of Hallow, near Worcester, tells of a bored young boy who wandered away from church during the All Hallows service. In the graveyard there he saw a gaggle of children in masks playing with hobby lanterns, so went over to join them. Laughing, the costumed infants got up and ran away, with the grinning truant giving chase. On and on they ran, giggling and playing, until they reached the adjoining village of Grimley, and the remains of an old earthwork that the locals called Grimhill. Finally, the children in their death's head masks stopped running and formed a circle, beckoning the boy to join them. As he did, he began to notice something was wrong, details off. The children weren't... right. Arms missing, legs backward, fingerless hands. To his horror, the boy realised that the creatures before him didn't have masks on, and weren't children at all – those were just the costumes they wore. The boy fled, screaming – ran all the way back to church, and never strayed from the service again. This behaviour-correcting fable was found written in the back of an eighteenth century school Bible in 1910 (note the otherworldly role of 'Grimhill', likely a burial mound, with 'Grim' an alternative name for Woden)

These are especially interesting taken in conjunction with the church porch divination customs discussed in earlier chapters, as is the following from the old Church of St Peter's at Barnstaple in Devon. There is reported, from midnight at All Hallows Eve until midnight on 12th November, the spectre of a beautiful young woman inside the church, or on the porch at night, with lights emanating from inside. She is said to produce a feeling of joy in any who see her, and warm laughter has been heard by witnesses. She is believed to be the spirit of eighteenth-century Elizabeth Burton, whose memorial tablet in the church reads as follows:

> Underneath the library of this church resteth, until the Archangel's trump shall summon her to appear on an immortal stage, the body of ELIZABETH BURTON, comedian; formerly of Drury-Lane, but late of Exeter Theatre; who exchanged Time for Eternity on All Souls Day [1st November], 1771, aged 20 years [...] This small tribute, to the memory of an amiable young woman, an innocent cheerful companion, and most excellent actress, was placed here by J. FOOTE, manager of the theatre.

We should all be so lucky to receive such an epitaph.

Happy Halloween.

EPILOGUE

I finish this book abed, with food bubbling away, at midnight 'twixt the Eve and Day of Midsummer, 2024, on Empress Road, Lyndhurst.

I would like to thank and acknowledge all the usual suspects: Hesper, Gordon, Nori, Myrtle, James Carney Thompson, Laura Romer-Ormiston, Tim Grieveson, Will Ashcroft, Alexander Larman, Richard Reeves, Elizabeth Lopes, Avi Esther, Georgie Unwin, Beth Redwood Pain, Ben and Emma Tyrie, Dave Ruis, James Woodhead, Zoe Reilly, Lucy Mills, Jess Haydon, Zanni Knights, Dwight Hendrickson, Shana Cooper, Aoibhin O'Connor, Megan Moriarty, Holly Alder, Maia Giacomelli, Jo and Tony, Rob and Alison, Northern Jordan, Richie, Liam, Clive, Charlie, and everyone else at the Fox, and the History Press. Above them all is my all-hallowed Mother, without whom I would be nothing, and my Grandfathers: Peter Brice and Graham Stratford.

If there is a conclusion to my book, it is that continuity matters. In a world where so much divides, and so many feel so alone and unimportant and disconnected, the enaction of culture, heritage and community is everything - engaging together with the same landscape, seasons, ritual and ceremony that those before us did, and passing it forward so that those after us can do likewise, and engage with us in turn. This intangible inheritance is powerful and brittle, and if we allow it to collapse then we rob the future of something we cannot begin to understand, that is rarer and more important than we can know.

Sing the songs, then; eat the food and tell the stories, celebrate the seasons as they come and go and come again. Invite neighbours, give gifts, touch grass. Remember the dead. Very few people can fix the world; everyone can help their home.